ABOVE THE ASH

THE COAL ELF CHRONICLES

ABOVE THE ASH

MARIA DEVIVO

4 Horsemen
Publications, Inc.

DEDICATION:

For Husband—Words cannot express just how lucky I am to have you. Thank you for forever.

For Sissy—"Tell me you're sisters without telling me you're sisters." Our connection is too scary to explain away. We saw Him that night, you can't tell me otherwise.

For Child—It's always for you, and always will be for you.

TABLE OF CONTENTS

The No

Lapis
Hall
Norland
Ice

Headquarters
West Bar
West Bank
Town Square
Mon
Valley
Lumber District

chPole
and
Frost Weather Outpost
Tir-La Dunes
Stixx Manor
Tir-La Treals
Skye Manor
ir-La Rise
East Bank
East Bank Town Square
The Inn
Plumm Stable
ch of Cave
Nessie Fruit Groves
ishing District

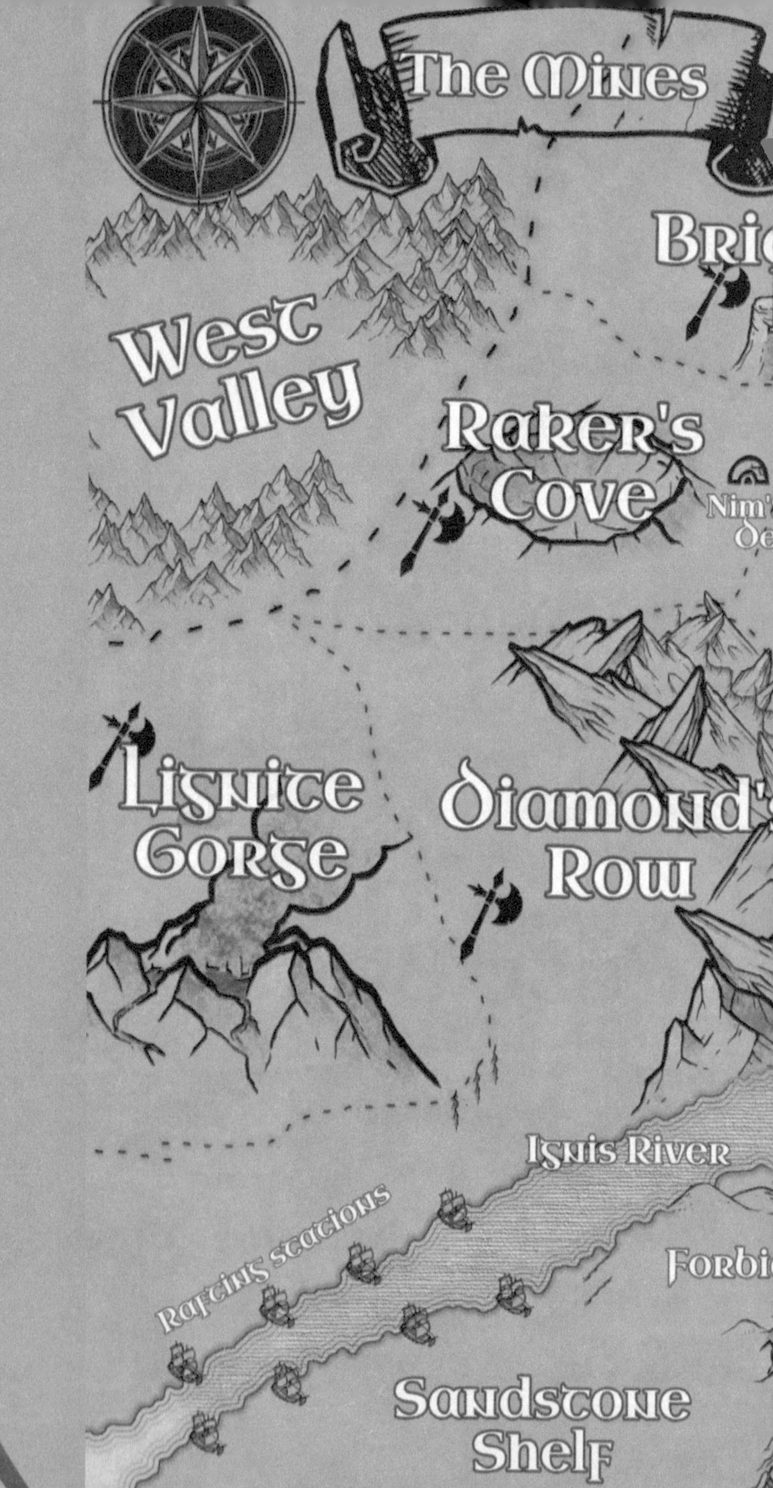

The Mines
Bri
West
Valley
Raker's
Cove
Nim'
de
Lignite
Gorge
Diamond'
Row
Ignis River
Rafting stations
Forbi
Sandstone
Shelf

Durkuss's Den
Ebony Crag
Ember's Den
Crystal Cave
Bommer's Den
Rock II
Tannen's Den
Stoker Cove
Onyx Alley
Banter's Den
Banter's Office
Welfort Den
Sturd's Den
n Corridor
Barrier Holt

CHAPTER ONE

"Santa Claus is not real!" little Ryan Black taunted from the back of the yellow school bus. "He's not real! It's just your parents who put all that junk under the tree and in your stupid stockings."

A few of the other kids around him chuckled and nodded in agreement, but Jennifer ducked her head down and closed her eyes as if to drown out the evil words that came from his sour mouth.

For her whole life, all seven glorious years of it, she had never once doubted the existence of Santa Claus. Why anyone would was unfathomable to her. All her friends believed. Her sister believed. Heck, even Ryan had believed not too long ago. It was just last December when her first-grade teacher, Mrs. Dunbar, took the class on a field trip to Christmas Lane. Jennifer remembered that Ryan had been the first child in line to happily sit on Santa's lap and rattle off his wish list of toys. So, what had changed?

What had happened in the span of a year? Why was Ryan, and some of the others, saying these horrible, hateful things?

They're just teasing you, she thought. *They just want to make you cry.*

Yes, those kids did that quite often—pull her hair, tell her to look down at the spider on her shirt, then flick her nose when she did, rip the pages out of her notebook, and other second grade torments. And it usually ended the same way—Jennifer would start to cry, and her tormentors would naturally laugh. She hated it when she cried in front of them, but sometimes she just couldn't help it. She hated it even more when they laughed at her. It was cruel and made her feel like a caterpillar trapped inside its stuffy and thread-filled cocoon. Her second-grade teacher, Mrs. Johanson, had shown them pictures at the beginning of this school year of what the inside of a cocoon looked like, and she often wondered what it felt like to be in that little enclosure.

The bus gently came to its next stop—its squeaky brakes jerking in rhythmic motion so as to not slip and slide on the icy road. Jennifer opened her eyes and looked out the window. The snowdrifts on the sidewalk were at least three feet high, and she watched as the children exited the bus and tried to plow through the dirty snow.

She took a deep breath. *Two more stops,* she assured herself. Two more stops and she would be off this bus and ready to start her Winter Vacation. She would be away from all the creeps at school, away from all the monotonous school-work, and Santa would be making his way to her house very soon! Oh, had she been a good girl this year! She smiled to herself as she went over her mental checklist—*kept my room clean, was always nice to my sister (well, tried to be), respectful to my parents, ate all my vegetables, got good grades in school, and…*

"If you believe in Santa Claus, then you're a baby!" Ryan continued his oration.

"Yeah!" one of the other kids chimed in.

Jennifer cringed. She certainly was *not* a baby!

Ryan sauntered down the aisle and stopped at every seat. "Do *you* believe in Santa Claus?" he asked as he pointed his finger in each of the passenger's faces. Jennifer heard the frightened mumbles of the other kids. "No," each responded hesitantly.

He made his way to Elizabeth Stockton who sat across the aisle from Jennifer and who was in Jennifer's dance class after school. Elizabeth looked over at Jennifer, her big brown eyes opened wide with terror. Ryan leaned over and got directly in Elizabeth's face, blocking Jennifer's view. "Do *you* believe in Santa Claus?" he sneered.

"N… n… no," Elizabeth stammered.

Jennifer froze and clutched the thick straps of her overstuffed My Little Pony backpack. She was next on Ryan's hit list, and she knew the question he was going to ask her was a tough one. If she lied and said she didn't believe in Santa, then he would leave her alone and move on. But she wasn't supposed to lie. She never lied. She couldn't lie. She *did* believe in Santa and if she lied about it, He would know! She couldn't risk losing a present off her list… or even worse… *coal in her stocking!*

Her heart beat so frantically in her little chest she could feel it through the thick padding of her winter coat. Ryan swiveled his body around to face her, and a hot tear escaped from the corner of her eye. She couldn't stop it from forming or rising or swelling over and onto her cold cheek. His eyes locked on hers, and he gave a half smirk when he noticed the small streak glistening down the side of her face. Just as he was about the move in closer for the kill, the bus's brakes began to pump. Ryan lost his footing, grabbed onto the high-backed seat, and jerked from side to side with the motion of the bus.

The door hissed open as a cold wave of air blasted its way inside. Jennifer closed her eyes in thankful prayer and breathed a sigh of relief. She wouldn't have to answer his questions, nor would she have to decide to lie or not because this was Ryan's time to get off the bus. Her body relaxed at the thought of not having to see him or hear his voice for the next few weeks. He gave her one last narrowed-eyed glare as if to say, "I'll be back for you," and turned to leave.

Jennifer stared at the back of his red coat until she could no longer see it down the aisle and turned her head to look out the window again. All she saw out there was gray sky and mounds of dirty snow heaped recklessly along the sidewalk. It was the same thing she saw at every bus stop, every time it snowed. The three other children who had gotten off the bus with Ryan had scooped up handfuls of dirty snow in their mittens and smashed the filthy concoction of snow and gravel on each other's backs. Ryan leaned forward to pick up some snow in retaliation but lost his footing and fell face-first into the snowdrift. A roar of laughter echoed against the gray sky until the bus was out of earshot.

Jennifer smirked in delight at seeing her arch-nemesis take such a tumble. *Serves him right for saying Santa isn't real*, she thought gleefully.

That night during dinner, Jennifer remained quiet and pensive. Normally, she would have blathered on and on about Mrs. Johanson and her wonderful day at school, but the gravity of Ryan Black's claims still hung heavy in her mind. She opted to let her sister do most of the talking. She didn't even realize she was spinning her peas around with her fork until her mother snapped, "Jenny! What on earth are you…?"

She looked up from her plate as if she had been yanked out of a dream. "Oh, sorry," she meekly responded.

"Spacing out, kiddo?" her father asked with a smile.

Jennifer nodded.

"Thinking about what Santa is going to bring you?" her mother prodded.

Jacey, Jennifer's older sister, giggled. Jennifer shot her a puzzled look. She inhaled and muttered, "Ryan Black said Santa isn't real."

Her parents quickly glanced at each other peculiarly. Jacey choked a little on her soda. Jennifer's eyes went wide. "Well?" she begged her mother. "Is he right?"

Her mother reached her long arms across the table and placed her hands on top of Jennifer's. "Sweetie, do you believe that Santa is real?"

Without hesitation, she responded, "Yes! Of course!"

"Then he's real," her mother assured.

"But… but… but Ryan said that…"

Her mother tilted her head forward and narrowed her eyes. "What exactly did Ryan say?"

Jennifer thought for a moment—wanting to get his exact words correct, needing exact confirmation on the situation at hand. "He said, 'Santa is not real. It's just your parents who put all that junk for you under the tree.' Is he right, Mom?"

Jacey giggled again. "Jacey!" their father scolded, and she cleared her throat first before stopping.

"Yes," her mother declared. "He is right."

Jennifer swallowed hard and the world around her felt fuzzy—like being trapped inside a threaded cocoon. "He *is*?" she squeaked, the desperation in her voice hollow and grim.

"Santa doesn't come to your home if you don't believe in Him. Ryan probably stopped believing, and now his parents have to give him all his presents. So, technically, he's kinda right. But if you believe in Him and you're a good girl all year, Santa knows where to find you and He will bring you whatever your heart desires."

"Within reason," her father butted in.

Her mother smiled and pulled back her arms. "Yes, within reason," she continued. "Have you been a good girl, Jennifer?"

Jennifer's face lit up, and she wildly nodded her head.

Her mother smiled. "Then I don't think you have anything to worry about."

"Yeah, but you never know! You could get coal in your stocking from the Coal Elf, ya know. She's the crazy elf! She'll give you coal if you just look at Mom the wrong way!" Jacey teased and giggled again.

Jennifer bit her lower lip and tensed up. Her mother shook her head and said, "Don't pay her any mind. She's just being silly."

Jennifer breathed out heavily and relaxed.

The next few days were pure torture. Jennifer's home was all abuzz with preparations for Christmas Eve and Christmas Day: cookie baking, food making, setting up the guest room for Aunt Jill and Uncle Mark, gift wrapping, and card writing. The anxiety bubbled up inside of Jennifer so much that she thought she would burst. Even at the first sight of presents under the tree, she couldn't wait until she could dive right in and tear across the glittery paper to reveal her treasures beneath.

Christmas Eve was a nightmare. It seemed as if her entire family had gathered in her home with their loud stories and trays upon trays of food with names she couldn't pronounce. Aunts, uncles, grandparents, cousins, and even friends congregated in every nook and cranny of her parents' home making her feel anxious and small and trapped. *Here's my cocoon, again…* The night dragged on and on. It started with appetizers and Uncle Mark's disgusting stories of working in the ER. Then the grown-ups washed dishes while Grandpa Mac smoked his pipe. Then they sat down to eat dinner while Aunt Jill complained about her job as a Vice Principal. She used big words that went over Jennifer's head. Then the grown-ups had to wash more dishes while Grandma Tessie fell and gave all the adults a heart attack. Then all the children had to sit around and wait for the adults to finish their coffee and cake. Grandpa Mac smoked another pipe before they could begin opening presents from each other.

Torture. Anxiety. Sweaty palms of anticipation.

Amid the happiness, and family-time, and gift-giving, and laughter, Jennifer had only one thing in mind — *Santa Claus*. And because of that, a night that would have normally been a lot of fun with her sister and cousins ended up being unbearable.

But it wasn't until the family left that the real torment set in. This was the worst time.

"Santa will know if you're not asleep, and He doesn't come to houses where the kids are awake," her mother warned as she tucked Jennifer into bed. "Make sure you close your eyes and try your hardest to get some rest."

"But what if I have to go to the bathroom?" Jennifer said in fear.

"Then call for someone to get you. They'll make sure the coast is clear."

"But what if I get coal in my stocking?" Jacey giggled.

"I'm sure that's not going to happen, Jenny."

Jennifer still wasn't convinced. "What if I can't fall asleep?"

Jacey huffed and shifted restlessly under her covers in the neighboring bed.

"Just go to sleep, Jen!" she whined.

"Come on, Jace," their mother pleaded, "you know how it is." She ran her hand across Jennifer's forehead. "You'll be fine. Just keep your eyes closed, keep your good thoughts flowing, and you'll eventually fall asleep. You've been so good this year. Daddy and I are so proud of you."

Jennifer smiled and her mother kissed her forehead and left the room.

Try as she might, she just couldn't get her mind to calm down. Jacey had fallen asleep as soon as her head hit the pillow. *How can she do it?* Jennifer thought. *How can she fall asleep so fast?*

She tried shifting her position in bed in order to get comfortable, but that didn't help much. She tried singing songs in her head to take her mind off her anticipation, but that didn't work either. She even tried counting sheep, but the sheep morphed into reindeer pulling Santa's famous sleigh, and that got her even more anxious.

"I know I've been good this year, I know I've been good…" she whispered to herself over and over as if in prayer. But her agonizing brain took her to other places. To darker places. "What if Ryan *is* right? What if there really is no such thing as Santa Claus?" To say the words out loud scared her more than the clown-monster in her closet.

The wind outside picked up and violently beat against the house. The initial howling sound made her jump at first. Curious, she sat up and leaned over to the window next to her bed. With her middle and forefinger, she opened up two slats of her vertical blinds and stared out at the gray night. She scanned the horizon for any signs of His greatness—maybe a glitter trail of His sleigh, or a silhouette against the streetlights. Her heart beat fast with anticipation, and hope, and desire to see something…anything that would prove Ryan Black wrong and end Jacey's incessant giggling.

And then, in the distance, right above the crest of the tree-lined street she saw something.

It.

A flash. A dash. A streak across the night sky that was too thick to be a shooting star and lingered too long to be a trick of her own imagination. Grandma Tessie had told her sometimes angels fell from the heavens to help people on earth, but this was no angel. This could only be one thing—*Santa Claus!*

She pulled back her hand from the blinds and quickly covered herself up in her blankets. She closed her eyes tightly, in fear that *He* had seen *her* watching Him and would punish her by passing over her house. "I've been a good girl this year… I've been a good girl this year…" she repeated to herself until she finally fell asleep.

The sun had barely peaked its head over their side of the world when Jennifer and Jacey shot out of bed and ran down the hall to wake up their parents. Christmas morning was upon them, and the excitement was electric all through the house. Their mother moaned as she wearily kicked her legs from underneath the covers and slid off the side of her bed.

"Get up! Get up!" Jennifer squealed as she shook her father's legs. "What time is it?" their father grumbled.

"Girls, go downstairs," their mother commanded, "but don't open anything until your father and I get there."

Jennifer and Jacey raced out of their parents' room and flew down the stairs. Before them was a glorious sight of mountains of presents wrapped neatly in glittery paper. Jennifer jumped up and down with excitement as she took in the wonder and beauty of this Christmas morning.

I was a good girl; I was a good girl… she thought over and over as she impatiently waited for her parents to make their way to the room.

Once her parents arrived, it was on! Jennifer and Jacey happily tore through their presents like uncontrollable savages as Mom and Dad looked on. Dolls, clothes, clothes for her dolls, video games, reading books, coloring books, art kits, board games… it went on and on in a never-ending frenzy of gifts. Jennifer didn't even mind the new packages of underwear as long as it was something to open up! It was thrilling and sent a rush down her seven-year-old spine.

"Oh, thank you, Santa!" Jennifer exclaimed as she clutched her new fashion doll—the one with the curly blue and pink hair and the cut off shorts.

When the gifts were just about finished, her father stood up in the sea of torn wrapping paper. "There's one more thing," he announced with a smile.

"Stockings!" Jacey screeched as if she had forgotten the family ritual of saving their stockings for last.

The stockings were always so much fun. Her mother would hang them with brass hooks right next to the fireplace, and Santa would always leave the cutest little chachkies in them—lip-gloss, candy coins, gift cards to their favorite fast-food restaurants, jewelry. They always saved the stockings for last because it was a nice way to wrap up the craziness of the morning.

Dad unhooked the stockings and handed the one that said "Jacey" to Jennifer and the one that said "Jenny" to Jacey. The girls laughed and said, "Daaaaaaddddd!" with a unison eyeroll before passing the correct stocking to each other.

Dad laughed. Mom laughed. The girls laughed.

As Jennifer reached her hand up to the mouth of her stocking, she noticed a slight black, ashy smudge on her fingertip. She thought nothing of it and proceeded to stick her hand into the depths of the sock. Her face twisted when she felt something hard at the bottom.

Her mother gave her a puzzled look. "What's wrong, sweetie?"

Jennifer pulled out her hand to reveal an ash covered palm. Jacey's face fell in horror, as she too experienced the same black soot hand.

"Mom?" Jacey asked in terror.

"What's the matter? What's going on?" their mother said with heightened concern. She quickly looked over at their father who had a look of horror in his eyes. "Hun?" she asked him, bewildered. "Did you…?"

Her father shook his head in silence.

Jacey plunged her hand back into her stocking, digging around for something, anything. "There's a note! I got a note!" She pulled out her blackened hand, clutching an ashy scroll. She untied the black ribbon and unfurled the paper. Jennifer quickly put her hand back into her stocking to see if she, too, had a note. She moved her fingers against the hard, ashy substance, and sure enough, there was a little scroll for her as well.

"I got one, too," Jennifer announced.

"Well, what do they say?" their mother pried.

Jacey looked at Jennifer, tears starting to form in her eyes. "You first," she commanded, and Jennifer untied her note.

Jennifer swallowed hard, trying to dissolve the tight lump in her throat. "'Dear Jennifer,'" she finally squeaked out. "'I understand that you tried to be good this year, but you used your sister's hairspray and never replaced it, and you laughed at a classmate when he fell in the snow. Please be better next year. Sincerely, Ember, The Coal Elf.'"

There was a collective gasp in the living room. Jennifer nearly choked on the words she read. How could this be? They *saw*? They *knew*? How could this be happening? She actually had gotten *coal* in her *stocking*?

Her mother motioned for Jacey to read hers, but Jacey clutched it to her chest. "No!" she yelled. "I'm not reading this!"

Her mother extended her hand. "Give it here then!"

Jacey quieted down and reluctantly handed the scroll over.

"'Dear Jacey,'" Mom began to read, "'Your name has been grayed in the Book for some time now. Please don't ruin the day for others. There is still good, and hope, and the *spirit* in this world. Help keep it alive.'"

A deep silence hung heavy in the room—a silence that seemed to last forever.

Finally, their father stood up and wiped his dirty hands along his pajama pants. "Well," he huffed. "At least we know one thing for sure."

Mother, Jennifer, and Jacey all tilted their heads to hear Father's explanation.

"That Ryan kid is totally wrong!"

CHAPTER TWO

Ember always enjoyed the view of the world beneath her whenever she rode in her sleigh or atop her reindeer, Asche. There was a calm serenity in the thin air that made her swoon and feel exhilarated. It was almost like taking a long, deep draught of the finest grulish, and feeling its dizzying effects right before sleep stretched out her loving arms, wrapped her up nice and tight, and carried her off to slumber. Riding above the world gave her a terribly similar sensation—as if there was true magic coursing through her veins.

She poked her head over the side of her sleigh and gazed at the scene below her. A gray fog blanketed the top of the dome, and the bright stars speckled the inky black sky. But, somehow, something looked different. Off. New. Woven throughout the gray haze was a subtle glow pulsating and growing, almost like a shift in consciousness awakening on the horizon.

Could it be? Could my plan be working? she thought.

She patted an empty coal sack next to her on the bench of her sleigh and a small sensation of sadness sprung up in the pit of her stomach. Every child, everywhere, would wake up on the Big Day to a stocking-full of coal and a note about their specific transgressions. Ember's heart sank for all the Brittanys, and Tylers, and Taylors, and Jennifers of the world who may or may not have truly deserved it. She imagined their little hearts breaking as they reached into their stockings only to pull forth a handful of soot. Coal was reserved for the naughtiest of naughties, the Sturds of the human world, if you will. But now, to quote Sturd, in these *dire* times, in order to stop the names from being blackened in the Book, in order to save the entire elven race from vanishing from existence, the human world needed a wake-up call.

How many human hearts would be crushed at dawn?

Most.

But how many fires would that coal re-ignite in those hearts?

All.

If there was one thing Ember knew best, it was that a little disappointment in life never killed anybody!

She inhaled and closed her eyes, absorbing every second of the calm.

The calm before the storm.

"We did good tonight!" she called to Asche and Boptail, the two Shadow-Deer who had escorted her throughout the human world that evening.

Both loyal beasts neighed and grunted in agreement. Ember smiled and tugged at the reins. "Not done, yet" she yelled. The deer stiffened against her pulling. "One more stop to make before we can rest."

Asche shimmied his thick head side to side like a boxer getting ready for a fight.

Boptail's tail flittered up and down in anticipation. The two picked up the pace and sped off against the black night sky, and the stars whizzed by in a fast motion tail-light haze. Ember tightened her grip on the reins and planted her feet firmly on the sleigh floor.

"*Alfreight onla Lapis Hall!*" she screeched in Elvish, and the deer dipped below the clouds on their final descent.

Lapis Hall: The home of the Claus, a castle shrouded in magic on the highest mountain in Norland, unseen to the naked elf-eye. Only a select few had the privilege of approaching its gates and entering inside. And even then, it was said that once an elf leaves the domain, they are stripped of the memory of how they got there. Ember had an advantage tonight—she had not one, but two Shadow-Deer who not only understood Elvish, but who had an inherent ability to navigate the most mystical, magical, and most secret avenues of the land. The castle was surrounded by blueice archways that sparkled from within—the essence of the ice glowed, creating natural lit pathways to the blue iron doors of the castle. Boptail and Asche slid up to the doors—the blueice path unfamiliar beneath their hooves. Ember hadn't even hopped out of the sleigh when the iron doors flung open, and a frantic elf raced out of the castle.

"What are you doing here?" she shouted in panic. "You are absolutely forbidden to be here!"

It was Senara Calix, Madame Claus's trusted assistant.

Ember slid out of the sleigh, patted Asche on the nuzzle as if to command him to stay put and approached the hysterical elf. "I'm here to see the Boss," she declared as she adjusted the black cap on her head.

Senara's eyes widened. Her black eyes jutted out like two pieces of coal freshly mined from the cavern. *I've had enough coal for one night*, Ember thought as she studied Senara's face.

"Ember!" Senara pleaded. "You must leave! Right now! Go back home this instant!"

Ember stopped in her tracks and hunched her shoulders forward. "Listen, Senara, it's been a very long night. Don't give me any static, okay? Let me in to talk to the Big Guy, and I'll be on my way."

Senara exhaled, and a thick white puff of smoke circled around her face. "Nope. I can't let you in. You need to leave."

Ember rolled her eyes. "Well, that's not going to happen. I can stand out here all night if I have to."

Senara's face twitched as her arms crossed in front of her chest and grasped her shoulders.

Norland was cold this time of year. Lapis Hall, the home of the Claus, was even colder. Ember knew Senara wouldn't be able to guard the door all night; she knew Senara wouldn't be able to meet her challenge. Ember smirked as Senara shifted her weight from side to side, bravely keeping her stance and bravely taking on the frigid blast of nighttime wind. It was only a matter of time before she broke.

Suddenly, a tall figure materialized at the open door and called, "Senara! What's going on?" It was Docena. Madame Claus. Her black silhouette sharply outlined by the candlelight from within the hall.

Senara spun around and ran to her. "Madame! I'm so sorry, but Ember…"

"Ember?" Docena repeated in disbelief. "Ember? What is she…"

"She's demanded to see the Claus, Madame. She said she won't leave until she does."

Docena craned her neck over Senara's head to catch Ember's gaze. With part of Senara's body blocking the light, Ember could see Madame Claus was dressed only in a red silky night gown. Her white hair tumbled over her shoulders in snowy waves nearly touching the floor—a stark contrast from the no-nonsense business attire and tightly bunned coiffure she normally wore. Ember's smile and wave was first met with Mrs. Claus's initial eye roll, and then her hesitant hand motion to come in.

"Good evening, Madame!" Ember said cheerily as she walked over the castle's threshold and into the front hallway.

Senara closed the heavy doors behind them, and Docena's eyes narrowed, glaring hard at Ember. "That'll be all, Senara," she said, holding her stare on the Coal Elf.

"But Madame…" Senara stuttered.

"It's okay, dear. Go to your room and warm up. You'll freeze to death if you don't. Thank you. I can take it from here." Senara nodded fervently and click-clacked her way through the icy hallways.

Docena turned her attention back to Ember. "Poor girl. She can't stand the cold. I set up her chambers on the warm side of the palace, but she still needs to wear layers upon layers," she chuckled. "I find most of my attendants have a low tolerance for the cold." She ran her long fingers down her pale-skinned arm, and Ember noticed the dark purple veins pressed closely to Docena's skin gave her a violet skin tone, as if there was pure ice coursing through her.

There's magic in those veins, Ember thought.

"Not cold, child?" Docena asked curiously.

Ember jammed her ash covered hands deep into her pockets and looked down at her attire—she had on her filthy black jumpsuit, and the hat given to her by Tannen's wife Holly on top of her head. That was it. That was all she needed. "Um, I guess not," she stammered, taken off guard. "It could be that I've been working double time tonight and my blood is pumping extra hard. I mean, it's chilly, but not any more than I'm used to." Yes, the extra work could explain her indifference to the frigid temperatures surrounding the ice structure of Lapis Hall, but come to think of it, the cold never bothered Ember much at *any* time in her life. She remembered playing in the snow as an elfling with little more on than a tunic! In fact, there was something about the splendor of Lapis Hall that made her remember a very particular time in her elflinghood…

A time when the snow drifted down slowly from the heavy white clouds.

Each paper-thin flake had felt like a soft icy kiss caressing the tips of her pointed ears. She stuck out her tongue and outstretched her arms, embracing the frigid air and onset of a mid-March North Pole snowstorm. Coatless, hatless, gloveless. It didn't matter, for there was an anticipation burning in the pit of her stomach like the spark of a wildfire ready to grow and consume. An ember. Like her name. *Ember.* This frantic feeling of flame from within made her stir with jitters and little kid excitement, like that feeling she got every Big Night when the Boss would make His grand ride across the sky delivering presents and treats to the good kids in the world. That feeling made her skin hot to the touch, completely unaware of the sub-zero degree weather in which she so mindlessly played. Nothing could ruin that day. Not the impending storm, nor her Nanny Elf hollering from the second-floor window for her to bundle up. That day was special. That day was going to change the rest of her life—the day of her ninth elfyear birthday.

"Emmy!" Nanny Carole had called, yet again. "Emmy! You get in this house right now before you catch your death! Didn't you hear your father calling for you?"

Ember had tilted her head back once again to meet the descending snow with an opened mouth. "Two more minutes!"

"No, no, no!" Carole replied. "Your mother will have a fit if you get sick! And don't you go expecting me to take care of you when you do. Now git, you ornery girl!"

Ember's tiny shoulders slouched in defeat, and she exhaled loudly. Of course, her daydreams would have to be interrupted by the agitated voice of her caregiver.

"Stop your huffing and march your elfling self in here right now!" Carole's voice echoed across the courtyard.

"Okay, okay," Ember muttered as she dejectedly made her way back to her family's sprawling manor in Tir-La Treals.

Nanny Carole was waiting at the back door with a plush pink bathrobe in hand. She had held it wide open, and when Ember had stepped over the threshold of the back patio door, Carole engulfed her with the oversized garment.

Ember turned up her nose. "I don't need this. It's too hot!"

"Oh, you quit your complaining, Emmy! Your poor parents are as nervous as chinchis sitting in that there parlor, and you're outside all wild-child dancing in the snow without a care in the world."

Ember's face twisted. "Nervous? Nervous about what?" What did her parents have to be nervous about? This was her special day! Her nineth elfyear birthday! The day that she was going to start preparing the rest of her elflife!

Carole huffed in disbelief. "You can't be serious, child. Today is one of the most important days of your life!"

True, it was. And of course, Ember was feeling the tell-tale symptoms of excitement, but nervousness? That wasn't quite the word for it. Anticipation? Yes. But nervousness? That would indicate some sort of fear, and fear was the last thing that she had racing through her mind. Life for Ember had been good.

Charmed.

She had wanted for nothing. Had no worries or doubts or fears. She had been certain that the news from the Council would be nothing but wonderful, and it perplexed her that her parents had been a bit unhinged by the day's major announcement.

Ember had tugged the bathrobe tightly at the waist and spun around the kitchen floor. Carole shook her head side to side and made a *tsk tsk* sound with her tongue. "Wild-child," she remarked under her breath and under a small smile. "You'll certainly be the one who retires me, now won't you?"

Ember had giggled gaily as she went whirling past Carole and nearly collided with the sharp metal edge of the wood burning stove. Carole gasped as she instinctively stretched her arm out to block Ember's near-miss crash. "I'm okay!" Ember had said with slight defiance. "You can't protect me forever, you know!"

Carole sighed deeply and gave Ember a tight squeeze. "Can't protect you forever, this is true," she began, "but I have one more year left to do my best."

"Ember Autumn Skye!" her father had roared from within the living room.

Ember heard the urgency in his voice, and she stiffened a little. She clutched tightly on to Nanny Carole's apron as Carole lovingly stroked Ember's hair and whispered words of comfort. Ember scampered into the living room where the rest of her family had been gathered.

The light from the eager sun had been trying to punch its way through the white-cloud sky. It cast eerie shadows in the room—*scary* shadows across the floor and furniture. Mother and Father had looked like elongated ghostly figures hovering sternly over the candy cane striped sofa. Ember's older sister, Ginger, had been sprawled out on the floor—her tummy resting comfortably against the fluffy rug while the heels of her bare feet rhythmically tapped against her rear end. Father had held the letter from the Council in his chubby hands and motioned for her to sit next to him on the candy cane striped couch…

"So," Docena said breaking Ember from her memory, "what brings you here, to my home, on the busiest, most important night in the entire Elven Realm?" The sarcasm was thick in her voice.

Ember balled her fists inside her pockets, readying them for her verbal altercation, holding herself steadfast in preparation for what was to come. "While seeing you is always a pleasure, Madame, tonight I'm here to see your husband."

Docena arched her throat and gave a forced laugh. There was nothing funny about the situation at hand; the both of them knew that all too well. "Oh, my!" she said in mock surprise. "That is *some* request, child."

Ember inhaled deeply through her nostrils, her anger rising at Madame Claus's obvious derision. "Yes, I know," she said calmly, composing herself. "I am well aware that it is a very large request—a very *unorthodox* request. But I'm afraid that this can't wait, and…"

"The Boss needs his rest," Docena interrupted. "He will have His grulish and mustn't be disturbed for a fortnight. That is the way. You know this. And as you know, any formal requests for audience with the Claus must be presented to the Council in writing, so if there isn't anything else I will gladly escort you…" Docena motioned her armed toward the front doors.

Ember looked over her shoulder at the doors behind her but did not budge. She looked back at Docena and crinkled her nose in defiance. "No," she said casually. "I don't think so. I need to talk to the Boss. Tonight."

Docena smiled and stepped forward. She wrapped her arm around Ember's shoulder, sending an icy chill throughout her body, even through the thickness of her burlap jumpsuit. Ember shivered from her touch.

"This simply can't happen," Docena said in a loving way. "He's tired. He needs His rest. And so do you. You've had a busy night, too. You need at least a week for down time. Take my advice— go home, drink some of the finest grulish you can get your hands on, and sleep until you can't sleep anymore. It'll do you good. Trust me, I've been around the Claus for an extremely long time, and He's always His best and sharpest and wittiest and most productive right after His two-week sabbatical." She smiled and began waltzing Ember closer to the front door.

Ember stopped in her tracks and wriggled from under Docena's arctic grip. She gave a small chuckle. She knew it was a dead end with Mrs. Claus, so she needed to change her game plan. Time for a full-blown confession. Now or never. "I suppose you're right, Madame," Ember said, returning the sarcasm. "Just look at me!" and she gestured her hands, motioning them up and down the front of her body. "I'm a filthy mess! Filthy! Awful! Tired, too. Oh, so very, very tired!"

She stretched her arms high above her head and feigned a yawn. Ember knew Docena was no idiot, and that she would see right through the sarcastic charade.

Docena crossed her arms in front of her chest. "Speak true, child," she said, narrowing her eyes.

Ember shrugged her shoulders. "I've just been *busy*."

"Yes, I know. Go on. What exactly does that mean, girl?"

Ember swallowed hard. The knot in her throat almost took her voice away. She knew that this confession was probably the only thing that would allow her to come face to face with the Claus. She paused—hesitated for a split second, and for the other half of that second, mustered up her courage to say, "They all got coal, ya know. All of them. The whole lot of those kids."

Docena's face twisted to the side. "Excuse me?" she asked.

"All of them. Ya know. Like, the whole world. Every kid. I gave them coal."

Docena's chest rose out in front of her as she breathed deeply. She shut her eyes and quickly shook her head side to side. "Are you telling me that you delivered coal to every child in the world? Bad *and* good?"

"Mmm hmm," Ember said.

Docena's hands shot up to her head, and she gathered her hair away from her face in exasperation. "What?" she screamed, her voice echoing throughout the palace. "What did you do, Ember?

You can't be serious!" Unhinged, she paced back and forth across the ice floor with anxious strides.

Ember took a step back, scared of what Madame Claus's rage might bring out, scared of what Madame Claus was capable of. "I had to!" she argued in her defense. "Something *had* to be done! Those kids needed to know what was up! The blackened names in the Book were getting out of control and…and, well… I think it worked! There was a different kind of energy in the air. You just wait! When the reports come out tomorrow, when you get word from the Council members at Headquarters, I will almost guarantee that the Book will have calmed down, and that the Blackened names will have stopped. I'd be even willing to bet that some of those grayed names go colorful again, and…"

Docena stopped in her tracks. "That was not for you to decide! You went above the Council, above the Law, above the Claus! How dare you think that you matter enough to go out on your own!"

The blood in Ember's veins got hot and pulsated through her body. "Well, it didn't seem like your husband was doing anything about it!" she spat.

A long finger glided up and into Ember's face. "Watch your tongue! My husband, your *Boss*, is not a well elf. He's lucky He was able to make it out of His chambers to ride tonight. Could you imagine if that were to happen? And here you are—belligerent, obstinate, wishing to disturb an old elf on the precipice of convergence with the Mists. How dare you! How dare you think…" Docena's voice trailed as tears rose to her eyes.

Ember hung her head low, absorbing the reality of Docena's words. She felt sorry that Docena would soon be losing the man she loved so dearly. "I'm sorry," she said. "Yes, I am belligerent, and obstinate, and ornery, and all those other words you and the others have said about me for all these years. I am all those things only because I am desperate. I am sad for the Boss. I feel very bad that He is in the twilight of His years, but He has completely given up! The elves all feel it—Above and Below!"

Docena waved her hand in the air as if to silence Ember. "There are still rules, young lady. Rules that we have followed for many a century. The Council will want to see you once they find out about what you've done tonight. You might face banishment, or even worse. You, and everyone else who helped you in your plot."

Think again, lady! That's not happening. 'Almond tall struthers' before I let that happen!

"You do know The Council is corrupt, right? I don't understand why you refuse to see that!"

Docena wiped her tear-stained cheek and inhaled. "It doesn't matter what I see or don't see."

Ember balled up her fists again as the rage inside her grew. Confusion and frustration ate away at her, and she did everything in her power to remain calm and composed. "I don't understand. You and the Claus are above the Council, are you not?"

"Yes. And no. You see, child, the ancient elves long ago created this system of checks and balances in service to The Mists of the North. The Claus was instated as the figurehead, or rather, the Hand of the Mists. The Council was created as a support system for the Claus. So yes, while in the hierarchy of power, the Claus is technically Law, it's the Council who dominates the operation."

"So, it's totally okay for the Council to give Sturd free reign to come and go as he pleases, to create his own agenda of chaos and…"

"As his elfwife, you were supposed to get him under control."

The silence in the frozen foyer filled the space between Docena and Ember with a sharp buzzing noise. The sound rang in Ember's mind like a bomb had been detonated right next to her head. She walked toward the door and opened it. A gush of pure Norland wind raced passed her, nearly blowing her cap off her head. "That's not my job," she said looking at her boots. "It was never my job to be your pawn. Whatever sick game you're playing with the Council, leave me out of it." She turned her head and faced Madame Claus. Tears ran down Madame Claus's face, but Ember had no more sympathy for her. "Instead of worrying about proper coal deliveries and ancient decrees, maybe you and the Boss should be worried about your people—ya know, the Elven race! How about the fact that I quite possibly stopped the names from being blackened in the Book. How about a 'Thanks Ember, whoo-hoo!' Remember that unfortunate Coal-less Night disaster? Yeah. I kinda fixed that, ya know. Or how about this one—the groups of twins that are currently being held captive by Sturd and his weirdo army known as The Brotherhood waiting for Claus-knows-what to happen to them. Groups of twins who are supposed to be candidates, replacements, for the Boss. What about all that?"

Docena had no words. She stared straight ahead at Ember.

"Let me ask you one thing. My Life Job. My Assignment in the Mines. Did you have anything to do with that?"

"No," Docena answered quickly and quietly.

"Oh, so it was the Council then?"

Docena seemed as if she was deep in memory. "No," she said in a faraway voice. "The Claus and your father…" her voice trailed.

"My father?" Ember shouted. "What do you mean, my father?"

Docena snapped back into the present and waved her hands in the air. "You need to go, Ember. This has been quite enough for one night!" She swiftly glided over to Ember and ushered her closer to the door.

Exasperated, Ember's shoulders fell forward in defeat. It was no use, and she could longer deny her own fatigue. "Tell your husband, the great and powerful Claus, that I'll come back to talk to Him after His fortnight siesta." And with that, Ember slammed the blue iron doors behind her.

CHAPTER THREE

The old abbey was nestled deep in a clearing of evergreen trees in West Bank in an area known as Mon Valley. Mon Valley was the home to many woodland creatures of the North Pole, and no elf resided in the center of its natural beauty and wonder.

Surrounded by overgrown brush and hidden from the comings and goings that took place in the city on a daily basis, the house of worship, The Mon Valley Abbey, had once been frequented by many elves who came to the structure and prayed to the Mon—*The Mists of the North*. All modern-time elves believed in the existence of the Mists, but there were some who held on to the old ways of ancient Elven society when the Mists of the North were revered and feared—the highest of the high in their spiritual culture.

Elves made sacrifices to the Mists to appease them, prayed to them constantly, begged for their mercy and forgiveness when they sinned, and conducted their lives in accordance with their laws. Over time, the old ways went to the wayside, and the Mists of the North became things of fairy tales and children's songs. But there were some who still believed. Some who held on fervently to the old ways. The devout elves built the abbey out of the evergreen trees and continued with their traditions—away from the modernized clans who might have shunned them or laughed at them.

However, even with good intentions, the elves were not true Builders, and when the plague of Nessie Sickness made its way to West Bank, the rickety church had been abandoned by its parishioners. This allowed the already unstable structure to grow weary and hollow. A snowstorm the next winter caused the roof to partially collapse, and when the Council had announced its plans for reconstruction, the once sacred place had taken a spot so far down their list it had been forgotten. Out of sight, out of mind. But Sturd knew. Sturd knew all about the reconstruction plans for every inch of the North Pole. His job as Field Data Collector gave him access to all that information.

So, it was here, in this dilapidated abbey, that he instructed the Brotherhood to round up all the twin-elves at the Pole.

Out of sight. Out of mind.

Sturd lurked in the shadows just outside the back of the church and crouched down low. The tips of his pointed ears crept up slightly above the sill of a broken window, but he knew the frantic elves inside wouldn't even notice he was there watching and listening to their conversations. The wind blasted in his face, taking his breath away with a desperate gasp for air. *That's what it must feel like to be strangled,* he mused as he covered his mouth with his ferret-like hands and inhaled the sweet smell of gasoline. He smiled to himself, proud that his plan was coming to fruition—unfurling in front of his eyes like a glorious present slowly revealing itself from its colorful wrappings.

Sim Nim'sim rounded the corner and joined Sturd in his huddled position underneath the window.

"We good?" Sturd asked.

Sim nodded; his clipboard tucked firmly under his arm.

Inside the abbey, the twins were restless amidst the chaos and confusion. Nim, Sim's brother, and Bulder Dwin'nae, *Sturd's* brother, were inside the church handing out blankets and passing around a tray of cookies trying to keep the peace. When the murmur of the masses began to swell, Nim stood up in the center of the group and held his hands up high. "It'll be okay!" he declared. "This is for your safety!"

"Yes, you've all said that! But why are we here? Why won't anyone tell us anything?" an elf called out in frustration.

A buzzing and humming spread throughout the church, and Nim raised his hand high again to get their attention. "There are Enforcer Elves combing the streets of East and West Bank tonight.

They are trying to find the elf who so heinously murdered the Book Keepers—Orthor and Ogden Castleberry, and the Reindeer Judges—Roderick and Gorlick Twist."

The crowd collectively gasped:

"*Oh, my Claus!*"

"*How could this be?*"

"*What is going on?*"

"*I still don't understand?*"

Bulder's small voice spoke out, "It's okay, really, it'll be okay," but he was unconvincing, and the crowd's cries got louder than before.

A middle-aged male elf stood up and took a step toward Nim. "What does this have to do with my brother and me? Why are we in danger?" He motioned to the crowd. "Why are Brynlea and Rylea Gale here? What danger could these poor little elflings be in? They never did anything to anyone!"

The crowd buzzed again:

"*Yeah!*"

"*Why won't you tell us?*"

"*Let us go home!*"

"*What did we ever do wrong?*"

"Brothers! Sisters!" Nim raised his voice. "We wanted to make sure that every twin was accounted for before we got into all that."

Outside, Sturd nudged Sim on the arm. "Are they? Are all the twins accounted for?"

Sim nodded.

"My nephews? The Dwin'nae boys? They were found?"

Sim looked down at the clipboard in his hand and flipped the pages over a few times. "Uh… yeah…," he fumbled a little. "Sid checked them in a few hours ago. Says here they were picked up in West Bank."

Sturd snatched the clipboard away from Sim in disbelief. "Give me that!" he growled. "I don't trust any of your cronies!" He feverishly scanned the papers. And yes, sure enough, there were check marks and notations next to the names Bambam and Juju Dwin'nae. "Hmmm," he huffed, still not trusting the paper, "I need to see them for myself!"

"Sturd!" Sim exclaimed with fear. "You can't go in there!"

Sturd lowered his head and peered at Sim with his blood-red eyes. "You can't be serious," he muttered and arched his back up higher so he could get a glimpse of the inside of the church undetected. Sim followed suit and scanned the congregation.

"See? There they are!" Sim whispered and pointed out the backs of two heads of carrot-capped curls sitting cross-legged on the wooden floor. The twins huddled together, encased in a brown burlap blanket. With the candlelight inside of the church giving off wild shadows and their heads side by side so close, it was hard to tell where one began and the other ended.

Sturd gave a quick nod. It was confirmation enough. "What about the reindeer trainer?"

Sim shrugged and lowered his head. "Nowhere to be found."

"Whatever. It doesn't matter now, I guess. I don't fathom she would have been considered a candidate anyway because of her dead sister and all." Sturd ducked back down and continued listening to what Nim was saying inside.

"So, yes… you all know that being a twin at the Pole is very special and very rare."

"Yes!" Bulder tried desperately to interject. "Look around you. This is not a large group by any means."

"Large enough!" an angry elf shot back, silencing the timid Bulder.

"I know, I know," Nim coaxed. "Listen, by a show of hands, how many of you can speak Elvish?"

Most of the elves raised their hands. Little Brynlea and Rylea Gale and a few of the other elfling pairs did not.

"According to an ancient text called the *Dublix Santarae*, once all living twinsets in any one particular generation are granted the gift of Elvish, they are then considered *candidates*, and it will be time to choose a new Claus."

"A new Claus?"

"No! How can this be?"

"Does this mean that…?"

Another concerned voice spoke up, "So, are you saying that someone doesn't want a new Claus to be chosen? Is that what this is about?

Someone is killing off the twins so there can't be a new Claus?"

"That is the theory we are working under," Nim confirmed.

A thunderous cry rang out:

"I bet it's the Boss Himself!"

"That lazy old geezer probably doesn't want anyone else to take His place!"

"I want to go home!"

Sturd chuckled. "They sure have spirit, don't they?" he said jokingly to Sim.

Sim gave a little snigger in return. "Yeah," his voice trailed a bit. "Maybe they're right, though. Maybe this truly is the Boss's intent?"

Sturd closed his eyes and inhaled a deep and irritated breath. *Stupid fool,* he thought, *if you only knew the real truth!* He pursed his lips and gathered some composure. "Ya know, Sim, that thought hadn't ever occurred to me," he said with an air of mock surprise.

Sim smiled a soft grin in spite of himself, and Sturd nearly vomited at the thought of Sim's stupidity.

"Brothers! Sisters!" Nim's voice once again elevated to bring order in the church. "That is where we, the Brotherhood, come in to help. We are here to protect you and the interests of our race. For the last two years, we elves have faced many trials and tribulations, and the road ahead is still not paved. We are on the verge of a new era here at the Pole! We elves deserve a bigger voice, and a bigger say in how we live out our days.

We demand our freedom from the oppressions of our rulers. We work so hard at whatever job they *tell* us to do, but what about what we *want* to do? How is that fair? Aren't we entitled to live how we see fit?"

The crowd applauded. Outside, Sim smiled at his brother's rousing speech.

Nim continued. "What you are witnessing now, my friends, is a new dawn, a new day. Yes, my brother and I started out as disgruntled coal elves, and during a very introspective time in our lives, we came to realize that our frustrations are the frustrations of elves everywhere. We started the Brotherhood to unite the voices of those Below with the voices of those Above. We will unite all Brothers *and* Sisters, and create a Pole that we can be happy with. A Pole that we can all be proud of. Together! When this is all said and done, we hope you will join us on our crusade for a stronger, more peaceful existence!"

The crowd was wild with cheers and applause:

"Thank you!"

"Bless you!"

"We stand with the Brotherhood!"

Sturd licked his lips in anticipation. "He's good."

Sim smiled. "Yeah, he was always good in front of a crowd."

"It's such a shame to have to see him go."

Sim stood up at attention. "Huh?"

Sturd stood up as well, straightened out his back, and let the popping noises of his body fill his ears for a second. He reached into his pocket and handed Sim a pack of matches. Sim's eyes grew wide with both terror and confusion, as if his brain was unable to process Sturd's command.

"Light it up," Sturd said nonchalantly.

"What? Huh? I… I… I don't…" Sim stammered.

The night wind howled and whipped in between them. Sim lost his balance for a second, and Sturd naturally snickered. "Do I need to draw you a picture on how to…"

"What? Huh?" Sim repeated in disbelief.

Sturd reached out, grabbed Sim's hand, and deposited the matches in his palm. "The. Church," he said. Each word slow and with deep emphasis. "Light. It. Up."

"No!" Sim protested. "I can't! I couldn't! I won't! This… this is insane! My… my brother is in there! He would…"

Sturd put his hand lovingly on Sim's shoulder. "He would be collateral damage. Think of this," he cooed, "my brother and my nephews are all in that abbey. I stand to lose far more than you."

Sim jerked away from Sturd's touch and swatted at his shoulder where the ferret-paw had been. "No! No way! This is crazy! No one has to die!"

Sturd's blood boiled and bubbled. He knew he was taking a gamble by enlisting the aid of this rag-tag group—*The Brotherhood* (whatever *that* was supposed to mean!). But there was no other way, and he knew he would have to remain calm and poised and ramp up the charm. Behind his eyes, all he saw was rage and anger and hatred and *red,* but he was slick enough to understand he was alone in these thoughts and feelings. In order to get what he wanted, he was well aware of the amount of finesse it was going to take. He paused and took a step back to let Sim breathe and absorb what was being asked of him. Sim bent forward and put his head between his knees. He took deep, panicked breaths—one after the other, quickly, frantically.

"It's okay, Sim. You know this is for the greater good." Sturd grimaced as he patted Sim's back to calm him down. "You heard what your brother said. We need a united front on this. If there are no candidates for the next Claus, the entire North Pole playbook has to be re-written. That's hissss-tory!" he hissed.

Sim stood up. A glazed look washed over his face, and he swayed back and forth.

It was as if he were in some kind of trance—the thought of taking control of his life obviously resonating in his brain.

"Do you want to be part of history?" Sturd continued. "For years, you despised being forced to work in the Mines like a slave. For years, you resented never being given an elfwife to have as a companion, or the luxury of a family to fulfill you. If we do this—if *you* do this—you will be re-writing your destiny. I'll be the one in control. And I will need someone by my side. Someone strong." Sim's back stiffened. "Someone wise."

Sim turned to Sturd at attention.

"Someone who's not afraid to make big moves or execute the hard decisions for the greater good."

Sim looked down at the matches in his hand with a pained expression.

"I'll need a right-hand elf. A supreme adviser. And I've had you, Sim Nim'sim, in mind all along. I want you to be my General. My most trusted confidante. I know you can do this. Now burn them all."

Without further coaxing or nudging, Sturd walked off into the thick of the evergreen forest and waited for the sounds and smells of what was to come.

In moments, a heat wave swelled out of the clearing, and an orange glow danced fiercely among the trees. Sturd stopped in his tracks, enticed to watch the glorious blaze behind him. He turned to see the flames from the old abbey stretch high against the dark horizon—so high it was as if they were building their own fiery staircase to the moon. Blended with the sound of the roaring fire was the harsh cacophony of moans and cries and screams of the elves trapped within. The smell of burnt hair and flesh flooded the cold air of the forest like a foul stench wafting offensively on sacred ground. He closed his eyes, inhaled it all, and listened with joy as the rest of the roof tumbled down upon those inside, silencing the cries and allowing the thunderous inferno to dominate the landscape. It couldn't have been more than a few minutes before the timeworn building was completely engulfed in flames.

Soon, Sim came rushing into the forest—screaming, crying, hobbling, stopping every moment or so to lurch forward and vomit.

Sniveling idiot! If you knew how many family members I've…

Sim shouted, "I did it! I did it!" And Sturd wanted desperately to shut him up, to tell him to keep quiet, to punch it into Sim's little pea-brain that *nothing* was *done*, that this *accident* just *happened*.

But he couldn't.

Try as he might, Sturd was paralyzed—frozen still in his place, unable to move a muscle. His vision shot in and out of focus, and the roar of the fire and Sim's incessant screams sounded as if they were miles away, universes away. A dizzying wave descended upon him, and a searing pain took root in the pit of his stomach. Something began clawing its way into his belly, tearing at his insides, opening his soft spots through and through.

I'm being attacked was his only thought as the assault on his paralyzed body continued.

His abdomen was hot and sticky with his own blood; he felt his intestines open like a font and empty out onto his boots and snow. He started to panic—a fever heat so strong that he couldn't even open his mouth to yell. The clawing sensation worked its way from his stomach, up to his throat, into his cheeks, and behind his eyes.

The pressure behind his eyeballs was blinding! If only he could close his eyes, or cry out, or move, or double over in pain! Every fiber of his being separated, danced in front of him, and then reorganized back together like a jigsaw puzzle out of blood and tissue and organs and flesh and…

His head spun, and for a split second he was able to move his eyes. He almost didn't want to look down at himself because he feared he would see a mangled, bloody mess of an elf being tormented and tortured by some unseen, diabolical force with horns and claws and teeth shredding through his flesh. But he knew he had to; he knew he had to make sense of these sudden, torturous feelings. Sim was still blathering on in the background, and Sturd still felt as if he were spinning. He finally managed to slowly tilt his head forward to get a glimpse of his body. And there was nothing—no blood, no entrails, no claws—just Sturd, intact, in his work clothes and coat.

Sturd's eyes closed, and he crumbled to the ground in a heap.

CHAPTER FOUR

"Do you think she's dead?"

"She has to be dead!"

"I know, right? It's the only explanation, and…"

Kyla balled up her hands. Her sharp nails dug into the flesh of her palms. "Ember is *not* dead!" she scolded the twins for the skatey-eighth time. "How many times do I have to tell you two that?"

Bambam and Juju looked at each other wearily. Their gaze was more than a fleeting look. It was just as Ember said—the boys spoke Elvish telepathically, and witnessing it first-hand gave Kyla the creeps. "What are you boys doing? What are you saying to each other?"

They both smirked—Bambam from the right corner of his mouth, Juju from the left—and continued to stare each other down. "I'm hungry," Bambam whined.

"I'm thirsty," Juju said.

"I want to go home," Bambam moaned.

"I think Ember forgot about us," Juju said.

"Maybe she died," Bambam chuckled.

Kyla rolled her eyes. "You know she said she would come back for us as soon as it was safe. She has a lot to take care of, but she certainly didn't forget about us, and she certainly didn't die. Remember what she told us—*she's* in trouble, but *we're* in danger, so it's important that we sit tight as long as we can. We've only been down here for a little bit. Just hold out a little longer, and this will all be over."

Bambam put his hands on his hips and frowned. "She said there would be snacks down here!"

"Are you serious?" Kyla said, exasperated. "You're eight elfyears old! Can't you two just sit quietly for fifteen minutes? Talk to each other about whatever, but just do it so I can't hear you, please."

The twins looked at each other, exhaled, and said, "Alright, Kyla" in unison.

The secret room beneath Skye Manor had probably seen better days. The wooden spiral staircase had creaked and cracked when they walked down its steps and onto the concrete floor. The stone walls were covered in a thin layer of spider-webbing, and the weak halogen lamps that hung from them gave off a candlelight glow throughout. It smelled wet—like wet stone that had been saturated from a winter blast and never given the opportunity to dry out.

Creepy and cold—Kyla thought as she sat down on one of the heavy, black-lacquered chests stacked neatly across the floor.

Juju sat on the swivel chair attached to the large drawing board in the center of the room as Bambam perused the bookshelf along the back wall.

Juju blew a puff of dust from the desk and up into his face. He coughed wildly and Bambam looked over his shoulder and laughed at him.

"Okay, boys. Just behave," Kyla sang in her eternally optimistic tone. "This is Ember's father's workplace, remember? We need to be extremely careful with all of his things."

"But," Juju said wiping his forearm across the desk to clean off the excess dust, "that would really only matter if he was still alive."

"Yeah," Bambam piped in, "isn't Ember's entire family dead?"

Juju snickered, "Maybe she's dead, too!"

Kyla stiffened, took a deep breath, and responded as calmly and gently as she could. "Yes. Most of Ember's family is dead. My family is dead, too. My twin sister Tyla, in fact. And if memory serves me correctly, some of your family members are dead, as well."

The boys stared back at her.

"Just be a little more respectful, okay? You never know what kind of pain someone has gone through in their elflife. Everyone has a story. Everyone has had some*thing* happen to change them or shape them. It's not something you want to joke about or make fun of."

They hung their heads down in shame and said, "Sorry, Kyla," before continuing their fiddling and investigation of the secret room.

Kyla closed her eyes, imagining what was happening Aboveground: *Did Ember succeed in the All-Coal mission? Where were the twins? Was she able to get them home and safe? Did she get to see the Boss? What about her deer at Plumm Stable?* The thought of them thinking she abandoned them sent a shiver right through her. She clasped her arms to hug her shoulders and looked around the small space. She wondered if this was what the coal elves felt like every day—cold, damp, with no natural light to come through the terrain, enclosed in a tight, cramped space. Was it that feeling that drove them to near madness? Could *she* endure living in the Mines? Would she have been able to survive if that had been her Life Job?

"Hey! Hey! I found something!" Bambam exclaimed. He held a shoebox in one hand and small silver packages in another.

Kyla stood up. "Bring that here, let me see it!"

The boys huddled around her as Bambam presented what he found. "Look!" he said. "It's Nessie Nibs!"

"Oh! I love Nessie Nibs!" Juju squealed.

Nessie Nibs were a gummy snack made from Nessie fruit. All little elflings enjoyed them in their lunch boxes or as a special treat. Kyla, too, had loved Nessie Nibs. They were sweet and chewy and stuck to the roof of her mouth whenever she ate them. She remembered when she and Tyla would have Nib competitions to see who could fit the most in their mouth at once. Tyla usually won, to which Kyla would declare, "It's because you have a bigger mouth, big mouth!" And of course, the two would go into fits of hysterics.

"Can we have them? Can we have them? Please, please. Please!" the boys begged.

"Give them here," she said, snatching them from Bambam's hands. The silver packaging was undisturbed, and Kyla turned them over and over in her hands, examining them. "There's no date," she finally said. "I don't know when they came out, or when they were set to expire."

"So? Who cares? Uncle Barkuss eats expired food all the time!" Bambam said.

"No way, buddy," Kyla explained. "Not this. There's no way to tell when this was made. Who knows if it was from that bad batch of Nessie back in the day. Ya know, the *infected* Nessies. I'm gonna say absolutely not. I don't need you two getting sick on me."

"But I'm soooooo hungry!" Juju complained.

"It's only been a few hours!" Kyla reiterated.

"Our Momma says we're growing boys!" Bambam declared.

Kyla rolled her eyes again. "Look, maybe you two should rest or something. Calm your brain down. Maybe when you wake up, we'll be ready to go."

The boys stared at each other as if they were talking, then nodded. Kyla took off her wool coat and sat down on the concrete floor with her back against the black-lacquered chest. "Here," she said, patting her legs. Bambam rested his head on her left thigh and Juju rested his head on her right. They both curled their legs up against their chests. Kyla fanned out her coat and laid it across the both of them. She patted their curly orange hair. "There, there," she said lovingly. "Just rest. Recharge. It'll all be okay."

Within minutes, their quickened breaths became long and deep nasally snorts of sleep. Kyla relaxed her back, trying not to move the lower half of her body. For the first time in her elflife, she was grateful she had not been assigned an elfhusband. Elfhusbands meant elflings, and elflings meant all *this*: whining, complaining, teaching, grooming, playing, feeding, and all that other Elfmomma jazz. She was glad she wasn't a part of it. Give her a stable of reindeer any day, and she would be comfortable and right in her element. But put her in charge of elflings? Nope. No way. It was like a foreign language to her—one that she didn't want to begin to decipher.

She watched the boys as they slept on her sprawled-out legs. The tops of their carrot-capped curls rising and falling with every deep breath they took. Even in sleep it was as if they were still talking to each other—their movements and breathing patterns in perfect harmony. Bambam inhaled as Juju exhaled. Juju sighed, and Bambam responded with his own sigh. Bambam's fingers twitched, to which Juju's leg jolted. It was like their brains and bodies were hardwired to each other. Could it be possible they even shared the same dreams? What would happen to them if they were ever separated? Would one be able to exist without the other?

Kyla remembered when she and Tyla were elflings. And while they never had the gift of telepathy like Bambam and Juju, they were still very much in twin sync. Each girl had acted in accordance with the other, often completing each other's thoughts and sentences, speaking in unison, dressing alike without planning to, and other acts that bound them together as being one entity rather than two. She even remembered the moments of silence between them when they could *read* each other's thoughts. Her heart ached for Tyla, and sitting there in that cold cellar with the twins curled up in her lap made her ache for her sister even more. A part of Kyla died with Tyla, but their first true separation came on their Assignment Day…

Kyla and Tyla had been stuffing their mouths with Nessie Nibs all morning. It had become sort of a tradition at their home—their mother Lyra had allowed the girls to eat anything they wanted on their elfyear birthday. It didn't matter what it was or when it was. Whatever their little hearts desired, it was okay for that one day. Their father Otto was against the idea at first, but Lyra had convincing opal eyes and appealed to Otto's soft heart. So, on that morning, the twins chose to eat handfuls upon handfuls of Nessie Nibs. Plain

Nessie flavored, grape flavored, strawberry flavored, apple flavored, even the hallyhack flavor that tasted so bad that it was kind of good. It didn't matter—they kept shoving them into their mouths, gummy piece after gummy piece.

Kyla had finally figured out a way to nestle the gummy pieces into the spaces between where her elfling teeth had fallen out and where her adult elfteeth were poking through. The little white buds of the new teeth served as little pikes in her mouth, and she was able to stack the Nibs kebob style along her bottom jaw. "I'm gonna win this time!" she sang with a mumbled tune.

"No way! I've beaten you the last four rounds!" Tyla said.

Kyla bopped her head with confidence. "Nuh-uhhh! I got this! Just watch me!"

The girls froze when they heard the knock at the front door. Looking at each other, they were able to get each other's message: *The letters are here, run downstairs now!* The girls spit out their mouthfuls of Nibs and sprinted down the stairs. Lyra and Otto each held onto the intricately designed envelopes with proud smiles across their faces.

"Lemme see! Lemme see!" the girls clamored around their parents, jumping up and down.

"Hold on! Hold on!" Otto laughed. "Seems that I have a letter for Miss Kyla Plumm."

Lyra waved the other letter in the air. "And seems I have a letter for Miss Tyla Plumm. Oh, wait?" she paused with a confused look on her face. "Is this for Kyla?"

"Hmmm…" Otto scratched his head. "This one might be for Tyla, but…" Father traded letters with Mother. They looked at them with puzzled faces, swapping letters again, then again.

"Oh, come on!" the girls chanted. "Stop messing around and give them to us!"

Mother and Father giggled, and they handed the girls the correct letters. Kyla and Tyla tore open their envelopes with excited fury. The two had had many conversations about the possibilities of their future. Would they be kept in the family business of Reindeer Training? Would they be sent to West Bank to be Builder Elves? Would they be sent off to do something exotic in the northernmost territory of Norland? Kyla fumbled with her letter before screaming out, "Reindeer Trainer! I got Reindeer Trainer!"

Mother and Father cheered with delight and hugged her. "That's wonderful, Kyla! Absolutely wonderful!" Mother gushed.

But Tyla was quiet. A look of terror washed over her face.

"Ty? What's wrong?" Father said in a low voice.

"I… I…" Tyla stammered.

Mother turned to her and took the letter from her hand. "Grove Elf?"

"Grove Elf?" Father repeated.

"What does that mean?" Kyla asked. "Why didn't she get Reindeer Trainer?"

For all their talks and suppositions, being split up was never discussed. Tears streamed down Tyla's face. Kyla froze, the reality of their impending separation hitting her hard like glass shattering on ceramic tile…

Bambam and Juju shuddered awake, their heads perking up simultaneously.

Kyla's eyes shot open when her brain registered the crashing noise that jolted her out of her sleep.

Juju grabbed Bambam's hand. "What was that noise?"

Bambam was practically paralyzed. "I don't know. Maybe they're here for us." There were more rustling noises coming from upstairs.

"Shhh!" Kyla warned. "Just be quiet."

"Maybe it's Ember."

Kyla tilted her head and tried to listen to the sounds. "I don't think so. Doesn't sound like elf-feet." She stretched her legs out, shaking off the fuzzy feeling in them from where the boys had been resting, stood up, and walked over to the spiral staircase.

The boys followed right behind her. "What if it's Sturd? He doesn't have real elffeet, does he?" Juju cried.

"Stop it. Sturd has no idea we're even here. How would he know that?"

"What if he got to Ember? What if he made her tell him where we are?" Bambam said.

"Yeah, and what if he killed her!" Juju continued.

Kyla raised her hand to silence them. "Just stay here and stay quiet," she instructed. "I'm gonna go have a look upstairs."

"No! No, don't do it! Don't go!!" they begged.

"Shhhh! I'll be fine. Just don't make any noise down here. Besides, while I'm up there, I'll have a look around. Maybe look through the kitchen for some food. Just stay put!"

Juju ran over to the drawing board and picked up a dusty protractor. He opened it at both ends and handed it to Kyla. She nodded briskly and began her ascent up the creaky, crackly stairs.

"Be careful," Bambam whispered to her back.

"Be good!" she whispered back.

"We're in a secret cellar filled with books, how much trouble can we get in?" Juju asked.

Kyla rolled her eyes and continued up the stairs. *Smart alecs*, she thought, but her grip on the protractor remained tight. She opened the heavy bookcase and lurked about the dark office. Slicked with sweat, her hands fumbled with the metal device. Her own footsteps sent shivers down her back as she prowled through the main floor of Skye Manor.

"No one's here. No one's here," she said out loud, trying to calm her nerves. The wind howled outside and beat heavily against the hollowed-out mansion.

Glass rattled in the window casements. Down the hallway, a door swung on its hinges, and Kyla decided it would be best to investigate there first.

"There's no way anyone would be able to find us. No way!" she said, like a mantra, over and over again.

She entered a bedroom. A broken window had allowed the air to rush in and had caused the door to open and shut with its icy rhythm. The walls were decorated with fancy paintings, a green and pink floral coverlet was spread on the bed, and a sitting chair was underneath a broken window. It was an older person's room and had been left undisturbed for a long while. On the nightstand to her left was an old picture in a frame. Kyla picked it up and smiled when she saw an older woman with gray hair fastened into a bun holding the hand of a sweet-looking elfling with blonde pigtails and a teal pinafore. *Ember. Little Ember and her trusted Nanny*—the faraway memories of a bygone era.

Broken glass littered the floor and as soon as Kyla walked closer to inspect it, something darted across the floor and under the bed, stopping her heart for a second.

She jumped back and screeched—her hand over her heart in terror. She extended the pointy end of the protractor in front of her and crouched down to get a better look at what had scurried past her. Two glowing red eyes stared at her from under the bed. She paused. There was only one explanation for red, glowing eyes, and her heart stopped again.

It's Sturd! she thought. *He's found us! He's going to take us away, and…*

With a stabbing motion, Kyla cried, "Get out of here, you wretched thing!"

A white snow-kit scampered out from under the bed, hopped onto the sitting chair, and pranced out of the broken window.

Kyla's hands shook, and she dropped the pro-tractor to the floor. She laughed out loud with relief. "Yeah, Sturd!" she chuckled. "You sneaky fox, you!" And she continued her laughter as she relaxed and made her way through the rest of the house.

There were some cans of food left behind in an old, dusty cabinet in the Butler's pantry: tur-nip-bean mash, salted hallyhack slices, cream of cremmle soup, and an unopened bag of tater-skin chips. Not what she would have preferred to eat, but Kyla figured this would be enough to hold the boys over for a little bit until they got word from Ember.

"Hey, boys!" she called as she made her way down the stairs. "I found something for us to eat. It's not the best selection, but..." She stopped in her tracks when she saw Bambam and Juju sprawled out on the concrete floor sitting in a sea of papers. The black-lacquered trunks were open, and blueprints and folders spilled out of them haphazardly. "What in the world?" she scolded and dropped the cans to the floor. "What are you boys doing? I thought I told you to stay out of trouble!"

"We're not *in* trouble, Kyla," Bambam said matter-of-factly. "We had to do something to pass the time."

"Yeah," Juju said in awe. "Just look at all this stuff. This is amazing." He held up a folder and fanned the contents out in front of Kyla's face.

"Put all this stuff away, okay? This is the property of Elden Skye, Ember's father. We need to be respectful and…"

Bambam grabbed her hand and dragged her to join them on the floor. "But, Kyla! This is just so *cool*. Look. Look at this design he was working on. It's a piece of metal that you stand on, and it flies! It flies! I can't read his handwriting, but he called it a something-board."

Kyla raised her eyebrows. "A something-board? Really?"

"He had tons of blueprints. Tons of plans," Juju said.

Too bad none of them would ever come to fruition due to his untimely death, she thought. "All right, all right. Enough!" she finally swatted at them to get away from the papers. "This is too weird. You wanted food, I brought you food. Go. Eat. Get away from here and let me clean this mess up." She scurried them away and began organizing the Toy Designer's paperwork and returned it to the trunk.

After a few minutes, Kyla noticed that the boys were quiet. Too quiet. Not the usual little-elfling-stuffing-their-face quiet, either. They were *twin* quiet—the kind of quiet that happens when they were using their secret code, their secret language, their secret telepathy gift that only they had. Sensing something was up she said, "All right guys, what's going on?"

When they didn't answer her, she looked up from the mess on the floor. The boys were huddled together at the foot of the staircase, gesturing to each other. "Bambam? Juju? What's going on? What's up?"

Juju stood up and walked over to her with a piece of paper in his hands. "Um, remember how you said Ember wasn't dead?"

Kyla's eyes flashed, and her face bloomed with red heat. She put her hands on her hips and exhaled like a raging dragon. "Yes, Juju, for the five-millionth time, Ember is *not* dead."

He held out the paper to her, his hand shaking like a leaf in the winter wind. "Well," he hesitated, "not according to this."

She snatched it out of his hand. "Let me see that."

The top of the paper read "Certificate of Death." "'On this elfday, March the fourteenth,'" she read aloud, "'the year of the Claus 306VIII, we hereby acknowledge the death of Ember Autumn Skye. Signed Elden Skye, Carole Frost, Jack Frost, and Jolenir M'Raz, the Claus.'"

The paper slipped from Kyla's hand.

"You shouldn't have told her," Bambam said.

"We had to," Juju yelled at him.

"But now she's all weird."

"I told you Ember was dead!"

They spoke to each other in Elvish, and their voices sounded far away and mumbled. She could barely make out her own thoughts when she shouted at them, "I can speak Elvish, too, have you forgotten?"

The boys went silent at Kyla's harsh tone.

She bent down to pick up the certificate and looked it over again in disbelief.

How could this be?

Ember is dead?

CHAPTER FIVE

It hadn't been all that long ago when Ember had been called to the Council's Chamber to discuss the Coal-less Night. She had committed to memory every inch of the waiting room at Headquarters—the cream-colored walls and shaggy beige carpet, the desk in the corner with the nervous secretary, the large brown couches, and of course, the snarky Enforcer Elf with the high-pitched voice who pulled and pushed her around. Nothing about it had changed. Even now. Even as she sat side by side with Tannen, his hand on her knee, squeezing it for reassurance.

Who is he trying to calm down? Me? Or himself? she thought.

The inside door to the Chambers flew open, and Kipper Gulch emerged from the darkness within. "Ember Ruprecht. Tannen Trayth. The Council will see you now," he announced, his voice squeaking at the last syllable.

Ember and Tannen stood up and gave each other a nod before entering the beige-colored door to the side room. She walked over the threshold first and extended her arm behind her as if to guide him through. Kipper Gulch followed right behind them. She remembered the anxiety and anticipation she felt when she first confronted the Council here, and she could only imagine what was going through Tannen's mind. Was he nervous? Scared? Overwhelmed? All three? She thought it unfortunate that his first time in Norland had to be under these circumstances, much like her very own years ago when she was called before the Council as a Defector.

He just needs to stick to the plan and keep his mouth shut, and we'll be good.

For all her comings and goings back and forth to Norland, Aboveground, Headquarters and the Mines, this was only Ember's second time in the Chambers, yet she quickly saw that it was set up much differently from the last time she had been there. The long table in the center of the room was still there. At it sat three principal members of the Council—Una, Zelcodor, and Quisto. Cerissa and Trelson were not present as they had been regulated to oversee the Book.

Una sat at the center with the other members to each side of her. Next to Zelcodor was Madame Claus, and next to Quisto on the other side was Balthasar Hollis. Balthasar was a Judge Elf in East Bank who dealt with petty elf squabbles and disagreements. Ember remembered him from a long time ago when her mother had a falling out with one of the neighbors over the property line between Skye Manor and Windell Manor. Judge Hollis was swift and fair in his verdict, pleasing all parties involved, but to a young elfling, those types of things don't really matter. What Ember had remembered most was the Judge's long pointed nose and his mismatched eyes—one ice blue and the other pitch black. She narrowed her eyes, wondering why a County Judge would be called to a Council Meeting.

But who was she kidding? This wasn't a Council Meeting in the sense of a *Council Meeting*. This particular meeting was unprecedented simply because the events that had transpired had been unprecedented. A slight burning smell drifted across the room, and Ember swiveled her head to the right. There in the corner was an elevated platform, and upon the platform, Sturd and Sim Nim'sim sat on hard wooden chairs next to each other as if they were on stage getting ready to perform a musical number or dramatic piece.

On stage? More like on trial.

Kipper motioned his head in the direction of the platform, guiding Ember and Tannen to take a seat next to Sturd and Sim. They walked up the small staircase and took their positions, but before she sat, Ember scooted her chair a few feet from Sturd. He had a square bandage taped to the side of his forehead and he reeked. The smell of burnt clothes and hair and wood and flesh made her stomach do flip-flops. She also noticed something off about him and it wasn't the stench or the blood stains seeping through the white gauze on his head. He looked different, something about him *felt* different—like his shoulders lurched forward a little more noticeably, and his eyes glowed a little more piercingly, and his horns poked out a little more menacingly... *horns?* Ember studied his face for a few moments and saw poking out from the top of Sturd's former hairline there appeared to be two small nubs, like black stalagmites jutting out from the ceiling in Onyx Alley. But she brushed it off as the shadows in the room playing tricks on her. Sturd *tsked* with agitation when she moved away from him, to which she replied by shrugging her shoulders.

Ember looked over at Tannen who fidgeted with his hands. She reached out and touched his knee, like he had done to her before, and squeezed her hand tight around his kneecap. *Who am I trying to calm down? Him? Or me?* she thought. He looked up and gave her a soft smile.

From the vantage point of the stage, Ember could see the transmitter on the Council's table was blinking its green light, and she automatically knew that the Boss had His ear on the other end somewhere over in Lapis Hall. She shook her head, bewildered. *He needed His rest so badly that He couldn't meet with me, but He can sit in on this Inquiry with no problem. What a coward!*

"Before we begin," Mrs. Claus announced, "because the Council is short-handed, we have brought in Judge Balthasar Hollis of East Bank to help preside over the Inquiry today. I will be acting Council member on behalf of Cerissa Lux.

Judge Hollis will step in for Trelson Castleberry. Councilwoman, you may proceed." She waved her hand in Una's direction.

Una cleared her throat and swiftly tapped her gavel on the table three short times to bring order and silence to the room. "We are here today to determine whether or not the actions and incidents that have transpired over the last few days warrant punishment for the four elves before us."

Ember and Tannen quickly looked at each other as she removed her hand from his knee and placed it in her lap.

"Ember Ruprecht and Tannen Trayth," Una continued, "you are here because it has been revealed to us that you were both involved in what we are calling the All-Coal Night. Sim Nim'sim and Sturd Ruprecht, you are here because of your proximity and possible involvement in the incident that occurred at the Mon Valley Abbey. We will start with you, Mr. Trayth."

Ember's muscles tightened when she heard Tannen's name called. She straightened up, readied herself for the onslaught of questions and accusations she expected to be thrown at him, and mentally screamed to him to remember the plan… *Keep your mouth shut!*

"Mr. Trayth," Zelcodor started, "what is your position at the Pole?"

Tannen fidgeted some more in his chair. "I operate the Catta-cars in the Mines, Your Honor."

"And were you called to the Mines as an elfling?"

"No, sir. I'm a Ceffle—born and raised there. My ancestors were the Tree Elves from Aboveground, but..."

Una waved a dismissive hand in the air. "Yes, Mr. Trayth. We know all about the Tree Elves and their history. Proceed, Councilman."

Zelcodor gave her a menacing side glance before he resumed his line of questioning. "How long have you known Ember Ruprecht, Mr. Trayth?"

"Ever since she was assigned to the Mines as an elfling," he said quickly without missing a beat.

"And what is your relationship with her?"

Tannen paused and looked at Ember with a pained expression. Her heart ached as he said the words, "We're friends," because at one time they had been so much more, and she had wanted so much more. She wanted to stop the Inquiry right then and there and profess her undying love for Tannen Trayth... *I-can't-believe-what's-become-of-us, Tannen. I-don't-know-how-I-can-pretend-anymore, Tannen. I-want-to-grab-your-sandy-blond-hair-and-smother-your-face-in-kisses, Tannen...*

"Friends?" Quisto questioned. He flipped through some papers on his desk. "There have been rumors, young man. Rumors of a *relation-ship* between you and Mrs. Ruprecht."

Sturd obnoxiously cleared his throat. Tannen turned his head to Ember once again, but she kept her gaze straight ahead on the Council's Table. "Just rumors," he replied, and Ember felt her heart sink into her stomach with painful reality.

"I'm married to Holly Adaire Trayth. She is my one true elfwife. Ember and I have always just been, and always will be, good friends. Just very good friends."

She closed her eyes for a second to let the words pierce her heart like tiny daggers.

Judge Hollis scratched his long nose. "Mr. Trayth," he said. His voice was unnaturally deep for an elf. Its bass tones shook throughout the Chamber. Ember felt it resonate on the bottoms of her feet from up the makeshift stage. "What role did you have in the All-Coal Night? The Council has surmised that the only way Mrs. Ruprecht could have gotten that much coal Aboveground would have been with your help using the trolley car system. So please, explain."

Tannen breathed in and opened his mouth to speak, but Ember, afraid he would say something to implicate himself, stepped in. "He didn't know," she blurted. All eyes from the Council's table were directed at her. "It was all me. I... I..." she stammered and gave Tannen a sideways glance, "I used him. I sneaked onto his train cars at night and stocked the coal under the seats. And every day, I would take a little bit to where they needed to be. He was none the wiser. He had no clue." She let out a small giggle for good measure and saw a tiny smirk develop on the side of Una's mouth. She knew her words made Tannen look foolish and idiotic in the eyes of the Council, but that was the only way they were going to believe the story. Tannen's body slouched slightly in his chair. She knew her words had pierced him through, too.

"But the notes? What about the notes? How did you manage all of that?" Quisto drilled.

Ember shrugged brazenly. "Easy. They weren't anything too crazy, ya know? Simple. I did it all myself. Been planning this for a while."

"Well, Mrs. Ruprecht," Zelcodor said, "You clearly disobeyed protocol. Going rogue is not an option for our way of life. And quite frankly, we're not sure if you can ever be trusted again."

Una exhaled and smiled devilishly. Ember stared at her for a moment before Judge Hollis broke into the conversation. "Mrs. Ruprecht, if what you say is true and that you acted solely on your own, then it is my judgment that Tannen Trayth be exonerated of any misdeeds."

Tannen's fists clenched and his lip tightened. Ember patted his thigh in quiet celebration.

"However, Councilman #3 is correct," Judge Hollis continued. "Ember Ruprecht, you shall be stripped of your title of Coal Deliverer and banished to the outskirts of the North Pole."

Ember's heart stopped and the room began to spin. *Banished? Wait. What did he say? Did he say banished?*

Una raised her gavel high in the air, but before she could bang it against the wooden block on the table, Tannen spoke out. "Wait!" he cried. "In Ember's defense, Your Honor, what she did was a good thing. The blackened names in the Book have ceased dramatically, which is more than can be said for the Christmas in July debacle."

Una's lips pursed in an angry sneer. "And how would you know this? You're a Trolley Driver in the Mines, Mr. Trayth. There's no possible way for you to…"

"Is there any truth in what Mr. Trayth says?" Judge Hollis said, addressing the entire room.

Ember sat still. Frozen in place. Paralyzed from the throat down, it seemed, because she couldn't even open her mouth to defend herself. Only the word *banished* echoed in her mind until a series of buzzes from the table transmitter came through like a coded message repeating over and over.

Docena's eyes widened, and she cleared her throat. "Actually, Your Honor," she spoke out, "the blackened names have stopped. And the frost beaches are freezing up again. And…" she paused to decode some more of the blips and bleeps, "the Lumber District is rebounding."

Una gasped and tapped her foot against the stony floor.

"Please," Docena continued, "banishment and title stripping is much too harsh. I have it on good authority that Ember Ruprecht will be counseled by the Claus, and her ways will be set straight. Remember, the timing of her Life Job change and her marriage to Sturd Ruprecht has all been sudden and rushed. Her intentions were good. She just needs time and guidance, not banishment."

Judge Hollis scratched his head, mulling over Lady Frost's words.

"Are you serious, Madame?" Una lashed out. "Time? Guidance?"

Zelcodor reached to end the transmission on the device, but Docena extended her hand to stop him. She wagged a finger in his face to tell him "no," and he retreated.

"I suppose you're right," Judge Hollis said. "It seems some provisions can be made on this matter." He looked over at Una. "For now, my ruling is to turn Ember Ruprecht over into the care of Docena Frost M'Raz until further notice."

The room waited for the clank of the gavel on the table. Judge Hollis cleared his throat, signaling for Una to bang the instrument. She hesitated for a moment before slamming it down in disgust.

Ember shook her head, confused. The Boss's wife—Madame Claus herself—had just intervened and saved her butt from banishment? It was all too much to process!

Tannen smiled and reached over to give her a quick shoulder hug, but she was still in a daze.

"Now, in the matter of Mr. Ruprecht and Mr. Nim'sim," Quisto said in a loud voice. "Would one of you please care to explain what happened?"

Sturd shot a look at Sim, and Sim slinked into his chair. It was obvious that Sturd was going to be the one to do all the talking. "We were simply trying to protect the twins," he said in a pleading tone, but Ember saw right through his façade. "They were all inside, and I guess one of their candles must have fallen down and…" He sighed and paused as if to prevent himself from becoming emotional. "Before they realized what happened, it was too late."

Docena leaned forward in her seat, her eyes blazing with anger. "Lives were lost, Mr. Ruprecht! Important lives!"

Sturd hung his head to feign sadness. "Yes, I know," he said meekly to the floor. "We lost some good men, too. Sim's own brother Nim was in that fire. My precious little nephews, Bambam and Juju Dwin'nae, were in that fire."

The fog around Ember's brain immediately lifted when she heard Sturd speak the names of the dead. *You're wrong! You're wrong!* She wanted to shout knowing all too well that the twins were safe from harm at Skye Manor. Sturd's lies were laughable. She couldn't wait to figure out his stupid plan and…

"My half-brother, Bulder Dwin'nae, was in that fire, too," Sturd said with an almost sly smirk.

"Is this true, Mr. Nim'sim?" Judge Hollis asked.

Sim nodded, and Ember stopped her musing. *Bulder's not dead. He can't be dead. Wasn't he Aboveground at the Mouth when they were loading up her sleigh?* Ember played back the events of the Big Night: yes, there was Balrion, and Tannen, and Holly, and even crazy Barkuss had made his way to the surface for the first time! But she couldn't remember if Bulder had been there or not. Everything had happened so fast that night—getting the twins to the Manor, the coal, almost forgetting the List, Holly getting home safely and giving her the black cap, Boptail and Asche… That night was all too surreal, and suddenly, she couldn't remember if Bulder had been there or not. Her heart felt heavy in her chest. If Bulder was truly gone, what about the twins? Had they gotten to them, too? And how were Barkuss and Bommer and Balrion going to react to the news?

Ember's attention was drifting in and out of focus. She scarcely heard the explanation of the night's events, but tuned in when Sturd proclaimed, "Sim was a hero! He pushed me out of the way when the church blew up. It knocked me out and burned my face. I would be dead if not for Sim."

"Aww, shucks," she whispered.

Tannen let out a chuckle.

"In the matter of the Mon Valley Abbey disaster, I declare there were no wrongdoings on the behalf of Sturd Ruprecht and Sim Nim'sim. It was strictly an accident." Leaving no time for argument, questions, or debate, Una raised the gavel and pounded it on the table in one swift motion.

Docena sighed. "This leaves the Pole in a great imbalance. There are no twins left."

Claus, I pray you're wrong.

Judge Hollis scratched the tip of his nose. "What will happen now? There are no more twins. What does this mean? Will the Boss have to choose for Himself? Will we have to wait for a sign from the Mists? Or will the Boss have to remain?"

He can't remain! Ember thought. *Mrs. Claus said He was near the end! He's ready to go with the Mists.*

Una and Zelcodor glanced at each other.

Una.

Una M'Raz Ruprecht.

The Boss's sister.

The Boss's *twin* sister.

The picture was starting to come together for Ember. Perhaps this was all a ploy to get Una into the Boss's position…

"I can check the ancient texts to see if there has ever been a similar situation," Quisto whispered down the table to Una. "I can have Trelson and Cerissa help out in the Book Keepers' Office."

Una nodded. "That doesn't solve our killer problem. Someone murdered the Book Keepers and Reindeer Judges. That elf, or elves," and she glared at Ember and Tannen ominously, "could very well still have a plan in mind. Maybe a plan to do worse. I think we need to guard the Claus. Make sure he's safe at all times. Lapis Hall needs to be protected."

"A guard?" Docena asked defiantly. "Lapis Hall has never had a guard before. We've never needed it."

"Not until now," Una shot back. "And I don't mean a guard, Docena. I mean a full-on army."

Docena stood up from her chair, her distraught hands flailing in the air. "An army? What are you talking about, Jolevana! This is crazy talk! We have no weapons for an army."

"We have tools," Zelcodor interjected casually. "Mining tools."

The transmitter on the table beeped frantically, and Docena made her way to the door and shoved Kipper aside. "No way!" she screamed. "Absolutely not! This goes against everything we stand for as a community, as a society, as a... a... moral race!"

Una slammed her hands on the table and forcefully rose from her chair. "We've never had a murderer in our midst!" she shouted back. "We've never had a period of time where there has been so much pain and suffering and tragedy. Our leader is in real imminent danger, Docena. Your husband. My brother. I will do anything to protect him and our race. I am deeply offended that you would think otherwise!"

The room grew painfully silent. The transmitter stopped beeping, and the light switched from green to red. Docena paused at the door and put her hand on the knob. She turned her head in Una's direction but never looked up to meet Una's eyes. She nodded, regretfully, then turned back to walk out the door.

Una clapped her hands with determination. "Excellent!" she announced. "We will have to set up a perimeter around Lapis Hall. Sturd, arm your men with pickaxes, chargers and scrapers, cobbing hammers, bucking irons... whatever you can get from the tool cache in the Mines."

Huh. She knows an awful lot about the types of mining equipment we use...

"Ember, I want you and Tannen to help Sturd with the transport and delivery of the tools. We must make it clear that no one gets near the Castle. No one! The Claus must be guarded at all times until the killer is apprehended, and then and only then, can we figure out the next steps for a successor."

Sturd shifted in his seat. "My men?"

Una blinked rapidly. "Yes, yes, your men. The Brotherhood, of course."

A snakey smile spread across Sturd's face, and Sim clapped his hands together wildly like a simpleton.

CHAPTER SIX

Without concrete proof, Ember couldn't believe a word Sturd had said about Bulder and the twins dying in the fire. After the Inquiry in the Council's Chambers, she and Tannen rode in her sleigh from Norland to East Bank to check in on Kyla and the twins. The two rode in complete silence the entire way. Ember barely even looked at Tannen as a rush of conflicting emotions invaded her heart. *I just want something I can never have*, she told herself, and tried desperately to keep her focus on guiding Boptail and Asche to take it easy throughout the duration of their ride. Tannen had never been riding before, and his fun-filled day of firsts was now ending in a white-knuckled, green-faced flight over the entire North Pole. Ember prayed to Claus that he wasn't going to vomit in her sleigh.

Darkness had just settled in, and a swarm of Graespurs was dispersing in the night sky. Their velvety bodies flitted like tiny strobe lights against the brightness of the full moon. It was

Night Tide, one of Ember's favorite times to be in the sky, when the moonlight washed over the land below, and the sky shifted colors as the Graespurs arrived. It was magical—energizing. It was unfortunate that she couldn't relish this moment the way she wanted to. The wind had picked up its pace, and Asche and Boptail fought against the gale on their descent to Skye Manor. Tannen's grip on the side of the sleigh intensified, and his breath hitched in his throat as the sleigh glided downward.

"*Claugh sonna!*" she called to the deer in Elvish, instructing them to slow down and take it easy. "You holding up okay?" she asked Tannen.

He quickly nodded. "Great. Never been better," he answered dryly.

"Okay. This wind is working against us, and the landing might be a little bit rough," she yelled over a blast of cold air. "Just hold tight."

"Not a problem!" he answered back.

Asche and Boptail jerked and bucked against the pockets of air gusts, and Ember tugged and steered as best as she could. It was a struggle to get them on the right track and not tumble head over hoof onto the snowy land. When their hooves hit the ground, they sped up to keep the pace of the sleigh behind them. "Whoa! Whoa!" Ember shouted, and they gradually slowed to a synchronized trot. "Good job, guys!" she said, relaxing the reins. "*Aylanz tensh. Aylanz tensh.*"

Tannen released his hold from the side of the sleigh and relaxed his body when they finally stopped. He brushed his hair from his eyes and exhaled loudly. "Phew! Is it always that rough?"

Ember smiled. "Not usually. Sometimes. It depends. I trust those two, though, so I never get freaked out. I did the first time, but I'm so used to it by now it doesn't really faze me." She hopped down from the sleigh and motioned for Tannen to join her. He stood up but fumbled forward a bit and landed back on the bench. Ember crinkled her face, "Ooops! Sorry," she said apologetically. "Forgot to warn you that it takes a few minutes to get your land legs back. I'm just so…"

Tannen put two hands on the side of the sleigh and propped himself up. "Used to it? Yeah, yeah… I get it," he smiled and hopped down next to her.

Ember giggled. "I promise. Next time I take you riding, it won't be so rough."

"Sure. Next time I go riding with you, I'll have to be in a grulish coma!"

She playfully punched his arm, and he swatted back at her, intentionally missing. He bent down and scooped up a handful of snow. "I swear, Ember Skye, this is going right down your back if you don't…"

He paused, and her eyes went painfully wide. The two of them grew still and quiet. He had called her *Ember Skye*. The sadness that washed over her face spoke volumes: *Ember Skye doesn't exist anymore. Ember Skye doesn't have time for laughter and playing and flirting. Ember Skye just wants something she can never have…*

"Come on," she said, shifting her tone and breaking the tense silence between them, "the house is just up this road, past that run-down guard house." She walked over to Asche and Boptail, instructed them to stay put, unless they sensed danger, of course, and began her trek up the windy path. Tannen followed 10 feet behind her.

Once at the Manor, Ember looked over her shoulder to make sure no one was around. It was more instinct than a precautionary action. She slipped the key from her jump suit pocket and opened the heavy door. "This way," she said and led Tannen throughout the dark house. No lights were on, and at first glance, nothing in the rooms had appeared to be disturbed or out of the ordinary. A cold draft blew in from down the hall, but she ignored it and made her way to the secret passage in her father's office.

The bookcase creaked open, and there was a rustling noise from the bottom of the spiral staircase. "Are you sure they're here?" Tannen whispered.

Ember swallowed. A flash of doubt raced across her mind. "They have to be. I just know they are," she whispered in return.

"What if they…"

Ember punched his shoulder again. "Shush! Don't even say that!" she scolded in a raspy voice.

"Sorry! Sorry!" he apologized.

She nodded and snapped her head for him to follow her down the stairs. "Hello?" she quietly called into the darkness. The anxiety in her chest barely allowed her to get the words out. "You guys here?" Their footsteps made popping sounds against the wooden stairs as they made their way down to the secret room, and it deafeningly filled Ember's ears.

Is that what the burning wood sounded like? Pop pop pop pop pop…

Suddenly, a dim light popped on. "Ember? Is that you?" Kyla called back.

Ember breathed a sigh of relief. "Bambam? Juju?"

"Here!" the boys sang out.

By the time Ember reached the bottom, Kyla rushed up to meet her and flung her arms around her neck. "Oh, my Claus, Coal Girl! Are we ever so glad to see you!"

The boys squealed with delight. Ember smiled as she hugged Kyla fiercely. "You have no idea how glad I am to see all of *you!*"

Kyla released her grip and pulled back a little. "Oh, Tannen?" she questioned. "Ember," she said, her tone of voice changing, "what's going on?"

"The Council needed to see us for an Inquiry of sorts. Everything's all figured out, for now."

"Ember, I really need to get back to the stable," Kyla said with a desperate voice. "Some of my girls will be Mommas soon, and I really ought to…"

Ember raised her hand to calm her down. "I took care of everything. Before Tannen and I rode up to Headquarters, we dropped Holly off at the stable. She agreed to take care of them for you. I told her that if anything were to happen, or if she needed assistance, to contact Fannie Brightly. I hope it's okay that I told her to stay there?"

"Oh absolutely!" Kyla gushed and sighed with relief. "I just didn't want them to be alone for so long. I was getting nervous."

"No worries, my friend. I got you covered."

Ember turned her attention to the twins and glided over to them. Seeing them alive and well in her father's basement filled her heart with warmth and relief. They were fine. They hadn't been at the church fire.

Confirmation on two, one more to go…

She bent down and opened her arms wide to receive them. She wasn't expecting Bambam and Juju to tackle her the way they did, almost knocking her to the floor. Their curly orange hair tickled her nose as they smothered her cheeks with warm kisses and nuzzled their heads affectionately into the crook of her neck. She smiled at the loving reception. "Are you guys okay?" she asked.

They nodded and hummed.

"Kyla taking good care of you?"

They hummed and nodded again.

Ember stood up. "Okay. I have to ask you guys something very important."

They both looked up and took a step back.

"Do you know where your Uncle Bulder was during the Big Night? I thought he was with me

Aboveground helping your Uncle Barkuss load up the coal, but I'm not entirely sure."

The boys looked at each other and nodded in agreement. "No, Ember," Bambam said. "We both heard him tell our dad that he was going to help the Brotherhood guys."

"Yeah," Juju said, "he was going Aboveground, but not to help you. He was gonna go do that stuff with the twins up there."

"Yeah, then everything got crazy, and well…"

"Yeah. You know…" their voices simultaneously trailed off.

Ember looked over at Tannen and shook her head. That was more than enough confirmation she needed, but just to be absolutely positive of Bulder's tragic fate she said to him, "Go to Barkuss," and he nodded in agreement.

"Ember," Kyla pleaded, "what happened?"

Ember looked at Kyla, bewildered, and then back at the boys. She knelt down beside them again. "Listen," she began calmly, yet firmly, "I have to tell you something. There was a terrible accident in West Bank."

Kyla gasped. Her hand shot to her chest and gripped the collar of her shirt. "All the twins," Ember continued, "they were being held in a makeshift church in Mon Valley. And there was an accident. A fire. No one survived."

Bambam's eyes widened. "Are you saying that…"

"Uncle Bulder was there, though," Juju finished for him.

Ember nodded reverently. "Yes. We're almost certain that your uncle was there, too. Tannen's gonna head back to the Mines now to get the story straight."

"I'm on it," he said. "We'll figure this all out, boys," he tried to reassure them.

Ember gave him a soft smile of gratitude. "Thank you, Tannen."

His emerald eyes sparkled, and he winked at her. "Anything for you, Em. You know that." And he turned, going up the stairs, and left.

"Uncle Bulder?"

"Dead?"

"No way. It can't be true."

Their breathing got heavy, and they both sniffled up sobs in their throats, trying very hard to hold back the tears from coming. Kyla opened her arms and gathered the boys at each of her sides. She rubbed their shoulders and backs in hopes of calming them down. "An accident, Ember?" she said accusingly.

"I know where you're going, Kyla. I'm already there."

"Sturd? Was he there? Did he make it out okay?"

Ember chuckled. "Why yes! Surprisingly so!" the sarcasm dripped from her tongue. "Sturd and one of his Brotherhood cronies were A-okay. Turns out they *are* working together."

"Wait! It *wasn't* an accident?" Bambam blurted.

"Oh sweetie," Kyla said, using her "child" voice, "we don't know that for sure. We sure do hope it was an accident, but…"

"I'm not gonna lie to you, guys," Ember interrupted. "All signs point to it *not* being an accident."

"Ember!" Kyla exclaimed.

"What? They need to know the truth, Ky. They're big boys."

"They're still elflings, Ember. Kid gloves, ya know?"

"No. The kid gloves came off the second they were put in danger!"

Kyla squeezed the boys closer to her in a defensive stance, and they tried to wriggle from her grip.

"But there's something good from all this," Ember continued.

Kyla scrunched her nose. "What's that?"

"I think we have a little safety net going on over here. We can't take any risks, and you guys need to stay here at Skye Manor. But you don't need to stay down here anymore. This cellar will only be if you run into any trouble. You can go upstairs for the time being. They're not looking for you anymore. They think the boys are dead. They think they died in the fire. Chances are Sturd and the Brotherhood are on to the next phase of their plan."

"Ten Lords-a-Leaping?"

"Exactly. Their attention is now turned toward General Una and her crusade to protect the Boss. As far as they're concerned, all twin candidates at the Pole have been eliminated. They won't be coming around here, that's for sure. But like I said, be smart about things. Don't make too much noise, no obvious lights on by windows, no playing outside. In fact, don't ever leave the home. I'll be coming back to check on you and to bring supplies if you need them. If the Council is doing what I think they're doing, it's even more important that the twins are kept safe … and hidden." She knelt down to meet their eyes and stared hard and deep, her eyes darting back and forth between them. "You're the last, boys. The last of your kind. Probably the first, too," she said to them telepathically in Elvish.

The boys giggled.

Kyla cocked her head to the side. "Did you just…?"

Ember stood up and nodded.

"How can you?"

Ember shrugged. The Elvish language was something that came very naturally to her. When Kyla had first introduced her to it, it seemed to flow and grow and expand within her. It was as if it was awakening, like it had been there all along from birth, and just a few key phrases and words unlocked the mystical floodgates. "I don't know. I just *can*. It's how I heard them and knew they knew the language."

Kyla scrunched her nose up again. "Isn't that kind of…weird?"

Ember laughed. "Yeah, I guess so. But *I'm* kinda weird, so I don't really put too much thought into it."

"You're also kinda dead, too," Juju announced.

Ember paused, jarred by his strange words. "Huh? What are you taking about?"

Kyla fidgeted. "Ember, I told them to behave and not get into anything. I told them that down here was your father's private workspace. But… well… you know how elflings can be."

Ember's eyes narrowed. "And…?"

"And, well…"

Bambam raced to the drawing table and snatched a piece of paper from it. "This!" he shouted, waving it in front of Ember's face.

Ember snatched it from his hand and looked it over. "What is this? Where did you find it?"

But none of them answered. They gave Ember a few moments to read it through and absorb what it said.

"Certificate of Death? What? Ember Autumn Skye. Yeah, that's me, all right. March 14? Sure is my birthday. Signed Elden Skye, Carole Frost, Jack Frost, and Jolenir M'Raz?" She shook her head in confusion. "I don't get it. I don't understand. Why would my father have a death certificate with *my* name and *my* birthday listed? And why would the Boss sign such a document?"

"Yeah, you're clearly not dead," Bambam assured.

"Clearly," Juju chimed.

"Clearly," Ember joined. She turned the paper over and over in her hand, the words like a confusing foreign language. Elvish was much easier to digest than this!

How could a living, breathing elf be holding her own death certificate? And the signatures? Carole Frost? Nanny Carole Frost? As in, Docena Frost?

"I don't understand," she said again.

Kyla broke away from the twins and led Ember to the drawing table. "There's more," she said in a small voice.

"What do you mean?"

Kyla retrieved a manila folder, opened it, and started thumbing through the paper within. "Ember, apparently your father had a working relationship with the Boss."

Ember rubbed her eyes. "I know. He was some big wig toy executive or something."

"No. I think it was more than that. After I came across the death certificate, I did some snooping of my own. And well, from what I could piece together, your father was close to the Boss. Real close. Like, BF close."

The boys collectively exclaimed, "Huh?"

"Best friends," Ember informed. "So, what are you saying? They were friends. So what?"

Kyla flipped through the pile and pulled out a letter. "He knew, Ember," she said as she handed it to her. "He knew about you going to the Mines. The Boss apparently needed some kind of favor, and He called for you to go there. Your dad agreed."

Ember flicked the paper out in front of her face. Her brows furrowed deeply as she read the words aloud, "'Dear Elden, I'm sorry, but the time has come. It has been brought to my attention that suspicions are growing, and I fear for our safety. You know what you need to do. I need you to be strong and uphold our agreement, not only as a loyal subject of the Claus, but as a trusted friend and adviser. Sincerely, Jole.'"

So that's what Docena meant about my father having something to do with my Life Assignment…

She remembered her father's words when she got her Life Job assignment, the day her charmed elf-life had changed forever: *This is what the Boss wants for you. Your mother and I never imagined you would end up o'er there in the Mines, but apparently the Boss has got it all figured out.*

Lies. Lies. Lies. And more lies. It was all a big, giant conspiracy! He knew! He knew the entire time! Not only did he know about her assignment to the Mines, but he also *allowed* her to go! *Allowed* her to endure! He practically arranged for it to happen! Rage swelled from the pit of her stomach and up into her chest. In one crumpling motion, she destroyed the letter and tossed it to the floor.

Kyla must have sensed Ember's anger coming to a head because she quickly put her hand on Ember's shoulder. "Wait, Ember, your father had a plan to get you back!" she muttered, trying to get the words out before Ember's fury could be unleashed. "Look at all these blueprints," she said, pointing to the scattered papers on the drawing table. "He was kind of a crazy genius, ya know?" and she forced a chuckle, but continued when there was no response. "He had this idea, this plan, to create an underground passage. It would start here, right underneath this cellar space, and run all the way to the Mines. *To you.* He either wanted to smuggle you home, or have a way to visit you, or…"

Ember's face was stone cold. Not a muscle moved or twitched.

"Ember, don't you see? He wanted to rescue you," Kyla pleaded.

"But he died before it ever came to be," Ember said matter-of-factly.

"And because no one knew about this place, the plans died with him."

"That still doesn't erase the fact that he let me go to the Mines in the first place! Doesn't excuse the fact that he was a willing participant in my assignment!" She clenched her fists. "He lied to me. They all lied to me."

Of all the elflings, the Boss chose you! Trust me, you'll be cooking and sewing and singing all day like a Nanny Elf. You'll probably get to come back to the manor on weekends and holidays. Her father's words from long ago echoed in her mind.

Lies. All lies.

Ember gathered all the papers from the drawing table into a pile. She folded the blueprints and stashed them into the manila folder, then tucked the folder under her arm. "Be good," she said to the boys. "I'll be back as soon as I can," she said to Kyla and began making her way up the stairs.

"But, Ember," Kyla said, "those are your father's papers. Shouldn't you leave them down here?"

"Yeah? He won't mind. He's dead." She held the folder high up in the air. "And according to what it says in here, apparently I am, too."

CHAPTER SEVEN

The uneven cracks in the bathroom mirror gave Sturd a monster-like appearance.

Each deep crack and crevice gave way to the jagged visage of evil that stared back at him. It was frightening to look at the way the webbed fissure of glass made his red glaring eyes look as if there were hundreds of them piercing through the glass itself. His own stomach turned at the sight of his repulsive reflection, and for a split second, he wished his father had replaced that stupid broken mirror a long time ago.

Oh, who was he kidding? Sturd relished the ugliness, and surprisingly embraced every aspect of his newest transformation. Because what else could he call his new set of physical changes but a transformation of sorts? As a child, Sturd had thick, jet-black hair that hung heavily in his eyes. His father, Corzakk, had always complained when it would get tangled up under his hard hat, so his mother I'len would constantly take the scissors to it. Sturd's eyes were once gray and had shimmered like light glinting off two pieces of pale coal. He was a healthy, strong, and curious young elfling with much potential. When his mother had defected, his hair had fallen out and never regrew.

Loneliness and solitude became his preference, and he chose to spend his free time hiding in the darkest places in the Mines without a light source. His eyes ultimately adjusted to the darkness, and the once pale gray hue transformed to a glowing red. His body began to arch downward, and his fingers grew crooked and worn.

But now? On top of his forehead, two little nubs rose up under his flesh, and along the side of his cheeks, a thin layer of gray hair had started to grow. He even noticed that the tips of his ears had come together into a razor-blade sharp point. This new change was much more than physical, though. Something different was stirring inside him. He could feel it deep in the very fabric of his essence, the very marrow of his bones. He was wakening, shifting.

He tilted his head from side to side, admiring how the mirror made his red eyes look duplicated—each red reflection representing to him all the lives he's touched, or rather, all the lives he destroyed. What was his body count up to? He chuckled to himself when he realized he had lost count of every elflife he had either ruined or ended. The surge of happiness he got at the mere thought of pallid elf faces gasping for breath under the weight of his hands, or the smell of elf-flesh singeing in the cold winter night air filled him with a delight unlike any other. The memories wrapped him in ecstasy and made him feel drunk with power and pleasure. But for some reason, he suddenly thought of his mother again and paused at his circus reflection.

Sturd left the bathroom and made his way out back to the remnants of his mother's old garden and graeviary. This sacred place had been the home of many a night-blooming flower and the sanctuary for many Graespurs. All that was left was a shell— skeletal bones covered in coal dust and overgrown kissle leaves. Chinchis had now made their home under the back porch steps and around the ruins of the garden. Their underground tunnels rose up from the ground in half-cylinders. He kicked at one of the tunnels, leaving a gaping hole at the top. Any chinchi passing through would be exposed to the open air of the Mines, something they did not like. He sniggered. "Guess you'll have to build another tunnel," he said contemptuously before sitting on the back steps.

Being in the garden only brought more memories of his past, of his mother. The path from his transformation to complete destruction had only begun when she had left him. Had she stayed, would he have traveled down the same road? Would he have these red eyes that struck fear into the hearts of all elves who caught their gaze? Would he have still pursued the title of King Chaos? What path would he have chosen for himself?

Probably the same one.

Because at the end of the day, at the end of the conversation, Sturd was always Sturd. He would always be Sturd—destined for something other than the miserable hand of cards he had been dealt. He was different. Weird. Unlike any other elfling—noticeably so from an early age. Not like the others, and not just because his father had always told him so. It was something he had always felt deep inside.

He remembered the last time his grandmother had come to visit them.

Grandmother Melithoro. His mother's mother. She was stern and cold and hard and calloused; I'len had none of her hard attributes. He never knew her first name, either. She was always Grandmother Melithoro. Once, when he was just learning how to speak, he had called her Granny Mel, to which she responded with a sharp snap of the back of her hand across his face.

She scoffed at him when she came into the garden and saw him playing Chyga Hunter with some Graelings. He had been growling and stomping in the yard, sneaking up on the babies in the graeviary and violently shaking their enclosure.

"What in Claus's name is he doing?" she had said to I'len with her nose upturned.

I'len waved her hands in the air. "Oh, Mother! He's just playing. All little elflings play like that."

"Yes, but, it's just so... so... *odd* the way he plays."

Sturd stopped for a moment in order to hear his mother's response. Satisfied with her answer, he had gone back to playing but distinctly kept his eyes and ears open and tuned into their conversation.

Grandmother sat on the patio bench, and I'len followed next to her. "Hmmm," she hummed, smoothing out her elfmaid dress. "I don't recall your other boys playing wild like that."

I'len lowered her head, and Grandmother placed her hand in I'len's lap. "Have you seen them, dear? Have you spoken to them?"

I'len shook her head.

"They are your sons, I'len! All of them! They are all brothers, too. *All* of them! And brothers need to be together. And children need to be with their mother."

"But how can I see them without seeing *him*. Corzakk would never allow it."

"Borthen Dwin'nae is your true love," Grandmother said with a fierce tone. "And true love can't be kept apart. Bommer, Banter, Balrion, Bulder, and Barkuss, they are all the results of your love for Borthen. But that one…" She lifted her old finger at Sturd.

"Mother!"

"I'len, you know it's true. I don't care what decree the Council made, I don't care what alliance he has or what unholy agreement he made with them. There are five other elflings who need their mother, regardless of whom she is married to."

"I do miss them terribly," I'len responded in a soft voice. "But Corzakk says it's not wise to see them. It will only confuse them."

"Confuse them? How can they be any more confused! This whole mess is confusing. I swear, I'len, you should just…"

"Shush, Mother! Don't talk like that!"

Sturd's body shook when he heard his mother raise her voice.

"It's the truth, and you know it!" Grandmother continued. "Look at those bruises on your arms. You didn't think I didn't notice them, did you?"

"Mother, I cook. I clean."

"Oh, no! Don't you tell me that! I took care of my elfhusband. I raised my gaggle of elflings. I know the normal bumps and bruises and scrapes and scars that come with the territory. What you have is more than just usual elfwife markings. He hurts you; I know he does."

"It doesn't matter. I have to take care of him, and Sturd, and…"

"You need to go."

Fear gripped Sturd. He had no idea what Grandmother was suggesting. "Where are you going, Mother?" he squeaked in a pleading voice.

I'len smiled weakly at him. "Nowhere, my dear. Keep playing, sweetie." She stood up from the bench and walked back to the den. "Enough of this, Mother," she barked at Grandmother, "we're not having this conversation."

It wasn't long after that Sturd had come home from the Mines with Corzakk to find the den empty and the ominous note on the kitchen table—*"I'm sorry."*

Sturd was so deep in thought, he scarcely heard the creaking of the door behind him. He looked up as Corzakk wiggled his body through a small opening of the door and made his way onto the rickety porch. His work suit was covered in thick, dark ash as if he had been mining all day, and he reeked of coal fire. Sturd opened his mouth to ask why his father, a Master Elf, would be hacking and slashing away at the cave walls, but Corzakk beat him to it. "How are things coming along, Son?" he asked.

Sturd stood up to greet his father. He shook his head as if to shake off the daydream memory, and stepped off the porch creating a few feet of distance between him and his father. "Okay," he answered. "The Brotherhood have commandeered the Catta-cars and are transporting the cache of mining tools Aboveground. They should have Lapis Hall armed and secured with over a dozen elves by week's end."

"Good. But that's not what I meant. How are things coming along?"

Sturd was puzzled. "I just told you…"

"Sturd, I'm not stupid. I can see through this façade of your plans and this alliance with The Brotherhood."

Sturd tightened his lips together, holding his tongue, biding his time.

"The Council is not stupid, either, ya know? They're well aware of…"

"They're well aware of nothing!" Sturd interrupted. "What have you been doing all day? Don't you have some elflings who need training?"

Corzakk wiped his forehead with the back of his hand and exhaled. "Never you mind what I've been up to." A rumble sound rose from his chest and out of his throat in a violent, heaving cough.

Sturd winced at the sound. "How many times do I have to tell you? Do you have Coppleysites, again?"

Corzakk spit a mouthful of blood over the side of the porch. "Again? More like still. They haven't gone away."

Sturd shook his head and clicked his tongue on the roof of his mouth.

"But that's not what we were talking about, Son."

Sturd clenched his fists and inhaled. "The Council is not inside my head."

Corzakk let out a rattled laugh that echoed against the cave walls with a demonic pulse. "Of course they are!" he exclaimed. "What goes on inside here," he pointed to Sturd's head, "and what goes on inside there," he pointed to Sturd's chest, "is written all over your actions. They practically have you figured out and anticipate every move you make."

Sturd sneered. *Not true,* he thought. They never knew about the *Dublix Santarae*. Never knew about how his twisted fingers wrapped tightly around his brother Banter's throat, how he squeezed until his eyes bulged forward in shock and surprise, how he inhaled Banter's last breath of life and filled himself with a swoon that made him feel light as a feather, light as a feather, light as… There was no way they could ever understand the riveting sensation of the kill—the thrill of it, the excitement of it, the *love* of it.

"They only know what I allow them to know," he growled defensively.

Corzakk's mouth screwed up at one side. "You've been promised greatness from a very young age. Your aunt and uncle have given you a certain degree of freedom. I'm so very proud of you. Proud of the independent elf you've become. Proud of your determination to shape your own future, and carve your own destiny."

Under the Fortieth Provision of Regulation Thirty, you are permitted, he recalled his uncle's cryptic words to him.

"You know I'm going to rule one day very soon, Father."

Corzakk hesitated and scratched his head. Sturd's eyes narrowed in defiance. "I don't doubt that, Son," Corzakk began, his voice lowering slightly. "But you see, there's just one little thing."

Sturd's eyes flashed, and a wave of hot rage bubbled up in his stomach. *How dare he doubt me! How dare he!* His mind screamed on the inside, but he managed to maintain composure and control. All he could mutter was, "What are you talking about?"

"That elfwife of yours…" Corzakk trailed. *Ember.*

The thought of Ember sent chills down Sturd's spine. He briefly closed his eyes to envision her face—her soft apple cheeks glowing with life, her piercing sapphire eyes twinkling in the torchlight of the Mines, her full, pink lips pursed in a capricious little smile, her long golden locks spilling over her shoulders as her strawberry scent wafted in the space around her. The thought of her enticed him and infuriated him at the same time. He thought of her precious face—that precious, angelic face—that could take all his anger and sorrow away and fill him with furious rage all at the same time. He wanted to nuzzle up to her glowing apple cheeks, bury his face in her long hair to inhale her strawberry essence, gently kiss the soft flesh of her pink lips, and gouge her eyeballs out with his bare hands! "I wouldn't call her much of an elfwife."

"Yes, yes," Corzakk conceded ruefully, "this much is true. You never truly had a chance to assert yourself in the marriage. There were many roadblocks and other distractions that prevented you from ever really taking up grievances with the Council in regard to her disobedient behavior."

Sturd nodded. Everything Corzakk said was true. Much had happened since they stepped over the pickaxe and said vows in front of Parson Brown.

Corzakk stepped down from the porch and met Sturd in the garden. "But you're beyond all that. Past it. And if you are going to rule someday like you say you are, you are going to have to eliminate any and all threats. Just the way you've been doing, Son. But now, you need to take it a step further. You are never going to reach your full potential with her around. I see that now."

Corzakk reached into his back pocket and retrieved a small blue vial. With his crooked fingers, he twisted the top open and dipped his long, sharp fingernail within. "Hold this," he said, handing it to Sturd.

Sturd screwed the cap back on and held the vial in front of his face, mesmerized by the marbled blue glass. Corzakk walked over to the chinchi hole that Sturd had destroyed moments before and reached his arm into the top of the opening Sturd had created. He pulled out one of the brown-furred creatures from deep inside its vulnerable den and held it out by its tail. With his infected fingernail, he cut a deep line on the underbelly of the chinchi that ran from its neck to its abdomen. The animal jolted and reared up, but Corzakk released it onto the dirt ground. The creature righted himself and tried to run away back to its hole, but it flipped over onto its back and squealed and screeched in agony. Its cries were deafening throughout the garden, and it twitched and spasmed uncontrollably for a few minutes until it gurgled up a bubble of blood, gave a final moan, and died.

Sturd's eyes widened with delight at the spectacle before him. He remembered the feeling of Moon Glow and Alcanthia poison seeping into the pores of his face all those years ago. He remembered the torturous burn of the plant secretions soaking into his flesh, mixing with his blood, and invading the very center of his soul. He cocked his head and gave his father a questioning look.

"The Apothecary Elves were testing a new salve. This was a round one and, obviously, didn't go as planned for them. It was to be destroyed, but I fortunately was able to get a hold of it. This is all there is, so it must be used wisely."

Sturd placed the vial in the palm of his hand and closed his fingers around it carefully.

"On vermin," Corzakk continued, "it's quick acting. But on an elf of a particular size and stature, the effects are much more different."

"Different how?"

Corzakk smirked. "Probably more painful. Could probably bring on some kind of hallucinations. Could linger for days, I suppose."

"And you know this because…"

Corzakk motioned his arms up and down the front of his filthy work suit. "Looks like I'm going to need a new apprentice," he said.

Sturd's eyes flashed once more as visions of murderous scenes danced in his head. He imagined Ember before him on the floor, doubled over in the fetal position, writhing helplessly while mumbling something incoherent and crazy. It was a peaceful thought, a marvelous thought. He smiled in spite of himself.

Corzakk touched Sturd's shoulder. "Come on inside, Son. We have some guests who are waiting for you."

CHAPTER EIGHT

Tension settled in the Mines like a thick, inescapable fog. As Ember rode through the Mines on the Catta-car, she saw it on the faces of the elves working below her and heard it in the grumbling sounds their voices made, bouncing off the cavern walls. There was a subtle silence throughout, but layered beneath it was a sad groan and, even further down, an angry wail. She was afraid that the angry wail would soon rise up and overtake the groan, bursting through the silence in an eruption of chaos and violence.

It had already begun.

As the trolley car hurtled its way through Raker's Cove, Ember noticed two Brotherhood members had cornered an older Miner. One was yelling in the Coal Elf's face, while the other was reaching for the Miner's pickaxe.

"But it's the only one I got!" the elderly elf yelped.

The trolley zoomed by but not before Ember was able to see the Brotherhood elf snatch the pickaxe away and shove the old elf to the ground.

"Next stop, Onyx Alley," called the trolley car driver. Ember's heart sank a little when she realized it wasn't Tannen's voice over the speaker. The voice belonged to Bradden Trayth, one of Tannen's cousins.

I'll get off at Brickrock Hill and walk the rest of the way, she thought.

Ember leaned her head back against the headrest and sighed. The rocking of the trolley was normally calming for her, but when she looked around at the other elves in the car, her anxiety began to rise. Hard faces. Angry faces. Deep lined faces of years upon years of sunless work. Dirt-stained faces. Sweat and tear-stained faces. Each one told a different story of toil and pain. Some of it she understood—she, too, had had her fair share of struggle and strife. But there were stories in those faces that were beyond comprehension to her. Stories she could scarcely begin to fathom. Stories she didn't necessarily *want* to understand.

Looking at these Coal Elves reminded her of when she was forced to leave her family to begin her trade on her 10th elfyear—her orientation to the Coal Miner's Guild. An official coach had been sent to Skye Manor to collect her, and her family stood outside anxiously waiting for her to begin her new journey. When the coach rolled up, Ember stared at the tear-stained faces of the boy elves through the panes of glass as they passed by her. She saw real fear in their eyes as they swatted at their descending tears and blew their noses. She stiffened her back and inhaled some confidence. *It's okay*, she thought, *they'll be doing the work, and I'll have to take care of them now.*

Reporters, looky-loos, and curious townspeople all gathered at the gates when the coach arrived. Even the Stixx family from neighboring Tir-la Dunes had their little elflings all lined up in a row to see Ember off, yet her own sister Ginger wasn't there. Ember's mother Amalia had rushed out of their home and threw her body at the bottom of the carriage steps in full dramatic style. A Reporter Elf shot one, two, three pictures, and Mother knew at least one would make the front page of morning news the next day. This made Ember feel a little like a celebrity. They were all there to see *her*!

Before stepping onto the carriage, Ember raised her tiny hand and gave a quick wave to the crowd. Some elves cheered and yelled things like: "Stay strong, little one!" and "Don't be afraid!" Others just glared. Nanny Carole rushed up and handed her a small velvet package and told her to open it when she got settled. She kissed Ember on her forehead, and with tears in her eyes whispered, "Be seein' ya real soon, Emmy." Ember smiled back.

The carriage was packed with 20 elflings from all the different parishes of the North Pole. Sad faces. Scared faces. Sniveling, tear and snot-stained faces. I-want-my-Momma faces.

I'll have to take care of them now, she proudly thought again and clutched the package from her Nanny.

Before they reached the Mouth of the Cave, the elflings were given a satchel that contained instructions and clothes. They were to put their own clothing and any personal items into the bag and dress in the black jumpsuit provided. *Jumpsuit?* Ember puzzled. *But, I'm not a worker! Oh well, maybe I just need it to protect my clothes from the dirty caves.* And with that, she stripped from her scarlet blouse and rose-pattern skirt and into the ebony one-piece worker's garb. She neatly folded her clothes and placed them into the bag. Curiously, she fingered the soft velvet of the box Nanny Carole gave her. Afraid that if she placed it in the bag with her clothes she would never see it again, she quickly unfastened the short chain latch on the front and glanced inside. Inside was a brown, leather-bound journal with a note attached: *When you get lonely, Emmy, write it all down!* She quickly unzipped the side of her boot and stuffed the book in the space between the thick leather and her scrawny ankle. Then, she took the box and placed it in the bag with her clothes and set it outside her cabin door. She would never see the contents of that bag ever again.

It felt like ages had passed since she'd even thought about her trusty journal. *So long ago*, she thought. *So very long ago.*

How much had changed in her life since that fateful day? How much had changed in *all* of their lives? A lifetime's worth of change. Had any elf, in the history of elfhood, experienced so many ups, downs, and twists and turns in the span of 10 elfyears? But the more she thought about it, about the changes that happened to her, the more she realized that so much had actually stayed the same.

So many elves had good intentions, yet so many executed those intentions very poorly. The Brotherhood was partially right about needing change in the entire North Pole system, but was being militant about it the way to go? *Man, if I were ruler, I'd…*

Her mind shifted back when she noticed one of the Coal Elves on the trolley car was looking at her with a twisted face. Quickly, she looked down, realizing in her daydream memory she had actually been rudely staring at him. She fidgeted with her hair—guilt and nerves getting the best of her. A long, gray strand mixed in with the blonde, and she plucked it out right before the trolley stopped and Bradden called over the speaker, "Brickrock Hill!"

Ember stood up, shimmied between the seats, hopped off the Catta, and walked the rest of the way back to her den.

When she got there, Barkuss and Balrion were sitting on her couch, and Tannen was at the dining room table. Barkuss's cheeks were red and puffy, and his eyes were bloodshot—tell-tale signs that he had been in a crying fit. She nodded at Tannen when she caught his eye—a gesture that was more of a "thank you" than a "hello." It was like a weight lifted off her chest knowing that Tannen had broken the news about Bulder to the others. She flung the manila folder onto the table and said, "Hey guys."

Barkuss was dazed, but he shot up from the couch and scooped her into his arms in a death-grip embrace when he realized she was there. "Oh, E!" he gushed, nuzzling his face in the crook of her neck.

She patted the back of his hair lovingly. "I'm so sorry, Barkuss. I'm so sorry." She looked at Balrion from over his shoulder. "Bommer?" she mouthed.

Balrion nodded. "He's out of his mind right now. Went storming off. Was saying something about not having a proper burial and all that."

Ember's lips tightened. "But, does he know about the boys?"

Barkuss released her, took a step back, and looked deeply into her eyes. "Yes. Yes, he does."

Ember grabbed his hands and squeezed to assert her assurance. "I promise you, Barkuss, they are all right. I just saw them. They are safe and healthy and alive."

Barkuss gave a small, soft smile. The news was probably bittersweet for him to hear.

"Kyla is the perfect one to watch over them. The fact that she speaks Elvish will be an extra layer of protection for them. They're okay. They're all okay."

Barkuss nodded. "I know. I know," he said solemnly. "I trust Kyla. She is a good and true friend."

She smiled and nodded. "We're lucky to have her."

Barkuss moved to the couch and sat next to his brother again.

"Bulder was weak," Balrion said angrily. "When our mother was re-assigned to a new family, it hit him the worst. It was like he had given up. He had his run-in with grulish, and we almost lost him then. He was always talking craziness about defecting…"

"Yes. He was very impressionable, too," Barkuss interrupted. "Always looking for something to hold on to. And when that Brotherhood came along, he jumped right on in." He huffed. "I think it gave Bommer some comfort knowing that maybe Bulder had some direction for once in a long while."

"Yeah, but look where that got him, the big dummy!" Balrion exclaimed.

Ember sat down on the chair next to the couch. She placed her hand lovingly on Barkuss's leg. "There was nothing you could do. Either of you. Bulder had a fragile mind."

"I could have been there for him more," Balrion said, his eyes fixed on the floor.

"I don't believe that," Ember said. "You did what you could for him. All of you. You tried to help him. You always came through for him when he needed it. Some elves can't be fixed. Change has to come from within, and only when someone wants it and is ready to commit. At least you know that Bulder finally thought he was making that change and doing what he thought was right in his life. He was picking up the broken pieces and trying to make sense of himself."

"You said it yourself, The Brotherhood gave him a sense of renewed purpose," Tannen added.

"Exactly," Ember continued. "His death was not in vain. He really, truly thought that he was doing something good for himself," she moved her other hand to touch Balrion, "for others," she looked back at Barkuss, "and for his family. What happened was a complete accident that was beyond anyone's control."

Barkuss's eyes brightened. She didn't have the heart to tell them she had suspected foul play in the Mon Valley Abbey fire. Telling them would solve nothing and only bring more anger to an already volatile situation. And if Bommer was in the state that Balrion said he was in, it would only unnecessarily stir the pot.

Barkuss and Balrion stood up, and Barkuss tapped Ember on the shoulder. She rose to meet another one of his tight embraces. "Thanks, E. What would we do without you?"

"Thank you, Ember," Balrion said as he reached the door. "Let's go, Barkuss. Let's go calm down Bommer and Jacinda."

With a final tap on the back, Barkuss left with Balrion.

"Barkuss is a good elf," Tannen remarked when they were gone.

"Yeah," Ember agreed. "He really is the best. Ya know, he was my first mining partner when I began working here. He got moved up to Coal Collector soon after, but we worked side by side in Crystal Cave for a little bit."

"Really? You never told me that."

"It was so funny. I remember the first time I heaved my ax up to pierce the rock, my hands were shaking so bad that I dropped it and it landed on my foot. I started crying and some of the other elves on the crew were snickering and stuff. But Barkuss comes strolling up to me, wagging his finger in my face, hand on his hip and says, 'Oh no! CUH-LAWZ no!'" Ember waved her finger in the air and sashayed her hips in her best Barkuss impersonation. "He said to me, 'Ain't no cry-babies on my crew! You pick up that ax and keep hacking, girl!'"

Tannen laughed.

Ember laughed, too. "The rest is history. He was so unlike any elf I had met in the Mines, and we just kinda... I don't know... clicked."

"Different. Like you."

"Yeah. Just like me. But *different*."

"So, Em, what's all this here?" Tannen motioned to the manila folder on the table.

Ember stiffened up. "Stuff from my father's workroom."

Everything but that death certificate junk, she thought as she touched her pocket.

"Anything good?"

Ember shrugged her shoulders. "I dunno," she said apathetically.

"Mind if I…"

"Knock yourself out," she answered with a wave of her hand.

Tannen flung the file open, and his eyes lit up. "Whoa!" he marveled. "Check out these blue-prints! Look at these plans! This is some pretty advanced work here, ya know."

Ember plopped on to the couch and rubbed her temples ruefully. "I guess. I don't really understand half of it. The twins seemed to get a kick out of that flying skateboard thingy, though I didn't see what the big to-do was all about."

Tannen's hands raced feverishly through the stack like an excited kid in a candy store. "No, no, no. You have no idea! Blueprints. Architecture. This is my *thing*. I was bred for this type of stuff."

She propped her legs onto the coffee table in front of her. "Well, better you than me. If you think any of that junk is worth something, well, have at it."

"Oh, Ember!" he gushed. "You have no idea. Ya know, legend has it that the very first Trayth to come to the Mines came by total accident."

"Oh yeah? You've told me plenty of sto-ries about…"

"Hmm," he rubbed his chin. "Not sure if I told you this one."

Ember smiled. She always enjoyed Tannen's stories, especially the ones about his family and their history. "Okay, I'll bite," she relented.

"Well," he continued, "legend has it that way back when elves were called one name…"

Ember waved her hand in the air. "Which was like thousands of thousands of thousands of years ago…" she interjected with a doubtful tone.

"Yeeeessss," he sang, "the very first Trayth. His name was just Trayth. Back in the olden times, when elves only had a first name, ya know? Anyway, he was a Tree Elf from Aboveground. Legend has it that he was so massive and mighty that he was more giant than elf."

Ember puffed in disbelief. "Oh yeah?"

"Are you gonna let me tell this story or not?"

Ember rolled her eyes playfully. "Go on, go on."

"So, legend has it that giant elf Trayth was sitting high up in tree. Well, he was a bit clumsy…"

"A Trayth family trait?"

Tannen paused for a second, smiled, and ignored her. "And he fell out of the tree. Well, he was so big that he caused a depression to open up, and he fell right through. Right down to the Mines. He came upon these caverns by sheer accident. So, he wandered around in the dark for about a month and made maps of everything he saw."

"No way!" she bellowed. "That's not what happened. The Boss hired the Tree Elves to build in the Mines."

"Yes, but legend says that Trayth's original plans were passed down through the Trayth family line and were the basis for the Catta-car system, the bridges and landings, the rafting stations, and all that when the Boss made the call."

"And then what happened?"

"I don't know. The story stops there, I guess."

Ember crossed her legs. "Not much of a story, then is it?"

"I guess not, but it's a fun little origin tale the mommas tell the elflings at Adam's Day parties and such." Tannen paused when he came to a large map in the stack of papers. "Hey, Em?" he called. "This is actually pretty good."

She perked up. "What is? What are you talking about?"

"Come here for a sec. You should see this."

Ember got up and stood over Tannen's shoulder. "What? What am I looking at here?" She paused. "Oh. The tunnel," she said unenthusiastically.

"You saw this? This is genius! This blueprint would directly connect Skye Manor to the Mines. If my calculations are correct, the tunnel would lead right... into... Crystal Cave. See? Right there." He pointed to a spot on the blueprints.

Ember sighed with disappointment. "My father's great escape plan for me."

"Really? Well, regardless, I think it could work."

"What do you mean? What are you thinking?"

"Well, for one thing, a connection like this would change the way coal would be delivered Aboveground. We could bypass the Ignis River. See here," he pointed to another spot and drew a line from one end to the other, "it's a straight shot through. It would definitely open the doors wide for trade and travel and…"

"Freedom?" Ember asked. Her face twisted as her mind began to unravel the multitude of possibilities.

"Yeah. Freedom," Tannen repeated with a smile.

She grabbed on to Tannen's shoulders and started shaking them with delight. "No Ignis. No Mouth. No Guards. No Passes. No rules and regulations. Tannen, can you imagine—Aboveground and Underground elves traveling between the two realms *freely* for like, the first time ever?"

"West Valley would get a make-over, that's for sure!"

They both laughed.

The implications were endless. The possibilities unprecedented. The thought of a free society where elves had the right to choose their destinies for themselves made her feel giddy inside.

Maybe this is the change we need? Maybe this is the change we have to commit to?

Maybe Father was right?

"You really think this is possible?" Ember asked excitedly.

"Possible. Plausible. Doable. However you want to call it. Your dad laid the foundation right here. It's pretty simple, actually. I could definitely pull this construction job off. I'm not just a Catta-car driver, ya know." He winked at her, and she blushed.

"But, what *if* elves had the power to choose where they wanted to go, or be, or stay? Do you think there would be a mass exodus of the Underground? Would Coal Elves just up and abandon their posts in favor of the Aboveground? And would any of the Abovegrounders willingly *choose* to leave their sunny lives up there for a much darker one down here? Wouldn't the balance get thrown off once again?"

"Maybe at first, but you'd be surprised. Think about it, Em. Look at Bommer. He has no desire to go Aboveground. But would he travel? Would he visit? Who knows? And the Trayths. They *chose* to stay here. They *chose* to come to the Mines. But would some go back Above if they could? Who knows?"

"How *would* we know? How would *they* know if they never had the choice in front of them?"

Tannen tapped his long finger on the tabletop. "This Blueprint can give them that choice."

Ember thought back to the boy elves in the carriage that day so long ago. How many of them had wanted to be a Toy Designer, or a Chef Elf, or a Fishing Elf? She thought about the hard faces of the Coal Elves on the trolley car that morning and the weary faces of so many she had come across during her years in the Mines. How many of them were truly content with what they had? How many had wished they were a Banker Elf, or even someone's elfhusband? She thought about Bulder—a tragic elf so desperate to make some kind of meaning out of his own existence—the very thing most of them spent their entire elflives doing, and she thought how very easily she could have ended up like him, or Nim Nim'sim, or I'len Dwin'nae, or even Pepper Brightly.

"If only I had the power to…" she began.

Ember still had a tight grip on Tannen's shoulders. He lifted up one of his hands and clasped it over hers. Electric waves pulsated throughout her body, and she closed her eyes, letting the heat from his aura surge within. She closed her eyes and did everything in her power to keep from crying.

I just want something I can never have, she thought, and she didn't know if she meant having power in the Pole to change things for her people, or the love of her life.

Or both.

CHAPTER NINE

It was jarring to see their living room filled with guests, as Sturd and Corzakk weren't the type to normally entertain. No one ever came by to celebrate the big holidays or successes, and certainly, no one ever came to visit "just because." But here they were—Councilmembers in the Mines at Welfort Den. Sturd's Aunt Una, Uncle Zelcodor, and Councilmembers Quisto Calix and Cerissa Lux sitting regally on his couch.

Immediately, his pointy ears perked up. In his entire elflife, his family members had rarely made the trek to the Mines. So why were they here now, dressed in their official Council Member garb— their black hooded robes with the purple braided cords around their necks, making them look like wizards and witches rather than elves.

"Aunt Una. Uncle Zelcodor. Councilmembers," Sturd said, tipping his head respectfully in each of their directions.

They all nodded back.

"Hello, my dear nephew," Una said, her voice deep and quiet.

"Forgive me for staring," Sturd continued suspiciously, "it's just that I hardly expected to see you all gracing us with your presence down here." He eyed them over again trying to make sense of this visit. "Your robes," he pointed, "if there was an important meeting to be held, why, you could have just sent for me, and I would have traveled up to Headquarters."

"We needed to speak with you, Sturd," Quisto said. "All meetings at Headquarters need to be logged in. Minutes need to be submitted for the records."

"This is more of a personal visit than an actual meeting," Zelcodor added.

Cerissa Lux crossed her legs then shifted uncomfortably and re-crossed them.

Sturd looked over at her, and even in the dimly lit room, he could see a blanched look of apprehension wash over her face like a white eclipse. She nervously twirled the frays of her purple cord around her fingers and struggled to find a comfortable position on the couch. Sturd knew her to be the gentle one on the Council, the voice of reason, the voice of morality. And here she sat in this dark domain nervous and scared. Sturd licked his lips and smiled at her terror.

"Okay," Sturd said to his uncle, "get personal."

Una motioned for them to take a seat on the chair, and he and Corzakk obeyed. "You see, Sturd," she began, "everything has been building up for many, many elfyears. Over three hundred, to be exact."

Sturd cocked his head to the side when he realized for the first time his aunt was ancient in her own right yet looked not a day over 40 elfyears. *Some great magics must enshroud her*, he thought.

Una continued speaking, but Sturd was distracted. Cerissa shifted in her seat again, and with every slight movement she made, the scent of her fear wafted in the air. Sturd inhaled the smell like a hound dog picking up the scent of its prey. It was a heavy metallic scent, like old, rusted iron. The blue veins under the flesh of her cream-colored neck pulsated with every quickened beat of her heart. They rose up and twitched against her skin so violently, Sturd was certain they would burst wide open. A thin coating of sweat formed on his palms. The veins delighted him. And he wondered: if he wrapped his hands around her throat, would those veins burst forth the metallic-smelling ooze within them?

Una cleared her throat "…as you know."

Sturd snapped back and looked at his aunt. "Yes, yes, of course," he said, breaking out of his murderous daydream.

"According to *The Dublix Santarae*, with which I know you are quite familiar, when a Claus is ready to dissipate into the Mists of the North, the twin sibling would naturally step into the position."

"But can you imagine what life is like for the twin?" Zelcodor interjected. "The twin leads a very long elflife because the Claus lives much longer than the average elf. And when the Claus goes back to the Mists, the sibling, who has lived alongside the first, would then be set to embark on *their* extended elflife as the de facto Claus."

Quisto nodded. "Double Santa. Double Life. Double Time."

Una sucked in a breath of air through her teeth. "Yes, but because of the special circumstances surrounding my brother and me, I was told early on that things would be vastly different in our case. While I would live alongside Jole for the duration of his Claus life, I would *not* be eligible to *be* the Claus when his time was up. I was told my second life would be a normal elflife. I would live. I would grow old. I would die. Like the rest of you. Like a normal elf. No grand finale. No glorious final exit. No riding on the wind with the Mists of the North. Just lights out. Exit stage left."

"And...?" Sturd said, urging her story along, wishing that the four of them would just get on with it and leave.

Una leaned forward and reached for the tops of Sturd's knees. "You, Sturd. You have changed all that. We always knew from early on that you would be something special." She turned her head to look at Zelcodor who grinned proudly.

"From before your birth, even," Corzakk reinforced.

Una smiled at Sturd. "Yes. And you've done splendidly well. You have been my champion all along, and I am eternally grateful for that."

Sturd pulled back from her touch. "Champion? What you mean 'champion?'" he snapped.

Zelcodor leaned forward to line up with Una. "You have put into motion a series of events that have positioned your aunt to claim her birthright and become the Claus."

Sturd's ears tingled and he clenched his fists. His sharp nails dug into the palms of his hands, mixing his sweat with pinpricks of blood.

"The Coal-less Night, The Double Coal Night, Christmas in July, The Twin Round-up. You know the rest," Quisto said.

"The Mists have no choice but to name Jolevana M'Raz Ruprecht the Claus once Jolenir is called back," Zelcodor said.

"I was born first, Sturd. It should have been me. *I* should have been called first. But the Mists denied me. They took my true destiny right from under me. I just want what is rightfully mine. And now, with the elimination of the twin candidates, my reign will be longer by at least an entire generation, if not more."

Sturd bit his lower lip, trying desperately to contain his rage.

Quisto ran his hands down the front fold of his robe. "Your efforts in our plight to instate the rightful ruler will be handsomely rewarded."

Una clapped her hands together. "Absolutely! You will take my spot on the Council when I finally ascend. This has always been the plan."

Sturd looked to Corzakk, who smiled and nodded. Sturd curled his upper lip in a silent sneer, and the smile quickly faded from Corzakk's face.

A pawn? They think I'm the pawn in their little power game? he thought and stood up from his chair. He paced back and forth across the living room floor. Cerissa squeaked in her throat every time his leg brushed up against her robe. "No, no, no!" he exclaimed with his head down. "That's not good! That's not what *I* want!"

Corzakk stood up and stepped in front of him. He placed his hands on his shoulders as if trying to talk sense into his son. "What are you talking about? Your aunt is the highest ranked Councilmember. Having her position would give you what you've always wanted—that high level of power and control."

Sturd jerked from Corzakk's touch.

Una and Zelcodor exchanged nervous looks. Cerissa remained silent, but her eyes were cast down, and she rocked back and forth.

"You would be in direct service to the Claus— above me, above Castleberry, above Cerissa, and even your uncle. The Council has much power and an extensive amount of control. You know this. You've seen what we've done," Quisto tried coaxing.

Sturd could no longer control himself. The cage of decorum had trapped him for too long, and his suppressed anger and fury was suffocating him. "What *you've* done?" he roared. "What *you've* done? You haven't done anything without me! I'm not your puppet! Those actions were mine. Those decisions were *mine*. If not for me, your little schemes and plans would have never come to pass. I don't want to be in direct service to the Claus. I'm going to *be* the Claus!"

Cerissa gasped as her hand flew up to clutch her chest.

"Sturd!" Corzakk reprimanded, but Sturd turned to his father with a fatal look, his red eyes silencing him.

Una and Zelcodor looked at each other again and chuckled. "Oh, Sturd!" Una gushed. "I do love your fire and your ambition. It's quite admirable, actually. But you have no claim. No birthright. There would be no way for the Mists to elect you, even if you begged them. Even if you offered them your soul."

Sturd's breathing came in labored pants, like a wild animal that was unsuccessful in the hunt. His body bent forward, and he placed his head between his knees trying to catch a full, solid breath. He closed his eyes tightly and the black shadows swirled in his mind's eye—gripping him, dizzying him. His head raced and pulsed, and his ears filled with a sharp buzzing sound. He didn't know if he was going to pass out or lash out.

Finally, he flung his head up from between his legs and opened his eyes. The first thing he saw was Cerissa sitting on the couch tightly clutching onto her purple cords. The fear in her eyes, the thin line of sweat dripping down the side of her face, the rapid pulse of her veiny neck, every aspect of her weak, pathetic self drove Sturd to the point of no return. With a guttural scream, he pounced on Cerissa and dragged her to the floor.

Cerissa bawled as Sturd mounted on top of her, pinning her with all his weight. "Please! Stop! No! Jolevana! Help meeee!"

Quisto grabbed on to Sturd's back, trying to pry him off his fellow Councilmember, but Una yelled for Quisto to stop. "Let him!" she instructed, and Quisto took a step back.

Cerissa's cries enraged Sturd even more, and he grabbed her by the collar of her robe and slammed her upper body against the stony floor, knocking her unconscious. The veins in her neck had quieted their throbbing to a slow, steady pace. With one swift motion, he clasped his boney fingers tightly around her throat and squeezed.

A collective gasp settled in the room, but all he could focus on was the white throat, his hands firmly gripped around it, the quickening of the blue veins under the skin. His head felt fuzzy, as if he were underwater, and he barely heard the voices yelling around him:

"Sturd, stop!"

"Sturd, get off her!"

"Sturd, let go of her!"

Male elf voices. Hushed voices. Excited voices. Jumbled voices. Soothing voices. Voices around him mixed with the sounds of his own discordant moans and grunts. Anger and fear and hatred and disgust and shock filled the air in the room, and he breathed it all in. Breathed in the panic.

Breathed in the chaos. Breathed in the violence. And breathed in Cerissa Lux's very last breath as she went limp underneath him.

As he stood up, the lifeless body thudded on the floor, and he wiped the sweat from his brow with the back of his hand. Horrified faces stared at him. Mouths gaped open. Eyes wide with shock. Sturd straightened out his back and moved his neck from side to side, cracking all the bones in his twisted neck and shoulders. He wanted to smile. Wanted to laugh. Wanted to relish all the different and electrifying sensations from the kill, but he couldn't. "What the…" he wanted to say, but something prevented him from saying anything. Corzakk's face screwed up to one side, and before Sturd could walk toward him, a body-rocking tremor arched his back behind him. The bones in his neck and spine crackled and separated, each one breaking apart and sending explosive shock waves throughout his body. His head snapped to face the ceiling, dangling behind him and barely hanging on to the muscles and ligaments of his neck.

It's happening again, he thought.

In an instant, there was the feeling of claws at his feet making deep cuts from the tops of his bones, up the skin of his shins, around his waist, and to the center of his chest. Hot blood oozed from the claw lines and saturated his boots and jumpsuit. It was sticky against his clothes. The open wounds stung like wasp needles piercing him over and over again. Pressure in his fingers and toes throbbed from within the nailbeds as the nails of his twenty digits forced their way out and into long jagged claws.

A sharp wind blasted through the room, and a cold mist enveloped him—raising him off the ground, keeping him levitated where he stood bent and broken and bleeding and changing and growing.

"What's happening to him?" Corzakk shouted over the roar of the unnatural squall.

"Step back!" Una answered. "Whatever you do, don't touch him!"

Sturd had risen two feet from the ground in his arched position when a stabbing sensation swept across his forehead. The nubs that had pushed their way up from the skin of his forehead were expanding and twisting and growing. They curled out in long, thick spirals with a sharp point at their ends.

Suddenly, the wind stopped, and Sturd fell on top of Cerissa's body. He moved his hands up and down frantically to feel himself. To his surprise, he wasn't bent, wasn't broken, wasn't bleeding. But his head felt heavy, and when he raised his hands to his forehead, he nearly gasped at the touch of his new facial addition.

Horns.

"It's happened!" Una declared in disbelief.

Corzakk quickly knelt down by the side of his son and put his arm around his shoulder. Sturd growled and jerked away. "I'm fine!" he said through gritted teeth, but the world around him was still fuzzy. He felt weak. Spent. Like he needed to sleep for a very, very long time.

"*What's* happened, Una?" Quisto said breathlessly as he surveyed the scene.

"It's the prophecy," she said. "The ancient Prophecy of Shadows. Sturd is transforming. He's becoming."

"Becoming what?" Zelcodor questioned.

"He's becoming The *Knecht*—the Servant of the Dark. This was foretold thousands and thousands of elfyears ago." Una lifted her arms into the air and closed her eyes. A strange smile swept across her face as she recited the ancient prophecy. "The Spirit of the Dark will come to be when the shadows descend upon the North in the form of a wild foundling. Bearing the Claws of Retribution, the Fangs of Contempt, and the Horns of Punishment, he will rise above the ashes to bring pain and suffering to the world below!"

Quisto and Zelcodor fell to their knees and bowed before Sturd. Corzakk hesitated at first but soon followed suit.

Sturd ran his tongue over the teeth in his mouth. A sharp fang pricked the top of it, and he hungrily sucked at the wound, letting the blood fill his mouth completely before swallowing.

"*Al freeg oft Krampusfrecht!*" Una chanted in Elvish.

Quisto, Zelcodor, and Corzakk repeated the unfamiliar words the best they could.

"*An daig unt Krampusnacht!*"

Again, they tried to repeat.

"Rise, Knecht Ruprecht," she said as she motioned her arms for him to stand. "Rise, and I will show you the way to your destiny."

Sturd shivered deep in his bones. He planted his hands on Cerissa's waist and tried to hoist himself up. In his mind, he was strong and able to sustain his weight on his feet, but such was not reality. He felt intoxicated and was barely able to put a coherent thought together, let alone coordinate his body! He stumbled forward, and his face landed directly on top of Cerissa's—cheek to cheek. The faint smell of her body's slow decay caught his attention, and he stared longingly at her wide eyes. Fearful eyes. Terrified eyes. Eyes that would no longer witness pain or corruption or chaos.

So sad, he thought tiredly. *So sad she won't get to see the hell I'm going to unleash on her friends.*

"Quisto, help him up," Una ordered. "We'll bring him to Norland to monitor his progress."

"And… her..?" Corzakk said, motioning to the dead body in his living room.

"Sim," Sturd muttered.

"Certainly," Zelcodor acknowledged. "I'll order some of the Brotherhood to come by and…"

"Oh," Corzakk interjected with a disappointed tone.

Zelcodor chuckled. "Apologies, brother. I leave her in your hands. I had forgotten about your *particular tastes.*"

Corzakk smiled and nodded.

Zelcodor and Quisto hoisted Sturd under one of their arms and led him to the door with Una following behind.

"Sim," Sturd repeated.

"What's that, Sturd?" Una asked.

"Sim. Put Sim Nim'sim on the Council. In her place."

Una huffed. "I'm not sure that's such a good idea right now, Sturd. Her family will need to process and…"

Zelcodor turned his head back to look at her. "Do what he asks, Una. I'll make sure everything is okay. If Sturd's going to take your spot, he's going to need to have a say in…"

"Fine, fine," she relented. "Let's deal with all of that later. First let's get him up North so we can prep him."

CHAPTER TEN

The halls of the castle were unusually chilly, even for Docena Frost M'Raz—The Ice Queen of Lapis Hall. Even here in her office, on the east side of the mansion where the sun touched the most, there was an unusual chill that filtered throughout. *Lapis Hall—the land of sunshine and rainbows.* This time of year, to the human eye, there was complete darkness at the North Pole. And rightfully so! With everything that went on there, it was only logical that her homeland would be shrouded in the most ancient of magics.

She exhaled a puff of smoky-white breath. While she normally would invite the frigid temperatures, the last few days had been a little too much to bear. Could she be feeling the effects of her age? Had the centuries worn down her natural immunities to the freezing drop of the thermometer? She was always one to embrace the bitter aspects of winter by prancing around in no more than a business suit while the rest of her staff—and even her husband, Jolenir—wrapped themselves in layer upon layer of heavy material.

She adjusted the collar of her fox coat to warm her neck with its fur lining and blew into the palms of her clasped hands. The only other time she could remember actually feeling the bite of the cold was when she was an elfling and a Thundersnow Storm ripped through the North Pole. But that was so many years ago, and according to her father Jack, storms like that only happened once every few thousand years.

Docena opened the drawer of her work desk, pulled out her Memory Book, and placed it on the granite surface next to the transmitter whose light was flashing green. She sighed as she opened her book and looked longingly at the transmitter—two symbolic elements of her past, present, and ultimately her future. The book was cream-colored and leather bound, tied neatly with turquoise lace. It smelled of old paper—crisp, with a hint of mold. Her heart fluttered as she turned each page and watched the pictures in the magic book come to life before her eyes. With a touch of the owner's finger, every image ever captured and stored in the book replayed a scene for nearly 30 seconds at a time. Like mini, audio-less movies to be watched over and over again. It had been some time since she had taken a stroll down memory lane, but for some reason, today felt like the right time.

An elf outside the window shouted and multiple voices were quickly raised in anger. She shook her head to block the noises out. Soon, Lapis Hall would be the center of attention with the armed guards of the Brotherhood on watch 24 hours a day. Docena just wanted this moment for herself to reminisce and relive some of her younger days in peace.

She certainly was not a young elf, that was for sure! On the first page of the memory book, there were pictures of her parents, Jack and Terralyn Frost, and all of her brothers and sisters—the entire Frost clan. She touched a family portrait, and the image sprang to life. Little brother Killian couldn't sit still if his life depended on it. Mother had to keep pulling him in line to stand next to big brother Gildan. Gildan was no help because he was so concerned about which side was his "good" side that he kept turning back and forth from left to right and ignored their mother's pleas to hold little Killian in place. Little sister Rora refused to let go of her Vixen stuffed animal. She kept cuddling the toy next to her cheek, which essentially blocked the elflings face from the shot. Big sister Maiza had to keep lowering the toy from Rora's face to her waist, and at one point even swatted the elfling's hand to stop. The eldest of her siblings Carole looked bored out of her mind, while five-year-old Docena kept moving in and out of the frame. In the last few seconds of the scene, Father threw his hands up in desperation and mouthed "Are we done?" Whoever had taken the picture that day must have either had a good ole laugh or wanted to run for the Cherry Blossom Mountains!

Docena smiled and turned the page. The array of pictures before her brought her back to times she had almost forgotten, times when things were simple and safe, times when she hadn't a care in the world but to play with her gaggle of siblings and swim under the ice-sheets of the frozen lake in their backyard.

But flipping through the pages was bittersweet because the memories of the past gave way to the events of the present. It amazed her how she had outlived the majority of her family. Her role as the Boss's wife gave her the same life extension as the Claus, and Docena had lived to bury her own mother, her brothers, her sisters (except for one), and many of her nieces and nephews. But when Jole's time was up, she would begin her second life in her ancestral home of Hailstone Peak on Ice Island, where she would grow old and eventually die. Her father Jack Frost still lived in his outpost on top of the mountain, but he had been a hermit for many a century. Would that happen to her? She wondered how he had felt about being alone, about having to bury his own wife and the lot of his children. She wondered how she would fair when Jole was no more and she would begin her second life. What would aging be like? What would it be like to die? She had lived for so long, her own death had never really been much of a thought, but now things were different. Her own mortality was within her reach.

A click-clacking sound against the ice stones in the hallway froze Docena's daydreams in their tracks. She knew it was her assistant Senara before the knock even came to the door. "Come in," Docena called when the clicking approached closer.

Senara burst into the office. Her chestnut brown hair was pulled back into a tight bun with frazzled strands framing her soft face. "I've tried, Madame!" she huffed, exasperated. "I've tried just about everything with her! I don't know what else to do! She's just so… so… *exhausting!*" She clicked her way to the couch across from the desk and plopped down into it. The purple velvet cushions sank deep with the weight of her fatigued body.

Docena slammed the memory book closed with an echoing *thud*. "Oh, Senara! How bad can it be? I've asked you to do one thing."

"But she asks so many questions! I brought her to the library like you told me to, but all she wanted to do was roam around and read what she wanted to read. I brought her the books like you instructed, but she slid them down the end of the table and insisted upon reading something else. And every five seconds she demands to see the Boss. I tell her 'No, Ember, that's impossible.' And then she says, 'Well, why?' and we go through that whole routine for at least five minutes. Then she wants to wander around the grounds, and I know she's just trying to snoop around. I know she's trying to look for Him."

"You know she would never find Him. You have nothing to worry about there."

Senara exhaled and blew a strand of hair away from her eyes. "I'm beat, Madame! Watching over Ember Ruprecht is worse than a schoolhouse full of elflings!"

Docena waved her hand in the air dismissively. "Oh, stop being so dramatic, Senara! Where is she now?"

"Outside. She said she wanted to see what the Brotherhood was up to. I figured it was the safest thing to let her do and would prevent her from…"

Docena closed her eyes and shook her head.

Senara sat up at attention. "Madame," she said in a low voice.

Docena opened her weary eyes.

"About the Brotherhood."

"Yes, Senara," Docena said with an aggravated tone. "What about them?"

"They're very… um… how can I say this?" Senara stuttered. "Um… they're very… brash."

Docena inhaled. "Well, dear, you'll have to remember—most of them have never been Aboveground before."

"Yes, but, the tools they carry, and the way they push and pull at each other. It's just a little… well, some of the servants are a bit frightened of them."

"Then you need to do what you do best. Damage control."

Senara bit her lower lip and hesitated sheepishly. "Well, you see Madame, *I'm* a little bit frightened."

Docena stood up and walked over to Senara. She outstretched her hands, and Senara stood up to face Mrs. Claus. "My dear, Senara," she sighed as she placed her hands on her shoulders. Senara's entire body tensed up. "There's no need for any of that. We are the elves the others look to in times of need and crisis. You need to try your hardest to keep it together, just as we've always done." She gave her a reassuring smile.

Senara breathed heavily, and her eyes went wide with fear and anxiety. "But, Madame, I have that whooshy feeling in my stomach and…"

"Honey, listen. You can't fall apart on me now. No panic attacks allowed, okay? I need you to be strong and alert, Senara. I need you to continue to be my right-hand elf and assist me like only you know how. How long have you been my assistant?"

Senara's shoulders relaxed and she smiled. "Many years now, Madame."

"Yes, dear, since you were but an elfling! We started out with your rocky apprenticeship, but I've watched you grow and flourish and become independent and strong."

Senara's face flushed with embarrassment. "I haven't spilled cocoa on you in a very long time."

Docena laughed at the memory. Yes, Senara Calix was a hard assistant to break in. The younger sister of Councilmember Quisto, Senara had frustrated her many, many times with her numerous panic attacks and nervous uncertainty. But that was long ago, and yes, Senara had outgrown those elfling-like tendencies. At the end of the day, she was the best assistant Docena had ever had. "I am so proud of you. I need you to stay strong. For us."

Senara breathed in through her nose and exhaled through her mouth. "Yes. Of course, Madame," she said calming down.

"Now remember, in the case of Ember, the answer is always 'no.' Let her run around the grounds a little. There's certainly no harm in that. Let her spread her wings and think she's exploring. But just make sure she goes back to the library to study. She needs an obvious refresher in the Codex, and I want you to put a lot of emphasis on the *Book of Traditions*. That's another important one she needs."

"Yes, Madame. Right away, Madame."

Docena stepped to the side of Senara and wrapped her arm around her shoulder. She gave her a quick squeeze and released her in the direction of the door.

Senara nodded her head tersely and scurried out.

When Senara's clacking sound had faded into the distance, the transmitter on Docena's desk crackled to life.

"Darling?" the voice on the other end asked.

Docena's heart fluttered at the sound of Jolenir's voice. "Yes, my dear?" She smiled.

"Your unwavering strength never fails to amaze me," He said.

"So, you were listening to that?"

"Every last word. I always said you should have been named the Claus over me. Your penchant for diplomacy is far superior to mine."

Docena laughed. "Oh pish-posh! You know just as well as I do that that lifestyle would have never complemented my figure!" She ran her hands down the sides of her hips feeling the svelte outline of her body through her heavy fox-fur coat. "And you can tolerate kids much better than I can! I was lucky I survived a houseful of sibling elves, never mind being head of the entire human world of kids!"

Jolenir laughed in agreement.

"Besides," Docena continued, "you have been the epitome of a perfect Claus."

"Ah, yes!" He mused. "I play the part quite well, don't I?"

"You *are* the part!"

"Yes, but for them… out there," His voice lowered with regret. "For my own—at the Pole—not so much."

Docena opened her mouth to counteract what He said, to deny his ineffectual non-actions, to tell Him "No, everything is totally fine," but she couldn't. She could never lie to Him. She could barely sugarcoat the truth. She hesitated for a moment before saying, "Well, dear, you've had an extraordinarily long run. It's only natural to let some things slip in your elder elfyears."

Jole sighed and let out a barely audible *harrumph*. They both knew good and well that what she said was a major understatement—that the last five elfyears or so had been nothing short of disastrous. "I'm ready, you know," He said after a few moments of reflective silence.

Docena's fluttering heart stopped briefly in its cage and a wave of icy dread froze her in place. In that split second, she wanted to race throughout the castle, find Him, and comfort Him until the Mists came. *He's leaving me now*, she thought frantically, but reality warmed her over before she could take flight. She knew very well that there was much to be done, now more than ever, before His time would come. And with that thought, a great sadness invaded her. He was ready. Willing. Wanting to leave this life. Done with His life work. Mission complete! And He was stuck. He couldn't go. Not now. Not until everything was put in order and made right. She could scarcely imagine how torturous that must be for Him. "I know you are," she said with a heavy heart and sat calmly at her desk. "Not much longer, my love."

The voices of the elves in the courtyard outside got loud again, and Docena welcomed the shift in attention. "The Coal Elf is here," she said to the transmitter. "And you know she's been asking to see you. To talk to you face to face."

"I know," He replied.

"I swear, she reminds me of someone I used to know so very, very long ago," she joked. "Headstrong. Independent. Ornery."

"Ah yes," Jole sighed. "Aren't all young elves like that? The fire of life blazing hot and wild in their souls. At that age, we all feel like we can take on the world."

"Yes, you speak the truth," Docena agreed and remembered their younger years. She and Jole had been on many adventures together, and it seemed like they were facing down and conquering the world together. There was a thrill when it didn't seem like Jole would make His rounds on a Big Night, and He came charging back to the Pole at the eleventh hour. Or the year when a conveyor line worth of bags never made it onto the sleigh and He had to valiantly make multiple trips for the cause. Or when her little brother Killian Frost had gotten control of the weather tower at Hailstone Peak and tried to foil Jole's Big Night run, and He single-handedly braved the bizarre weather patterns and prevailed. So many proud moments over the centuries. So many moments of goodness and valor. Those were the days of dashing adventure and heroic triumph when the Claus was fierce and fearless—a true champion of His people, a strong and respected leader. She fingered the cover of her memory book, but her heart was too heavy to open it. "Do you wish to see her?" Docena asked, breaking from her memory. "Do you want to see Ember?"

"No," he answered, His voice tired and sad. "Not yet."

Suddenly, there was a commotion in the hallway. The voices from outside had gotten louder and closer, and practically shattered the blueice pillars in the castle. Ember burst through the office door, quickly followed by two Brotherhood guards with large pickaxes, and Senara click-clacking her way not too far behind.

"There you are!" Ember yelled when she saw Docena sitting at her desk.

The guards stood at either side of Ember. When Senara finally clicked her way into the room, Docena peered over them and glared hard at her assistant. "One job!" she exclaimed at Senara. "I gave you one job!"

"I'm sorry, I'm sorry!" Senara muttered.

Docena locked her eyes with Ember's. "What can I help you with, Mrs. Ruprecht?" she said, addressing her formally and curtly.

Ember placed her hands on her hips and shifted her weight from side to side. "You know what I want. That's no secret. Your lovely assistant couldn't help me, so I figured you were the only one who could."

Docena exhaled. "Ember, you're here to study and learn. It's the terms of your release from Judge Hollis and the Council. It would behoove you to…"

"Fine. Fine. Fine," Ember relented. "I just want to talk to the Boss. Five minutes. I swear, five minutes, then I go study your books."

"He's in no condition to…"

"I know, I get it," Ember interrupted. "I'll be fast. I promise. I just have a couple of questions for Him and…"

"I've asked Him if He wanted to see you and…"

"He knows I'm here? Great! Send me His way!"

"He said 'no.' He doesn't want to see you right now."

Ember shifted again and wrung her hands together furiously. "But…"

"We've been through this, Ember. Please go back to the library to review the books you were assigned to review, and then you can go back home and start working on your coal deliveries, or whatever it is you need to work on."

"But…"

"But nothing!" Docena roared. "The Claus has said 'no!' And that is final, Ember! Now, you can go with Senara to the library, or I can have the Brotherhood guards escort you there."

Senara moved forward and gently gripped Ember by the elbow. "Come on, let's go now," she whispered.

Ember jerked her arm away, furrowed her brow, and lowered her chin. She huffed and grumbled something unintelligible, but never once took her blue eyes off Docena. The two stared each other down in a battle of wills before Ember reluctantly broke her gaze and growled, "Fine! Just don't touch me."

Is this what having a teenage elf is like? Docena thought and shook her head. *Thank the Claus I never had children!*

Senara led the way out of the office and to the library with Ember in tow. Docena gave a final nod to both of the guards, and they too followed after them.

CHAPTER ELEVEN

S turd woke up, but his eyes were still closed tight. He dared not move a muscle until he fully assessed what had been going on. From behind his eyelids, he surmised that wherever he was it was dark. He started at the top of his body and worked his way down his organs and limbs trying to evaluate his current situation with his mind's eye.

Dark room. Cold, hard table. Shackles around my wrists holding me in place.

His head ached. A throbbing sensation pulsated at the center of his forehead.

Horns.

His ears ached. Pressure and fluid pressed dully on his eardrums, like the way it did when he traveled back and forth between the Mines and Aboveground. Muffled sounds and noises from beyond the room he was in bounced off the walls like sounds in the caverns of the Mines. Only, he wasn't in the Mines…

I'm deeper below, though. Farther underground, yet somehow at a higher elevation.

His stomach ached. A low rumbling growl worked its way up from the vile depths of his gut to his chest. He swallowed the foul-tasting gas back down where it festered some more in his belly.

I'm hungry. How long has it been since I've eaten?

Sturd slowly fluttered his eyes open and tried to focus his vision on his surroundings. A needle protruded from his left forearm and was attached to a long tube. At the end of the line was a medical bag with clear fluids being pumped into his veins. He tried to move his arms, but he was barely able to move at all. The arms were weak and tingly and bound to the table with belted shackles at the wrists. He tried wriggling his hands back and forth against the restraints, but it was no use. He had all his mental faculties about him, but physically, he still didn't have it together.

The noises from outside the room grew closer. Voices. Elves. He remained completely still on the table and closed his eyes back half-way when the heavy door opened. A beam of light sneaked in, casting shadows from the objects all around the room—a bookcase, a desk, an oil lantern with a low flame, medical flasks and beakers with neon-colored contents, a skeleton body with an elf's head? The outside light shrunk when the group of elves entered the room and shut the door behind them.

Am I in the Medic Elf's room? There are far too many unusual objects here to be used by the Medics. Is this the Alchemist's chambers?

"Have you located any other materials about the Dark?" It was Una's voice, and Una only spoke openly and freely when in the company of the Council. They were all there.

"No, Ma'am," an unfamiliar elven voice responded. It was a low, hushed, whispered tone, and if Sturd didn't have amazing hearing, he would have missed what the elf had said. "Not much has been written or recorded. I've only found brief mentionings of the manifestation, but nothing complete, or resolved, for that matter. I've consulted all my resources, and there is extraordinarily little to go by. Half of what I've found is mostly conflicting tales. The other half is ghost stories told to frighten elflings in their beds." He moved over to the desk and turned up the dial on the oil lantern and a soft glow spread out evenly across the ceiling of the room.

Una sighed. "Those stories have long since passed, haven't they? Elflings have no fear anymore. When I was an elfling, we feared it all—Kaflaypors, Chygas, so many other unspeakable beasts who were said to steal your soul if you disobeyed or misbehaved. But we feared the Dark most of all." Her voice trailed off longingly.

"If we didn't worship the Mists, we were told the Dark would enter our hearts and change us for good," another elf said.

"Ah, Zelcodor! The good ole days. You remember. It was a different time back then for sure," Una responded.

"Yes," the quiet elf chimed. "The old tales. The old ways. These are the things that keep reappearing in all the texts."

"I guess this is all before Quisto's and my time," another elf said, and Sturd recognized the voice of Trelson Castleberry, Councilman #5, father of the Book Keeper elves Sturd had so viciously murdered.

Closed the chapter on those two, didn't I? A tiny smile crept at the side of his mouth, and he consciously straightened out his lips so no one would notice. His arm was no longer numb, either.

"When I was an elfling, the only tradition we were taught was the poem," Quisto said.

The Mists of the North come rolling by
As I spot them from the corner of my eye.
Changing yellow, to pink, to purple, to black,
I hope they soon will roll on back.

Just the thought of that sing-songy junk made Sturd's stomach do flip-flops. He hated that stupid little poem. He hated when the elves in the Mines would whistle a tune to it and sing it out high and loud as they worked. It meant nothing, with its nonsensical lyrics and ridiculous imagery. Every time one of his workers hummed it, or sang it, or recited it, or even referenced it, Sturd was flung into a rage where all he envisioned was smashing their pathetic little skulls against the sides of the rock walls.

He had even made up his own counter-poem: *The brain in your head comes oozing out...*

His finger twitched, and an electric wave shot down his leg. He turned his attention back to the conversation in the room. The whispery elf flipped through some pages in a book. "What I can gather, Madame Councilwoman, is that if Sturd did in fact spill blood in the holy place, it would be considered a direct affront to the Mists, and he would no longer be under their protection."

"Which would allow the Shadows of the Dark to descend and manifest itself within him," Una added. "I know the prophecy from my studies, but that was long ago."

"The connective ramifications are too hard to ignore, as well," he went on.

"Go on..." Zelcodor said.

"Yes, Magnus Scorpio, do go on..." Una said impatiently.

Una called the whisper elf Magnus. *The only elves who've ever gone by that title are the Alchemists. Solved that mystery.*

"The physical manifestation of the Shadows of the Dark is known as the Knecht. Characteristics of the Knecht include: misshapen body, preternatural eyes, strong odor. But most importantly, the Knecht must be a foundling—an orphan child with no mother or father, who was set out to roam free in a wide-open space with no supervision.

A lost one. One that is shunned and ultimately locked away."

"Locked away?" Quisto asked.

"That is just what the text said, I…"

"He *is* motherless," Zelcodor interrupted.

"And guidance from Corzakk has been minimal, to say the least," Una added.

"And what happened at the abbey would render him the perfect host for the Shadows of the Dark," Trelson said.

Sturd slowly clenched his fingers into a fist. Slow-burning anger seized his body. It incensed him that they spoke about him as if he wasn't even in the room.

If they only knew…

Una tapped her foot on the stone floor. "But what does this all mean? For me?" There was a worrisome tone in her voice, and Sturd knew she was only concerned with her end game.

"Well, Madame Councilwoman, in one of my sources, the actual word *knecht* translates to 'farmhand' or 'servant.' Some sources state the role of the Knecht is to punish children by beating them with switches, or poisoning them, or giving them coal."

Sturd's body uncontrollably twitched at the words. Rage flashed hot throughout his body again. The sound of the word "punishment" sent tingles of ecstasy down his spine, but "farmhand" and "servant"? *It'll be a hot day at the Pole before I would allow any of that!*

"You can interpret that however you like," the Magnus continued, "but I think it's safe to say Sturd becoming the Knecht is going to be a powerful force."

"What do you mean, *becoming*?" Quisto asked. "You mean he's not fully changed?"

"Yes… becoming," the Magnus stammered. "In my thorough examination of Sturd, I've concluded that the transformation is not quite complete."

"Based on what?" Una barked.

"Diagrams. Renderings. Piecing together all the hand-drawn ancient images. From the research, and my analysis of his bone structure, horn formation, ear elongation, I gather Sturd is nearing the final stage." There was a wild wonder in his voice—excited, disgusted, and awestruck at the same time. He moved to the desk and called for them to gather around. "Look. Here," he said and pointed to something in a book.

They all huddled together, hovering around the desk and the book. Sturd opened his eyes fully and craned his neck a bit so he could see what they were doing. One of them gasped, and he couldn't be sure who it came from.

"*Krampusfrecht,*" Una whispered in Elvish.

"*Doft algunis Krampusnacht,*" the Magnus responded, and he slammed the book shut.

Sturd's body inadvertently jolted when the sound of the book closing resounded in the room. In unison, all the elves' heads swiveled in his direction. He knew he had been spotted, so he moaned a little as if he were just waking up from his sleep, pretending that he hadn't been fully awake this whole time, listening, waiting, gathering his strength.

"I'll take it from here," Una said as she hurried the rest of the elves out of the room. Sturd turned his head from side to side and feigned another sickly moan as a second electric wave raced down the entire length of his body.

She approached him on the table and ran her hand along the ridges of his newly twisted horns like a mother smoothing the hair out the eyes of her newborn elfling. She looked down at him and smiled wickedly. "Nice of you to join us," she cooed.

Sturd stared back at her, his eyes squinted with fury.

"You heard everything, didn't you?"

He nodded.

"Awake the whole time, weren't you?"

He nodded again.

"Well, that's okay," she said with a sigh. "I'm glad you heard. I think it's important for all of us to know and understand what's going on."

"What are you doing to me?" he growled and motioned his head to the IV line protruding from his arm.

She held up the long tube attached to the fluid bag. "Oh, this?" she answered in surprise. "This is nothing. Just something to help you rest."

"Where am I?" His throat was dry and scratchy, and it hurt to form the words.

"You're in the Alchemist's Laboratory at Headquarters. Magnus Scorpio has been watching over you and taking good care of you while he researched the new developments in your... *behavior*."

Every instinct inside him screamed and thoughts of wrapping his hands around her neck flooded his mind. He ground his teeth together to try to gain control. "How long have I been here?"

"About a week."

Unable to hold back anymore, he thrashed wildly against his restraints. A new sense of power coursed through him, and he was quickly cognizant of the fact that, yes, he could easily tear through what was holding him down. With all of his strength, he regained composure, not wanting Una to witness the full extent of his power.

"What about Nim'sim?" he inquired.

"I did as you asked. He has replaced Cerissa Lux on the Council after her tragic *accident* in the Mines. I have to say, he's a little on the dim-witted side, but there's something about him that makes the other elves kind of fall in line. He's managed to mobilize the Brotherhood at Lapis Hall. Our fearless leader is now fully protected by our armed guards at all times."

Sturd contemplated the plan, thought about what the Alchemist said about his own transformation, pondered on why they had him chained up here for a week's time. He had things to do, plans to make... *elves to kill*... and all of this Una nonsense was putting a kink in his own end game. "Why?" he blurted after a few moments of silence.

Una cocked her head to the side. "Why? Why what? What do you mean, why? Why am I doing all this? Why have I spent half my elflife dreaming of being the Claus and the other half trying to figure out how to actually do it?"

He nodded.

She stood up, moved to the desk, and mindlessly flipped through the pages of the various books piled on top of each other. Sturd kept a close eye on her every movement and gesture—watching her, sizing her up, calculating every last flick of her wrist or twitch of her chin. "It's simple. I want what was stolen from me. And quite frankly, I'm not ready to die. Because once my brother Jolenir dies, I will start to die, too. Let me tell you a little story, dear nephew. Long before you were born, long before you were even a thought of being a factor in my grand equation." She sat at the desk and folded her hands together in front of her. "Over 300 elfyears ago, a pair of twin elflings were born to one of the most revered and prestigious clans in all of Norland. But these twins weren't just any old twin set. These twins were special—the most special pair all of the Pole had ever seen.

"When they were born, they glowed with golden magic and sparkled with silver dust. They were immediately presented to the Council, who at the time, declared that the twins had been kissed by the Mists of the North directly. Any elf who held them or were in their direct vicinity, even for a minute, could feel their divinity like the warm summer sun beating on their face. Hold one of the twins, and the golden magic would pierce your heart and bring a feeling of instantaneous joy. It was said to be the most beloved sight and feeling of all time!

"But, not only could the magic surrounding the twins be seen and felt, but also the twins could speak Elvish before they could speak anything else. They say the twins spoke to each other in the womb of their mother by ways of telepathy, and emerged into the world with the language fresh on their tongues. Elves came from all over the Pole just to be in the heavenly presence of the beautiful bundles of intrigue and fancy—Jolevana and Jolenir M'Raz.

"It was clear early on that these twins were the Chosen Ones—the ones who would take the place of the Claus when He was called back home by the Mists, but there was one pressing problem. One twin was obviously a girl, and the other a boy. This was unprecedented. Before my brother and I were born, there was never an issue in the selection process. The first-born twin would rule first, and his brother would serve as the Dublix. But my birth changed things. I was first-born, and I was a girl. A girl elf had never ruled as the Claus. Ever.

"As elflings, our glory was widely received and celebrated, but the older we got and the closer the Claus was to reaching His end-point, the more questions were raised about succession and validity. All of the divination tools in the universe couldn't prepare the Alchemists and Soothsayers for what was about to befall them.

"When the time came for the Life-Assignments, the Claus thought of a way to solve the problem of his successor. Instead of giving the Job to the rightful beneficiary, the first-born, he had us fight it out. He sent us to the Mines to live out our days until the Mists came for him. And whoever had the most profitable, and successful experience would be named his heir.

"You could only imagine what the Mines were like 300 elfyears ago. The conditions were far worse than they are now. For a female elfling who had only known light and love, the drastic change was too much to bear. The darkness snuffed out my golden aura. It obliterated the silver dust of joy from my soul and replaced it with ashes and soot. The cruelty of the environment itself etched its ashy markings onto my heart forever. And Jolenir, of course, adapted quite nicely. He was affable, and brave, and could fit in just about anywhere. I would have been strong, could have been strong, if he and I had stuck together, but the moment we got to the Mines, my brother shunned me, shut me out, and disregarded me like trash in the street. Concerned with his own self-preservation, Jole let me spend my days wallowing in pathetic tears, afraid for my life, lost and alone. I'd lost everything in my world, including my best friend.

"When the Mists finally came many, many years later, after I had endured the harshness and nightmares too unfathomable to speak about, they chose *him*. Him! And the consolation prize for me? A seat on the Council, a powerful husband from a respected clan, and the memories and scars of what they did to me.

"So maybe now you can understand why I've calculated and put all this into place."

"Revenge?" Sturd croaked.

Una chuckled. "It's so much more than that, though. Revenge. Retribution. Making a 'wrong' from the past 'right'. Restoring order, the way it should have been…"

"Getting your gold back?" he said sympathetically, trying hard not to sound too phony.

Una hadn't noticed because she inhaled and smiled. "Ah yes, getting my gold back is a wonderful thought."

Sturd's rage stirred again. She was stepping on his toes with her holier-than-thou story of sweet, cold revenge. This was *his* war. *His* plight. *His* time. His stomach growled a sad moan, and he shifted uncomfortably on the table. The poison vial in his pocket rubbed up against his leg and his mind raced with endless possibilities.

"I guess you're ready to take some food?" she asked after his stomach quieted.

He nodded, and she got up from the desk. "I'll be right back. I'll see what Magnus Scorpio can get for you."

Sturd watched as she left the room, taking note of her direction by the sound her shoes made on the floor. As soon as the door shut behind her, Sturd gathered all his strength—all his new-found, electric strength—and forced his arms up and through the leather buckle restraints. The clasps pierced his wrists and hot blood bubbled up to the surface of his flesh like tiny red jewels. Once free, he tore out the IV line in his arm and threw the needle to the floor. He crouched low by the door, listening for sounds of the other elves nearby. When the time was right, he creaked the door open and left.

CHAPTER TWELVE

Ember lowered her head as a blast of frigid air rushed at her face. Her tiny fingers felt the sting of the cold as they clutched tightly around her journal. All of East Bank was practically deserted now, as the shoppe keepers were making their last rounds of clean-up and locking their doors shut. Families were nestled deep within their dwellings—sipping frothy mugs of hot cocoa with mounds of marshmallows overflowing at the top, fires blazing in the hearths, and riding out yet another chilly night Aboveground. The night sky was decorated with giant amethyst-colored clouds that blotted out any sign of stars above. The desperate cold had even been too much for the Graespurs to handle. They huddled in groups one on top of the other and flew low to the ground.

Once the gust had passed, Ember opened her journal again and began scribbling down notes. Tannen had been strongly encouraging her to follow through with her father's plans, and she

159

had agreed whole-heartedly with his alterations to Elden's original vision. Initially, it appeared that her father had wanted the passageway to be secretive—a means for him to move back and forth through the Mines and Aboveground without detection, or as a way to smuggle young Ember back and forth. The original tunnel was narrow so that no more than two elves could walk side-by-side in the cramped space. Elden's idea was to have the focal point of the passage be his underground workspace at Skye Manor, but after analyzing all the particulars, Tannen had made many adjustments.

The new plan was to create a larger passageway that would serve as a bond of sorts. It would connect the Aboveground to the Mines, and by uniting both areas in the Pole, elves would be free to travel, visit, and trade freely without restrictions or barriers. The Mouth of the Cave would essentially be sealed off, making way for the new tunnel system. Of course, there were many details that needed to be worked out before they could even think about demolition and new construction, but Tannen's expansion of her father's first design was not only beautiful, it was also brilliant. His rendering started the tunnel at Skye Manor, but the entrance point was moved just outside of the home rather than inside. The passage then would run right through the heart of the Mines with many branches that would allow travelers to exit at different checkpoints. He was careful not to disrupt or venture into any of the mining areas so it would be safe for all coming and going. The long-term goal was to eventually set up a separate Catta-car system just for the tunnel. His enthusiasm for all of it sparked a wide variety of emotions in Ember. His passion for this project was infectious.

It was so infectious that she now stood in the heart of East Bank in the wicked cold of night making notations in her journal for him. She had volunteered to scout out the terrain of the Aboveground, observing all the land formations both natural and elf-made. Tannen had said something about land mass density and water-table elevations—things she had no real clue about—but she remembered what he said to look for and wrote everything down for him. Her journal had once been a means to help her sort out her own thoughts and feelings and problems, now it was being used as a tool to help her sort out the problems of her people.

"Kinda not my job, though," she said out loud to herself. And yes, she knew she was right. Just who did she think she was, by doing all this? How was it that she seemed to manage to get herself wrapped up in all these affairs that she had no business being in? It all led back to the Boss. If only she could talk to Him. If only she could sit Him down one-on-one, face-to-face, and tell Him everything. She would outline everything from the past three years, lay everything out on the line, and kind of verbally slap Him upside the head for being an absentee father to the elven race. It enraged her that she had just been there—at Lapis Hall, at His home, in the company of His *wife*—and still, He refused her requests to meet with her. It almost felt like He was *afraid* to speak to her. She huffed. "That's stupid," she said, mumbling the thought away.

She walked through the downtown area, passed the old Inn and the schoolhouse, and had planned to head up a little farther north to stop in at Skye Manor and check up on Kyla and the twins. Much of the landscape had changed since the Nessie Fruit Sickness and the reconstruction of East Bank, but the familiarity of it all hadn't gone away. Memories flooded her mind when she walked by the schoolyard. The jungle gym that stood there now was not the one from her elfling days, but she recalled many afternoons swinging on the tree swing with her old friend Hattie Candlewick and singing traditional elf songs with little Melody Grubbins. She managed to keep herself focused, though, and the whole time she jotted down her observations for Tannen.

By the time she had made it to the heart of East Bank town square, another gust of frosty wind blew so hard it took her breath away. She struggled and gasped for air against the chill. Town Square was deserted with only a few street lanterns glowing.

The wind howled and a swarm of Graespurs swooped down low a few feet in front of her. She jumped back at the sight of them, and at that very moment, the weight of her own solitude startled her. She tucked her journal under her arm and decided to continue the walk under the protection of the streetlamp light.

She hadn't walked far when she saw something move in the darkness across the street. She paused and tried to overcome the sense of dread that gripped deep inside her chest. She squinted her eyes and tried to make out the shape in the dark, and for the first time in a very long while, real fear began to eat away at her. There was a figure in the darkness, hulking and masked in shadow. She held her breath as thoughts of monsters and Chygas and all kinds of wicked nightmare creatures overtook her imagination wildly. The shape took a step forward in her direction, and that's when she saw the piercing red eyes.

Sturd.

She breathed a sigh of relief because it was just *Sturd,* but her reprieve was short-lived. If he *had* been following her, he could have made it all the way to Skye Manor and saw that the twins were still alive.

But no. She knew he wasn't following her. She would have sensed his presence long ago. Her senses were pretty sharp when it came to that. Sturd had been here in Town Square hanging out by himself, just lingering in the back alleys of the shoppes. But why? Then she realized there was something off about him. His shape, his posture, his aura were all unusual, even for him. "Sturd?" she called out. The shape moved closer with a menacing gait. She repeated, "Sturd? Is that you?" The shape moved closer still.

"Ember," he hissed. "My dear, beautiful wife."

Her instincts knew immediately that something was not right with him. His voice sounded different. Darker. Like shadows surrounded him and distorted the very sounds of his speech. Her instincts told her to flee. To run. To *defect* from his presence, but she was all too curious to figure out what was going on.

She struggled to keep calm and bantered back, "Semantics. You and I both know the truth about that!"

"Oh, I beg to differ," he replied. "We have been bound. We have been promised to each other in the most sacred of unions. I'm willing to bet that we'll be making good on that promise in the near future."

She chuckled. How could he possibly think that their sham of a marriage was actually going to work out, or come to fruition? It was comical, really. The only one who took her marriage to Sturd seriously was Barkuss, and that was only because her union with Sturd made her Barkuss's sister-in-law! "Don't bet too much on that one," she chided. "You'll probably be on the losing side."

"I never lose! Haven't you figured that out by now? Ancient elf laws contain serious power. We'll have to answer to it soon!" His voice was oddly inflected in a timbre she'd never heard from him before, like broken glass grating against his vocal cords. It piqued her interest and her concern.

"Um… are you okay?" she hesitantly asked.

"Of course I am!" he snarled. "Since when are you concerned with my well-being?"

She thought for a second with a dramatic pause. "True. But there's something going on with you right now."

"You're letting the cold air get to you," he said. "What are you doing here anyway? Shouldn't you be at Lapis Hall? House arrest, I believe."

"Yeah. Over and done with."

Sturd stuffed his hands in his pocket and started fidgeting. His movements were shifty and shaky—more so than usual. Overcome with curiosity, she took a step forward to get a better look at him, hoping she could figure out exactly what was *not right*. But it was no use because when she got a better view of him, he just looked jagged, like looking at a face in a broken mirror. For some strange reason, she had a hard time determining any of the features of his face. It was as if her own eyes were blurry. Like there was a smokescreen or a veil distorting her vision, or his visage—she couldn't tell which.

Sturd made a forward motion with his head. "Your stupid cry-baby book, I see."

Ember tightened up and looked down at her journal sticking out from her armpit. She quickly shoved it into her boot.

"Cooking up plans and schemes, or crying over your stupid, pathetic life?" he taunted.

"Let's get something straight—the scheming part is all *your* territory. Quite frankly, it's none of your business what I'm doing, but if you must know, you're not the only one with plans!"

"Oh no? I'm intrigued. Do tell."

She extended her hand and wagged her pointer finger at him the way she had seen Barkuss do so many times. "Oh, no, no, no. You'll just have to wait and see."

He opened his mouth and laughed, but it wasn't a normal Sturd laugh. It was haunting. Like a thousand rattling voices ringing out in unison. Ember's eyes opened wide for a second and she took a step back.

Run. Now. Go. Flee.

Sturd took another step closer. "Come on, lovely wife. We should be sharing everything." His voice was calm and steady, but eerily menacing.

She took another step backward. "I will if you will," she said trying to keep the conversation light, not wanting him to hear the fear in her shaky voice, see the terror on her blanched face, smell the panic on her skin. She tugged at the edges of the black scarf that dangled from her shoulders.

Keep cool, girl. Keep cool.

"As the husband, I get the privilege of your knowledge first, ya know. Wife tells the husband, *then* husband tells the wife."

"Um… I don't think I've ever heard that one before." She took a larger step backward, taking her out of the circle of the street light and into the opposite darkness, but this time, he matched her backward movement and glided up to her, bridging the gap between them. Under the streetlamp, she could make out his features more clearly.

When she looked upon the structure of his face, she couldn't help but bring her hand to her mouth and gasp with horror. "Sturd? W… what happened to you? Are you okay?" she stuttered through her hand.

He smiled. His jagged fangs cast downward shadows on his chin.

Run. Now. Go. Flee, she commanded herself on the inside, but she was too petrified and mesmerized to move. She had been afraid of Sturd when she was younger. He was mean and weird looking and a bully. But she had learned to deal with him. Learned to get over her fears of him. Learned to handle his disgusting personality and soul. *But this?* This wasn't even Sturd. What she looked upon now was not the face of Sturd from her elflinghood, nor was he the face of Sturd from her recent memory. This elf before her, this *thing* before her, was someone different. *Something* different. Something from her deepest, darkest nightmares.

He slid up next to her and wrapped an arm around her shoulder, and her heart nearly stopped beating. He whispered something into her ear. Something unintelligible but familiar. The words were like a song—musical and haunting, and neither in the common language, or in Elvish. The words were strange and beautiful, and they lulled her into the crook of his arm. Her shoulders relaxed, and she was at peace and comfortable, like in a dream.

He pulled her closer in, and his arm around her shoulder snaked up and around her neck. His hand caressed the side of her cheek, and she soon felt a pinch at her throat. Her head snapped back at the sensation, and she pulled away from him, clutching her neck. "What did you do that for?" she mumbled, but she suddenly was woozy and unsteady on her feet.

The world went dark, and she fell face down in the snow.

Ember lay helpless in the snow, unable to speak, unable to move. Her body twitched uncontrollably every few moments in forceful, convulsive waves.

If I close my eyes for just a moment, I might be able to block out the searing pain running down my neck and into my chest.

A stinging sensation rattled its way to every nerve ending in her body, and her throat felt like it was closing in on itself as if it had been pumped full of smoke. The smoke feeling had come on quickly, like a violent storm rolling across the horizon.

When she closed her eyes, all she could see were the colorful light orbs behind her lids transforming into the hundreds of butterflies flitting about the garden of her childhood home.

Home. I need to get Home.

But the beautiful butterflies didn't last for long. The image soothed her for a brief moment, but quickly gave way to the smells of burning coal and flesh invading her nostrils. The butterflies transformed into wicked little pixies with sharp claws and pointed teeth that nipped at her neck and face, slashed at her cheeks, and pulled her hair. She touched her face, and a warm wetness coated her palms. Was it tears from crying, or was it blood from the assault of the demonic creatures? If she opened her eyes, they would surely disappear, but she would also be met with the stinging and burning of the flesh smoke.

The pixies continued their attack. Their razor-sharp claws gauged her skin, and their metal studded wings lashed at the backs of her hands. They were relentless.

I'm losing so much blood. So much blood. So much blood.

She heard elves screaming in the distance. Screaming in agony over a roaring fire. She heard her mother screaming at her from the porch steps, "My daughter is dead!" as flashes of the death certificate with *Ember Autumn Skye* written on it came to her mind. Her hands cramped with pain from the cold. Her breaths came in short, labored pants. She crawled on her hands and knees looking for help from anyone, anywhere, but it was dark and damp and the threat of the pixies kept all the elves locked away in their homes.

Barkuss is crying somewhere. Crying over my dead, frozen body. Crying into the trail of the pink snow behind me. The pixies breathe fire. They breathed fire and scorched my legs so I cannot walk. Tannen cries, too. Don't forget to tell him the journal is in your boot. I should give it to the Graespurs overhead to bring back to the Mines with them. Kyla will take care of Asche. He'll be okay with her. And the sun is just rising. Just rising over the hilltop. Just making its way to greet the elves and say hello home. Home. Home. Home. Hello. Hello. Hello. Help. Help. Help…

Ember dragged herself up to the gate in front of her and mumbled something incoherently before plopping face down in the snow. Her legs were useless, and her mind was fractured. Unsure of what was happening and what was going on, she had sense enough to seek out help during her hallucination.

"Hey, lady! You okay?" an elfling said through the wrought iron fence.

"Dev! Look! Something's wrong with her!" another one shouted.

Ember lifted her face from the snow and tried to speak. *Please, help me,* she tried to articulate through the pain.

"What did she say?" one of the elflings asked.

"I dunno. We should call for help!"

"Nanny! Nanny!" they both started yelling. "Quick! Quick! Nanny Carole! Please, help!"

CHAPTER THIRTEEN

*S*ounds. *Voices. Lights. Darkness. Silence. Shadows. Screams. Laughter. Prayers.*

For Ember, a great symphony of noises and images passed forward and backward, side to side, in and out, from consciousness to unconsciousness. Dream to reality and back to dreaming again.

The sound of her mother crying. The sound of her sister laughing.

The feeling of her father's hand on her shoulder as she stares deeply into his sad brown eyes. When she extends her arm to wrap around his neck in search of peace and sanctuary, he turns from her, denies her a warm embrace, and walks away, abandoning her, leaving her scared and confused.

"Was I a bad elfling?" she calls to his back. "What did I do wrong?" she sobs.

"It's okay, Emmy-girl. I'm right here," a familiar voice whispers back, and Ember can't decipher whether or not it's coming from inside her head.

Songs. Questions. Flickers. Breezes. Chattering. Whispers. Squeals. Dampness. Cold.

She sits on the swing set at school, digging the heels of her black boots into the snow. She clutches the frozen chain and rocks her body side to side, practically twisting herself around in the seat. In the distance, the sunlight glints off the fine, white hair of Jordy Pines—sweet Jordy Pines from Tir-La Treals who holds her hand under the table during art class and who sits next to her at the lunch table. Jordy is playing catch with some of the other boys, and she can't help but stare at him. She gets butterflies in her stomach from just looking at him. She hopes to one day marry him and have a baker's dozen of elfbabies with sparkly white hair like his and sapphire blue eyes like hers. And a puppy. They would have a puppy and name him Jorber—part Jordy, part Ember.

Ember Pines has a nice ring to it…

He stops playing with the others when he realizes she's watching him. Her face gets bright red and her heart pounds as he walks up behind her. He grabs the back of the swing seat and begins to push, sending her soaring into the sky. Snow begins to fall and the flakes dust her eyelashes every time she gets sent up higher and higher. She blinks them away, but laughs wildly at the rush of the up and down, up and down, up and down. She's flying high above the world! It's a familiar feeling that gives her a rush of excitement and fear all at the same time. She was meant to fly—built to fly. Like her body was designed to handle the weightless feeling in her gut. She looks down at the world beneath her and smiles. She knows she has much work to do.

The snow falls heavier and now coats her hair with its white, sparkly dust. She wonders if she looks like Jordy now with her crown of pristine snowy locks. Suddenly, he pulls the swing to a stop and leans close to her ear. He whispers gently, "Almond tall struthers." Startled, she quickly turns her head around only to see Tannen standing behind her smiling.

Ember's eyes fluttered open. "Almond tall struthers," she mumbled incoherently.

"Did she just say something?" an elfling in the room said.

"I think so," another, younger voice responded.

"Go run and get Nanny! I'll watch her."

The elfling left the room and went screaming down the hall, his shock of orange hair blurred in the distance. "Nanny! Nanny Carole! She's awake! She's awake!"

When Ember was fully aware that she was conscious, she lay completely still on the couch. Her eyes darted back and forth to absorb her surroundings. She was in a brightly lit room with antique furniture and floral wallpaper—a living room decorated with expensive vases and a curio cabinet with a glass menagerie. It reminded her of Skye Manor, yet she knew it wasn't. Warm smells filled the home—food smells, comforting smells, familiar smells. Smells of home…

The elfling in the room stood over her and smiled a big toothy smile. Her bright red hair fell in small ringlets around her face.

I know you, Ember thought immediately, but she was still trying to make heads or tails of what was happening to her.

"You're awake!" the elfling said happily. She couldn't have been more than eight elfyears old.

Ember looked from side to side. "Yep," she said, her voice hoarse and scratchy. "I guess I am."

The other elfling came rushing into the room with an older elf following behind him, grasping his hand.

Ember thought she was looking at a ghost when she realized it was none other than Nanny Carole—*her* Nanny Carole. The Nanny Carole who raised her and cuddled her and sang her to sleep every night. The Nanny Carole who taught her to brush her hair and teeth diligently and to tie her shoes. The Nanny Carole who scolded her for playing naked in the cold winter air and admonished her to eat her vegetables and Nessie Fruit (but who hit her when she tried to eat it off the ground). Sweet Nanny Carole whom she loved like a mother. Sweet Nanny Carole whom she missed ferociously when she was sent to the Mines and whom she cried herself to sleep at night over.

"Emmy!" Carole sighed when she saw Ember was awake. She unlocked her grip on the elfling boy and raced to the side of the couch. She knelt down by Ember's side and stroked her hair from her forehead. She picked up Ember's hand in her own and brought them to her lips, showering her with a thousand kisses. "Oh my dear, sweet Emmy!" she gushed between kisses. "My lovely Emmy. Look at you! All grown up!"

Ember closed her eyes and embraced the warmth in her heart. Carole's wrinkled hands still felt smooth and warm on Ember's face. Her soft voice was soothing, like a comforting blanket on a chilly night. And she still smelled the same—like peppermint sticks and hot cocoa. The touch and smells opened up a flood of memories for her.

Wave after wave, she allowed everything to tumble back into her mind and her soul. She felt safe in that very moment. Safe and secure in the arms of her Nanny Elf.

This must be a dream. I'm probably still asleep…

"She looks old!" the boy elfling exclaimed.

"Shut up, Dev! That's not nice!" the red-head girl barked. "Don't you know that's Ember, the Coal Elf?"

"Sarrr-eee!" he whined indignantly. "But, just look at all her old lady gray hair. Why, she's got just as much as Nanny Carole!"

"Shush you, Devlin Verthar!" the girl repri-manded. "Shush your mouth right now!"

Lost in a sea of memories, Ember rubbed her temples. "Am I dreaming? Am I dead?"

Carole smiled lovingly. "No, Emmy. You're wide awake, and you're very much alive."

"You nearly died on us, though," the red-head said bluntly.

"Nanny saved you," the boy interjected.

"Wh… what happened?" Ember stuttered.

"Well," Carole said, "I was hoping you would be able to tell me that."

Ember propped herself up and tried to focus her thoughts, but the room spun when she moved. She winced, sucking in the air painfully between her teeth. Carole adjusted the pillows behind her. "Easy. Easy," she coaxed. "Let me help you. You're going to be woozy for a little while. Now think, Emmy. You came stumbling up to the Manor, dragging yourself through the snow, actually. You were clearly not in your right mind. Mumbling. Pupils big and black."

Everything was blurry, and Ember had trouble thinking.

"Were you hurt? Did you fall down and hit your head?" Carole prodded.

"No. Not that I can recall."

"Were you in a fight with someone? Did someone attack you?"

Ember rubbed her head and tried to piece everything together.

"Emmy, the way you were acting, I would swear to Claus that you had been poisoned or something."

Ember paused.

Sturd.

She remembered Sturd in the East Bank town square with his jagged face and twisty horns.

Sturd, but not Sturd. She remembered his fangs protruding from his mouth, and the way his voice sounded when he spoke—demonic and unnatural. She remembered the mysterious and musical words he spoke to her right before he scratched her neck with…

"Poison. Yes. I think I was poisoned," she confirmed.

But not enough to kill me. If he wanted me dead, why didn't he just do it? Because he didn't want me dead. He wanted me out of the way…

"Well, don't you worry, dear. I'll get you up and running in no time."

Ember gave a soft smile. *You usually did…* "Where am I, anyway?" she asked.

"Stixx Manor in Tir-La Dunes!" the redhead elfling exclaimed with great pride.

Ember nodded at the elf as it all fell into place. The red hair, the upscale home. The little elf was Juniper Stixx—the elfling Ember had spied on when she had come Aboveground on her Pass. Her brother-in-law Vonran had told her that Nanny Carole had taken a new charge at Stixx Manor, and Ember had watched the two jealously as they played games in the yard and sang the same songs Nanny had sung with Ember—like a second performance of a grand play, or a retelling of a grand lie. The happiness Ember felt from her reunion with Nanny Carole deadened a bit as she watched Juniper twirling her fire red curls between her dainty fingers.

"Junie, why don't you and Dev go run along and let me take care of Ember? She needs to rest up."

"Yes, Nanny," the elflings said in unison and scuttled along.

Carole moved to the serving bar on the other side of the room and poured Ember a glass of juice. "Sip this, dear," she said as she handed it to her. "When the Sickness hit, it devastated all of us, you know that."

Ember nodded and slowly sipped the pink concoction.

Carole sat on a rocking chair next to the couch. "I had been assigned to Stixx Manor for a few years before the Sickness came," she continued. "The only ones here who made it out alive were me and Junie. I care for her now. And the boy. We live here in Juniper's ancestral home. I thought it was the right thing to do to give her some normalcy. Devlin knew nothing from before the Sickness, so…"

"Devlin. As in Devlin Verthar? As in Devlin, Ginger's son?"

Carole nodded. "Ginger passed away from the Sickness shortly after giving birth. Vonran had been ill himself. He begged me to take care of him."

"Yes. I had heard that. It's just so strange to see him, ya know? He does kinda favor Ginger with his orange hair and all."

"Oh yes, but his disposition is more like his father's," Carole laughed. "He's not as snappy as Ginger was, or as vindictive."

"Yeah," Ember mused, remembering the cruel sister jokes from years ago, "Ginger did have a way of getting under everyone's skin."

"She wasn't my charge, but I still helped raise that girl. I couldn't refuse the wish of a dying elf, either. I'm the only family Devlin has ever known."

"He doesn't know I'm…"

"No. I didn't have the heart to tell him."

Ember sipped her drink, deep in thought. "You've cared for lots of elflings, haven't you?"

Carole sighed. "Ah, yes. A Nanny's elflife is a long and filled with lots of love because of it."

"You never had any elflings of your own, though. Never a family of your own. Didn't that ever bother you?"

"I never gave it any thought. They are all mine. All the elflings. All 350 elfyears worth."

Ember gagged a little on her drink. "Wait!" she exclaimed. "How is that possible? Elves barely make it to 150! Only elves like the Boss or his wife or the Council members get that life extension."

"And Nannies," Carole said matter-of-factly. "We're blessed with the same life extension as well. Who do you think cares for those integral elves of our society, or the potentially integral ones?"

Ember shifted on the couch and remembered the strange piece of paper that was still in her pocket. She paused briefly before saying, "Even dead ones?"

"Well, yes, unfortunately I've had to live through the deaths of many of my charges. It leaves a hole in my heart every time, that's for sure. But not ever a hole so deep and wide as the one that was created when I had to watch you go off to the Mines," she said with a regretful look on her face.

"Or how about when I died?"

Carole's face twisted with a puzzled look. "What do you mean?"

Ember reached down into her pocket and retrieved the Death Certificate. She held it up and Carole walked over to take it from her. Carole's wrinkled hands trembled, and the paper rattled quickly between her fingers. Her wide eyes scanned the document with a look of sudden fear. "Where did you get this?" she mumbled under her breath.

Ember sat up at attention when she realized Carole was having a real, physical reaction to the document. "My father's work room," she said, trying to control her excitement.

"This wouldn't have been in your father's workroom, Ember," Carole said with a condescending tone.

"The *other* workroom. Below the mansion."

"But... but... how?" Carole stammered.

"It doesn't matter how. I just need to know what it means. It's signed by my father, Jack Frost, the Boss Himself, and Carole Frost. I'm assuming that's you, right?"

Carole nodded her head.

"Funny. All these years. You've always just been *Nanny Carole*. Your family clan was never a thought for me. I guess I just assumed you were always part of *my* family. A Skye."

Carole's eyes swept the floor. "I was. I am. Nannies forsake their family names when they are called to their Life Jobs, so in a sense, we become a part of the families we work for. I have been a Skye, and a Stixx, and so many other names."

Ember felt a rush of energy surge through her as she started to realize she would finally be getting some answers. "But the signature here. Carole Frost. That *is* you, correct?" she grilled.

"It was," Carole said in a low voice.

"And the *Ember Autumn Skye* on the certificate? Well, that happens to be *my* name. And quite coincidentally, I was born on March 14, yet there it says that's when I died. So, you can kinda understand where there's cause for confusion. Technically, that should be a *birth* certificate, not a *death* certificate. That's gotta be a mistake or something, right?"

Carole folded up the paper, handed it back to Ember, and sat back down on the rocker. "Technically, it should be," she began. "But the paper you have is legitimate, my dear. There's no need for confusion. Of course you didn't die. That's impossible because you're living and breathing right here in front of me. That's not your death certificate, Emmy." She paused. Carole opened her mouth to say something, but she hesitated and stopped herself. Ember's eyes widened and she made a croaking sound in her throat, urging Carole on. Carole inhaled, and continued. "That's not your death certificate. It's the death certificate of the real Ember Autumn Skye."

Ember practically jumped up from the couch, but a dizzy feeling rocked her body back into its seated position. "What do you mean, the *real* Ember Autumn Skye? I am the real Ember Autumn Skye!"

Carole lowered her eyes, not able to look directly at Ember. A pained expression darkened her face. "All these years we went through great lengths to protect you. It was truly for your own good. You have to believe me."

"Protect me? Who had to protect me? Protect me from what? What in Claus's name are you talking about?"

"Emmy, it's not my place to say," Carole said firmly. "It's not for me to tell you. You'll have to get those answers from your father."

Ember's ears swelled with heat as the anger overtook her. "What?" she scoffed. "My father? Have you completely lost it? You know damn well that my father is dead! He died in a freak accident, didn't he?"

Carole looked up and locked her eyes on Ember's. "I know," she said calmly. "I know Elden is passed. I don't mean Elden. I mean your real father... the Boss."

CHAPTER FOURTEEN

It's not fair to keep these boys tucked away in this house, Kyla thought as she paced back and forth across the basement floor in Skye Manor. Yes, Ember had said it was okay to roam around the grounds. Yes, Ember had said they could stay upstairs for the most part. Yes, yes, yes. But no, no, no! Kyla was still fearful of getting caught. Even though Ember gave her the green light to relax a little, Kyla couldn't find it in her to ease up. Whenever the boys went exploring through the mansion, she held her breath and cringed at their every footfall. Whenever they decided to raid the cabinets for food, she made sure they did it at night and only by candlelight. If they played a board game in the parlor and got into a normal brotherly scuffle as to who won or who cheated or who rolled the dice twice in a row, she would snatch the game away and escort them back to the basement. They whined, and cried, and pouted, and stamped their feet, but Kyla stayed strong and determined. "I have to keep you safe" was her new mantra, yet all the while, she knew they only missed their parents and their home and their normal routine (whatever "normal" meant for young coal elflings), and it broke her heart every time she scolded them for being "too loud" or being "too wild."

The cold had been steadily increasing over the last few days, and with all the broken windows throughout the abandoned mansion, nighttime on the main floor had actually become colder than staying in the basement workroom. Each night they brought old sleeping bags and pillows and camped out on the stony floor. Not the most comfortable of choices, but at least down there, they were sheltered from the chill of the drafty hallways and, in Kyla's mind, safer from the outside forces.

The boys were fast asleep in the corner of the room. Each was in his own separate sleeping bag, yet they huddled close together for extra warmth. Their gentle snores were like a harmonious lullaby—while Juju inhaled, Bambam exhaled with a grunt, and when Bambam inhaled, Juju exhaled with a soft whistle. Kyla tossed in her sleeping bag, unable to find a semi-comfortable position. Her mind was more than unsettled, and she found it impossible to rest. Knowing the boys were deep into dreamland, she decided to get up and walk around the main floor to help clear her head and calm her nerves.

The howling wind screeched like an onslaught of ghosts invading the home. It rattled and shook the bedroom doors with their invisible hands. Kyla jumped every time the wind grated against broken window glass or fluttered the golden drapes in the parlor. Her walk-about was certainly not doing her anxiety any good, but she took comfort in the fact that all the spooky sounds of the main floor were inaudible in the basement, and that was something to at least be thankful for.

She headed for the kitchen in hopes of organizing what was left of their provisions when a violent blast of wind whipped down the hallway. It cried out, as if in pain, and sent shivers throughout her body. The moaning sound it made struck her deep. It sounded like an injured animal—a deer, perhaps—yelping out in pain from a hoof stuck in fencing debris, or crying out in the throes of giving birth.

She paused, thinking about her deer. She missed them all so much and had worried about how they were getting on without her. Her mind started racing again: Were they eating enough? Were they in good spirits? Ellavorn won't eat the lemongrass, Dunkel likes his mash warmed up, and Viella will not eat if she's close to Camden. Are they getting enough exercise? Are they practicing their drills? Was Holly making sure the stable doors were closed just right because there was a certain way it had to be jimmied in order to make them stay and…

And what about the four pregnant does? Merry, Jenara, Lumi, and Felice—all ready to give birth at any moment. *Those fawns will be here any day now*, she thought. *They might actually have already been born!* Kyla had always made it a point to be there whenever a fawn was born at the stable, and now, four would be coming into the world, and she wouldn't be able to help them or to make the most important bonding imprint on them.

Or can I?

Plumm Stable was fairly close to Skye Manor. The twins were fast asleep. It wasn't entirely out of the realm of possibility for her to sneak away for a few hours and be back before the boys woke up. They would never even know she was gone!

She crept down the spiral staircase to double check on the twins, and when she heard their lyrical pattern of snorts and whistles, she knew she was good to go. "I'll be back before you know it," she whispered to them, and left the mansion.

The wind stung her face as she moved through the city, and the surge of the howling sounds passed right through her pointy ears for she was determined to get to her deer. Nothing was going to stop her—not her fear or anxiety or the threat of monsters and ghosts lurking in the dark. She was focused and unwavering as she repeated over and over:

In and out. Quick. Say hello. Say goodbye. Pat their bellies. Head back to the twins.

If only things were that simple.

Kyla arrived at Plumm Stable to a scene she had not anticipated. Every light in the farmhouse and stable was on. Loud voices rang out above the wailing of the wind, and the stamping of hooves rumbled the very ground beneath her. Her stomach flipped as the absolute worst thoughts pierced her imagination.

She rushed up to the stable at a breakneck speed just as the wooden entranceway flung open. Holly's pink eyes were wild and frantic, and her hair was a tousled mess of a makeshift ponytail. She practically did a double-take when she saw Kyla standing there. "Kyla?" she asked in disbelief.

"Holly! What's going on?" Kyla answered, the panic rising in her voice.

"I'm coming! I'm coming!" a voice screamed from the farmhouse. "You tell that Momma to wait for me!" Fannie hobbled off the front porch with a silver basin of water in her hands and towels draped around her neck. Water splashed on the wooden floorboards and instantly crinkled and crackled into small ice puddles.

"Hurry, Fannie!" Holly yelled back. She grabbed Kyla's hands and pulled her into the stable. "Oh my Claus! I am so glad to see you!"

The reindeer were lined up in their individual corrals, and their neighing and whinnying got louder when Kyla walked in. For a split second, their reaction to her made her smile, and she wanted to smother all of them with hugs and kisses and apologize for having been away for so long.

"Look! They're ready," Holly said when she led Kyla to the last four corrals in the stable.

Sure enough, all four pregnant does were circling around in their enclosures, their pregnant bellies hanging low and grazing the hay on the floor. The poor does moaned pathetically and whinnied in discomfort.

Fannie burst through the stable door. "The Nessie mash is almost done, and I brought some towels and the water for Jenara 'cause she's the closest and..." Fannie stopped when she saw Kyla. She put down the supplies and gave her a quick hug.

"What's going on? What happened?" Kyla asked, trying to keep her voice calm and steady.

Fannie pulled back and smiled. She shrugged her broad shoulders. "I don't know, sugar! Jenara here went into labor, and Holly freaked out, so she sent for me to come help."

"Jenara started doing that circling thing," Holly said. "And then all the others started going crazy, so I went a little crazy."

"And no sooner had I gotten here," Fannie snapped her fingers, "the others followed suit just like that. I guess they decided they were all gonna have their fawns at the same time!"

"How long?" Kyla asked.

"A few hours now," Fannie answered. "But, how'd you know, Kyla? How'd you know to come? Is everything okay by you guys?"

"I... I didn't know," Kyla stammered as she walked around the stable inspecting the does.

"Everything's fine over by me. I…I guess I had a feeling something was up. I knew the girls were close, but not like this… not all at once."

"I know what you mean!" Fannie said. "It's a good thing you got here when you did. We're gonna need all the help we can get. I've never had to do four assists before."

"I've never even had to do one!" Holly chimed, and they all smiled.

Jenara let out a bleating wail, and the other deer snorted and stomped in unison. "It's okay. It's okay," Kyla said, quickly moving to her pen. "Everybody calm down," she called to the others in an authoritative tone. "We all have been around for a birth or two, so don't act like this is something new!" The deer listened to her direction and quieted down. "Fannie, it's about to go down over here. Toss me a towel. I think Lumi is next, so just stand watch by her."

Fannie threw a towel over the corral gate. "On it!" she replied.

"Holly, go back to the house and make sure the mash is done. Once these fawns are born, the mothers are going to want to have something to nibble on."

"You got it!" Holly answered, and she raced out.

The promise of hope and new life was in full swing at the stable, and Kyla was recharged with a sense of determined purpose. Any and all of her fears were squelched, and she had one goal in mind—help bring these fawns safely into the world.

Jenara lay panting on her side while Kyla cradled her head in her lap and stroked her neck. "You got this. You can do this," she coaxed the doe. "I'm so proud of you. You're doing such a good job." Jenara struggled to stay still. Her body jolted every few seconds with the pain of her contractions. "Good girl. Good girl," Kyla continued, nearly echoing what Fannie was saying in the adjacent stall.

With a deep groan and one last, hard push, Jenara's fawn was feet first in the hay. She immediately turned to groom him, and Kyla jumped up to make sure all was all right. "Is that Jaspar, the first treasure of the night?" she asked Jenara. "Is Jaspar okay?"

Jenara happily snorted and continued to attend to her newborn.

Just as Holly came back with the bucket of mash, Lumi bucked wildly in her corral. By the time Kyla made it over to them, a tawny fawn was already wobbling unsteadily in the hay. Lumi was too weak to groom the child, so Fannie rubbed the fawn down with the towel. Holly brought the mash over to Lumi and scooped small tablespoons of the food into her mouth. "It was like the baby shot straight up north on all legs," Holly said in amazement. "Almost like she was ready to fly!"

Kyla eyed Fannie to make sure the fawn was okay. Fannie nodded and led it over to Lumi so she could finish the grooming process. "So, name her," Kyla said to Holly.

"Huh?" she replied.

"Give the fawn a name!" Kyla repeated.

"It's part of the process, honey," Fannie added. "You say the name and get permission from the mother."

Holly hesitated. "Well… um… How about Northelyn?"

Kyla frowned. "Northelyn?"

"Yeah. Ya know. How she stood straight up north…"

Kyla held her hands up and shrugged her shoulders. "It's not up to me, Holly. You need to run it by Lumi."

"Oh… okay… um… Lumi? Is Northelyn an okay name for your baby?"

Lumi gave a weak snort in agreement, and Holly clapped her hands. "Northelyn it is!"

Another doe cried out in pain—this time it was Felice. Kyla hopped over the gate and into her pen just as the stark white fawn landed gracefully on her feet like a gentle falling snow. Felice was the strongest of the does and didn't need much assistance. When Kyla saw that she was well enough to groom, she called out, "Eira, the snowfall." Felice nodded her massive head, and Kyla joined Fannie and Holly in Merry's pen.

Merry was struggling something awful. Her abdomen was unusually large, and she could barely move. Holly knelt down by Merry's head and rubbed her snout.

Fannie bent over and examined the doe's underbelly. "Fannie," Kyla said, "you don't think that..."

"Twins. This here girl has got two fawns in there!"

Holly gasped. "No way! Are you serious?"

"Yep. And, from the looks of it," Fannie said prodding at Merry's fur, "I think... they're... stuck."

Without hesitation, Kyla knelt down beside Fannie and helped to massage the doe. Because the fawns were born feet first, it was critical to get them out as quickly as possible. Kyla had never assisted in a twin birth before, but she remembered her training exercises. It also helped that Fannie, another experienced Reindeer Trainer, was right next to her to guide her along the way.

After what felt like hours of pulling and pushing and tugging and massaging, the first of the gray-furred twins arrived. "Lucian, the light—to light the way for his brother to come," Fannie declared, and both Merry and Kyla nodded in agreement.

Within moments, the second gray-furred fawn seemed to shoot across the pen with no assistance needed. His wide eyes seemed to glow as he stood up and quickly righted himself. "Seren, the shooting star—to help guide his brother through the night," Kyla said, and Merry wearily snorted.

Kyla, Fannie, and Holly clapped vigorously when all the fawns were deemed to be well, and the deer in the stable stomped and whinnied in excitement.

Kyla wiped the sweat from her face. "What a night! I'm so glad everything went smoothly. Thank you, ladies, for everything you've done for my stable. You don't know how much it means to me."

Holly and Fannie smiled.

"I'm also glad that I won't have to do this again for a very long time!"

Fannie put her hand on Kyla's shoulder. "Well, not too long." She nodded her head in Boptail's direction. Boptail's head rested on the top of her corral's gate. She batted her long eyelashes knowingly at Kyla.

Kyla's eyes widened in surprise. "Wait!" she said in disbelief. "Are you saying that...?"

"That's right, sugar! Brightly and Plumm Stables are gonna have a common family member!"

Boptail nodded her head, and Asche stomped his hooves.

"Wow!" Kyla said under her breath.

"Certainly, wow! Five deer born on the same night, two of them twin brothers, a Shadow Fawn on the way... I'd say that's some team you've got here!"

Some team, for sure. A Main Team, perhaps.

Holly and Fannie went back to the farmhouse to call it a night while Kyla decided to stay with the group a little while longer before she had to make her way back to Skye Manor. Exhausted, she lay down on the hay next to Merry, and rested her eyes for just a minute.

Kyla awoke to Lucian and Seren licking the sides of her face, and a loud rustling sound passing overhead just outside of the stable. She froze as she realized where she was. A minute had turned into an hour, and an hour had turned into...

Graespurs heading back to the Mines.

Dawn was breaking on the horizon, and it wouldn't be long before Bambam and Juju would wake up and realize she wasn't there. She jumped up as an icy panic unfurled throughout her body. *"Aschen! Boptail! Fredale oust haglenshine!"* she called in Elvish.

Instantly, Asche and Boptail opened their eyes, ready for their next set of commands. Kyla knew she couldn't waste any more time, so she opened Asche and Boptail's corrals and hurriedly hitched them to Ember's sleigh. "We need to get to Skye Manor in double time!" she said as she fastened them to their harnesses. "Two deer are better than one, right?"

Asche and Boptail huffed and snorted, and Kyla hopped onto the driver's bench.

She gripped the reins tightly, and with a quick snap and a "Hee-ya," they rode out of the stable and soared into the twilight morning sky.

CHAPTER FIFTEEN

Ember prowled around the grounds of Skye Manor, making sure she stepped carefully over any of the downed topiaries. Her boots relentlessly crunched through the snow, and her nose crinkled up every time she heard the sound. She looked over her shoulder constantly to ensure she hadn't been followed or spotted. How could she have been, though? No one knew she had been with Nanny Carole at Stixx Manor, and for all Sturd knew, Ember could have been dead.

Of course you didn't die. That's impossible because you're living and breathing right here in front of me. Nanny Carole's words played back in her head over and over again. Yet, she couldn't believe her. She couldn't believe it when Carole said Ember was the daughter of the Boss. It was one of the most preposterous things she had ever heard. Even crazier than being Sturd's wife!

"You'll drive yourself crazy with all this, Ember," she said to herself as she pushed her way gently through the brush of the mansion courtyard. "Besides, it's impossible! The Claus doesn't have any children. I am the daughter of Elden and Amalia Skye. Elden and Amalia Skye. Elden and Amalia…"

But not too long ago, Amalia had sung a different tune. *"Get off my property, you imposter!"* her mother screamed at her when she had come to visit on her Pass. *"My daughter is dead! You're just a monster!"* Ember had just chalked the ranting and raving up to Amalia's depressed and drunken stupor, but was what she said the truth?

"Absolutely not!" Ember said out loud, trying to dismiss the memory, but the gnawing feeling in her stomach was too much to ignore. She inspected the palms of her hands to make sure she wasn't dreaming, or in some other weird, hallucinatory state. "But if I am, then…" she stopped as an overwhelming sense of despair took over her as she thought about her entire existence being a giant lie, one big joke, one big dark fantasy where the Sugar Plum Fairy doesn't exist.

The front door creaked open and echoed throughout the vacant home. It was strangely quiet for a structure that was supposed to be harboring two elfling boys.

There were signs of their presence strewn across the parlor floor—an empty cookie box by the couch, game pieces left haphazardly on the coffee table, and blankets and pillows out of place, but the deadened hush that filtered in the air left the house feeling like an empty tomb.

A jangling noise sounded outside, and Ember crept low beneath the windowsill so as not to be seen. She poked her head up cautiously when the familiar sound grew closer. "What the…" she gasped when she saw her two Shadow-Deer and Kyla driving her sleigh. She rolled her eyes and stood up in alarm. "You've got to be kidding me!"

Kyla told the reindeer to stay at their post in front of the house, and came bursting through the front door. Her face fell in shock when she saw Ember standing in the parlor with her hands on her hips. "Ember?" she asked, puzzled.

"Where were you?" Ember said, stern and threatening. She had never taken such a harsh tone with Kyla before. She had never had to. A twinge of regret ate at her, but Ember thought the seriousness of the situation called for her severe attitude.

Kyla stiffened at the anger in Ember's voice. "I'm so so so sorry!" she apologized. Tears swelled in her eyes. "I came back as quickly as I could, I swear it! I didn't mean to leave them alone all night."

"All night?" Ember roared.

"I just… I just had to see them… my deer. I was only going to go for an hour, maybe two. The boys were dead asleep, and I was going to be so fast. Really, I was," Kyla cried. "But when I got to the stable, all the does were in labor. I couldn't leave Fannie and Holly like that! I came back as soon as I could, I swear."

Ember's initial reaction was to yell and kick the legs of the couch. She envisioned herself grabbing Kyla by the shoulders and violently shaking her back and forth, shaking the sense into her, shaking the extreme gravity of the situation into her. "How could you be so stupid, Kyla?" she *wanted* to shriek.

But seeing the tears stream down her best friend's face made Ember take a step back and relax. *For all she's done for you…* she reminded herself, and clenched her fists together to help her calm down. "Okay," she said in a steady voice. "What's done is done. Now we have to move on and do what we gotta do."

Kyla smiled sheepishly and swatted at the tears on her cheek. "What do we have to do now?"

"I'm here for the boys. I'm going to bring them to Lapis Hall to see the Boss. He needs to see that they're alive, and He needs to see what they can do. He needs to anoint them as His successors, or whatever the process is for calling up the new Claus, and He needs to do it soon before any other craziness happens."

"Okay," Kyla nodded. "If that's what you think is best."

Ember looked out the window at her sleigh and deer, and smiled in spite of herself. "It actually works out well that you came back with my sleigh. Must be reading my mind or something."

Kyla's shoulders slouched forward, and she exhaled heavily. "I'll go get the boys," she said, and she walked to the secret door in the office.

"Bambam! Juju!" she yelled. "Bambam! Juju! Wake up and come upstairs!" Ember walked into the office and stood next to Kyla at the door. "Those two can sleep through anything," Kyla joked, but Ember's ears perked up uneasily when the boys didn't respond. "Bam! Ju! Let's go! Rise and shine! Big day ahead of us!" Kyla cheerfully called again, and a hint of panic tinged her voice.

But there was no response.

Ember closed her eyes, cleared her mind, and tried to listen for their voices—for their inside thoughts, or maybe even tap into the conversations of their dreams, but a deafening silence jarred her into action. She called in Elvish down the stairs, "Bambam! Juju! It's Ember! Wake up! We need you up here, now!" And when there still was no response, she flicked on the stairwell light and raced down into the room with Kyla right behind her.

Empty sleeping bags and pillows. Candy wrappers. Her father's books and papers scattered. "They're gone!" Ember yelled. "They're not here!"

Kyla gulped. "What do you mean they're gone?"

"They're not here!" Ember repeated frantically.

"Oh, Claus! This is my fault! This is all my fault!"

"Could they be upstairs? Are they hiding? Are they playing a game?"

"No! No! They've never done that! They know not to go through fthe house without me. Oh no, Ember. Do you think Sturd could have taken them?"

Ember inspected the room, searching for something—anything—that would tell the story of the boys' disappearance. "It's possible. I think he was following me the other night, but I can't be sure. He's different. Changed. I don't know, I can't explain it. I… I think he tried to poison me."

Kyla gasped louder. "Oh no, Ember! What if he has them?"

"Let me think, let me think." Ember started to run through all the possibilities in her mind—a long list of what-ifs and other end-of-world scenarios. She held her head in her hands, hunched her upper torso between her knees, and breathed heavily in hopes of stopping a severe panic attack. Before bringing her head up again, she opened her eyes and stared at the dirty stone floor. From the corner of her eye, she noticed something scribbled in the dirt and dust next to one of the boys' sleeping bags. "Kyla, come look at this."

Scrawled in the grime were Elvish words. It appeared to be written quickly and in a child's handwriting.

"Going to MV?" Kyla read.

"Do you think one of the boys wrote this?"

"I didn't write it!" Kyla proclaimed. "Does Sturd know Elvish?"

"Not that I know of."

No. He doesn't know Elvish, but he knows something else. Something older. Something darker…

"MV? What's MV? Is that somewhere in the Mines? Do you think the boys were trying to get back to their home?"

Ember thought. "No. I doubt it. They wouldn't know how to get to the Mouth without getting caught or noticed. They're too smart for that."

"MV? MV?" Kyla repeated. "You don't think it means Mon Valley, do you?"

"Where the old abbey was?"

"Oh, Claus! Ember, do you think Sturd could have taken them to the site of the church fire?"

Ember froze. The thought of Sturd dragging the twins to the ruins of the abbey to complete his sick ritual made her cringe in terror. "We gotta go. Now! I just hope we're not too late!"

Ember and Kyla hopped into the coal sleigh and commanded Asche and Boptail to take them to Mon Valley. The deer dropped them off on the outskirts of the clearing so they could lurk about among the evergreens and not be detected. The sickening scent of burnt wood and flesh still hung heavy in the air. There were voices coming from the clearing, and Ember and Kyla remained hidden behind the trees. "Don't look," she instructed Kyla. "Let me see if I can make anything out, and I'll let you know how we're going to play this out."

Kyla gave a curt nod of her head and leaned her back up against a tree.

Ember stealthily peaked around the side of an evergreen and saw the backs of many elves in a circle surrounding a pile of smoking rubble.

The elves held hands and were mumbling inaudible words. Ember squinted her eyes to focus. A female elf came into view, and placed a wreath of red kalinder flowers on top of the debris. A male elf with orange curly hair stepped out of the circle and raised his hands in the air.

Barkuss!

Ember sighed with relief, tapped Kyla on the shoulder, and gave her a thumbs-up sign. Kyla turned around and looked beyond the trees to see the sight that Ember was watching. She sighed, too, when it was clear that the boys were there and safe, each huddled at their mother Jacinda's side.

"Bulder," Barkuss began. "You were a brother, an uncle, and a dear friend. And all through your troubled life, we supported you and tried to help you find your own way. We are so proud of you for facing down and overcoming the demons you could. Your loss is felt deeply. We love you. You will always be in our hearts and minds."

Balrion moved forward and lit the wreath on fire. "For Bulder," he exclaimed.

"For Bulder," the others chanted back in unison.

"What are they doing?" Kyla whispered.

"A funeral," Ember said. "This is a makeshift funeral for their brother who died in the fire."

Because they couldn't send his body down the Ignis like they did for Banter. This is what Bommer meant by a proper burial.

"Bulder, as my younger brother, I had a responsibility to take care of you," Bommer said after a few moments of reverent silence. "Hell, as the oldest, I have a responsibility to take care of all my brothers—Banter, Balrion, you, and Barkuss. Two of the four, I let down. Two of the four, I failed. I couldn't save Banter, and I couldn't save you, but your loss hurts the most, though, because you were so fragile. I tried, little brother. I tried to get you on the right track. Please know that I tried." His voice crackled with sadness for a brief second. He paused, letting a wave of emotion pass through him before he continued with a darker tone. "The Dwin'nae family is cursed!"

"Bommer!" Barkuss cried out in protest, and Jacinda wrapped her frightened arms around the twins to bring them closer to her.

"We have endured more pain and suffering than any other family Above and Below!" Bommer continued, ignoring Barkuss's plea. "Will I have to bury my boys too? Am I condemned to witness every last one of my kinsmen reduced to nothing but ash?"

"Bommer, please!" Jacinda cried. "This isn't the time or the place!"

"Then when?" he snapped at her. "Haven't I been through enough? Haven't *we* been through enough?"

Ember feared the anger that poured from him. It was sharp and thorny, and it rooted itself at his very core. His anger was a dangerous tool that would surely lead him down a dangerous path, and she would have to try to diffuse the situation any way she could. She moved forward from behind her tree, but Kyla grabbed on to her jumpsuit, pulling her back. Her face was wild with concern. "What are you doing?" Kyla pleaded.

"I have to!" Ember said, jerking her arm away.

As she turned back, Ember noticed Tannen was there watching her in the distance, disconnected from the Dwin'nae family circle. Her heart jumped when she saw him, but she put her finger to her lip to signal him to be quiet. He nodded and quickly looked away.

Ember straightened out her jumpsuit and stepped out from the tree-line. "Oh my Claus!" she shouted, feigning surprise. "There you are, boys! What's going on? You nearly gave us heart attacks!" She waved her hand behind her, signaling Kyla to come out.

"Hey, Kyla!" Bambam said when he saw her. "Where'd you go?"

Bommer's face darkened. "Yeah, Kyla. Where did you go? Weren't you supposed to stay with the boys around the clock?"

Kyla put her head down and shuffled her feet. "I… I'm so sorry… I…"

Barkuss flounced around the circle to meet Ember. "Oh, E! You know how the Dwin'nae family is. Tied to tradition!" His eyes went unnaturally wide, and he nodded his head ever so slightly in Bommer's direction as if to make some kind of excuse for Bommer's behavior.

You're afraid of him, aren't you? You're afraid of your own brother, and rightfully so.

"I've missed you so much, Ember," Barkuss gushed as he grabbed her into a tight embrace. "It seems like we haven't been together in *ages*!"

"We're not gonna let that happen again, okay?" she assured him. "You know you're my number one elf!"

"And you're my number one gal," he said with a wink. "Sorry we took the boys away like that. We didn't mean to scare anyone. It's just, well, Bommer said the whole family needed to be here and…"

"Bulder needed a funeral," Balrion piped in. "He needed to be put to rest."

"And we couldn't have a proper one on the Ignis, so this was the compromise," Barkuss finished.

"It's okay," Ember said putting a hand on Barkuss's shoulder. "We're just glad they're safe. But tell me this—Tannen?" She nodded her head in Tannen's direction just beyond the debris by the opposite tree-line. "How did you manage to get him to come with you?"

Barkuss gave her a toothy grin. His puffy cheeks were reddened from the stinging cold and his hair was a mass of wind-blown gingery curls. "Girl," he said snapping his wrists forward, "who else was gonna guide this motley crew?"

She couldn't help but smile at him and all his bubbliness. "I'm actually quite proud of you, Barkuss! This is now the second time you've come Aboveground. Starting to have a newfound enjoyment for the fresh air?" she teased.

"Puh-leeze, child! Don't go thinking I'mma make a habit of it, either!" He clasped his hands together into a ball and blew into them. "Is it always this cold?"

"Not normally. No," Kyla said. "It actually is unseasonably cold for this time of year."

"Too cold for my blood," Balrion said, and Tannen walked over to join the group.

"Well, guys, it's about to get a lot colder where we're going," Ember announced.

Tannen gave her a puzzled look. "Ember?"

"I'm going to bring the boys up to the Boss," she said. "And I want you all to come with me."

Jacinda gasped, and the others mumbled in shock.

"Absolutely not!" Bommer shouted. "They're coming back home with me. There's no way I'm trusting you with them again. They're my sons, and I'll be the one to say where and when they go somewhere or do something."

Jacinda reached for his arm, but he pulled away from her.

"That doesn't make any sense!" Ember barked back. "You've got the biggest grievance and the loudest voice. You said so yourself, you're sick and tired of feeling like your family is cursed. Well, I'm here to tell you your family is blessed! I'm here to give you an opportunity to air out your grievances with the head honcho. We can actually do something instead of just sitting around talking and complaining."

Barkuss stepped forward. "Bommer, listen to Ember," he implored.

"Stay out of this, Barkuss," he snapped, and like Jacinda, Barkuss slunk back among the group.

"Just hear me out," Ember continued. "The Claus needs to see us. All of us. Bambam and Juju are extremely gifted. The Boss needs to know that they are alive and well. He needs to see what they can do so He can take the next steps and secure His heir. And Tannen… he has a solid plan to bring real change to the Pole. Not some stupid scheme to manipulate something in the human world, either—something that will start and grow with us all, right here. The Claus needs to see a variety of the elves He has ignored for far too long. He needs to see the lines of anguish on our faces…"

"And all the gray in your hair!" Bambam blurted.

Jacinda slapped him upside the head, his orange curls bounced forward and in his eyes. Juju laughed at his brother, only to be met with the same punishment.

Ember gave the boys a side-smile and continued. "He has many, many questions to answer."

Especially about me…

"Bommer?" Barkuss said in a gentle tone. "She speaks the truth. You know I've always vouched for the girl." He looked at Ember with a twinkle of pride in his eye. "I trust her with my life 100 gazillion percent! She's never done me wrong before."

Bommer grumbled.

"I vouch for her, too," Tannen spoke up. Ember's cheeks flashed with a pink blush. "I'd go to the ends of the Pole for Ember Skye."

And I would do the same for you, Tannen. Descendant-of-the-Tree-Elves, Tannen. Sandy-blond-hair-and-soft-glowing-emerald-eyes, Tannen. I-miss-your-sweet-and-salty-kisses, Tannen. Almond-tall-struthers, Tannen.

Kyla pushed her hair back from her eyes and looked straight up to Bommer. "Same here. Ride or die!" she declared.

Bommer looked to Balrion, who could only shrug his shoulders.

Jacinda took a side-step to her left away from Bommer, indicating that she, too, was on Ember's side. The twins gave their father a pleading look as he scratched the side of his head in deep thought.

"We're ready to go, Bommer," Ember urged. "I got two Shadow-Deer, a coal sleigh with enough room, and a first-class ticket to Lapis Hall. We'll storm the ice castle and get you audience with the Boss once and for all. What d'ya say?"

Bommer snorted a few times as he mulled the offer over in his head. The group waited patiently with bated breath.

"Come on, Poppa!" Juju whined.

"Yeah, Poppa, let's just go. You can do this," Bambam added.

Jacinda moved closer to him and placed her hand on his arm. This time he didn't pull away. "*We* can do this," she said, echoing her sons' pleas. "For Bulder."

Bommer grunted and groaned some more, and after a few minutes, he finally bellowed, "Fine! Let's ride!"

CHAPTER SIXTEEN

For a place that had been well hidden and kept a secret for hundreds of years, Lapis Hall was getting a lot of traffic lately. Sturd took a step back in the deep snow and eyed the ice castle before him. With amethyst turrets around its perimeter, the dazzling blueice palace glittered and glinted even under a partially hidden sun. It was a breath-taking sight to behold, even for a wretched soul like Sturd, and as he gazed upon the glory of the magical building he anticipated what it would be like when he took residence in the Crystal Keep.

Sturd grabbed the reins of his single passenger sled and forced Zyklon to one of the outposts on the grounds. Zyklon was the Boss's newest deer and had been living and training at Headquarters with the rest of the Main Team. Sturd was glad to have him. Zyklon was a strong buck, but young, and it was this that made Sturd believe he could groom the deer to do his will. And Zyklon's stark white fur allowed Sturd to travel between

Norland and Aboveground quite stealthily in this particularly nasty storm.

If there was one thing Sturd hated, it was the snow. When it landed on his face or clothes, it turned his stomach with a vicious jolt. He hated how it stuck and melted and turned to ice—cold and wet ice that left him with a deep chill in the very marrow of his bones. He hated how it attached itself to his ears and left stinging red marks all over his face. And most of all, he hated how the others reveled in it—how the little ones cheered and played and rolled around in it like feral animals on holiday. Disgusting! Despicable! Horrifying! But today's snow was different—it was bitter and sharp, and the sky was a depressing gray hue that was more suited to the feeling in Sturd's black heart. Today's snow brought with it a hint of miniature slivers of ice—just enough to pierce the spirits of those vile elflings and keep them indoors for the day.

Sim stood like a general in the center of the castle garden. His pointed ears poked out from his blue hat, and he tugged at his coat, forcing it to cover the exposed spots of his neck. Sturd could tell the cold bothered Sim—made him uncomfortable. With his foot, Sim gently tapped at a leather brown sack in front of him. "Shorgad! Halford!" he yelled for his men from across the gardens and they came bounding through the snow to meet him. "Make sure you get all the elves at their station points as soon as possible. I need Captain A on the east side rampart, and

Captain B on the west side corner tower with eyes and ears opened wide. You understand?"

With a boot stamp and a nod, the two Brotherhood elves responded, "Yes, Councilman!" in unison.

Sturd smiled slyly to himself. He was generally fascinated with Sim's command of the Brotherhood. Sim had taken charge and broken through as a true leader of what was once a ragtag bunch of Coal Elves complaining in the Mines. He had organized them, armed them, given them titles and duties, and had them under lock-step command. It was quite impressive to watch Sim push away the loss (killing) of his own brother, Nim—an act that would have surely sent other elves into an insane frenzy—pull his senses together, and dive deeply into this new role as chief. It's not every day that a lowly Coal Miner elf gets a seat with the highest-ranking group of elves at the Pole.

Sim pulled out two thick cobbing hammers from the brown leather sack at his feet and handed one to each of them. "Give these to Merck and Dauber first. They should be stationed on the south side behind the walk. The Boss thinks they're better suited to a weapon like this."

The Boss?

"Yes, Councilman!" they said as they took the weapons and trotted off.

The Boss? Sturd mused again to himself, his interest piqued. *Just exactly who did Sim mean?*

Sturd slithered up behind an unsuspecting Sim and hissed in his ear. "Hello, my friend."

Sim jumped back slightly, startled by the sound at first, but relaxed when he realized it was just Sturd.

"Protecting our Boss to the fullest capacity?" Sturd sang. "How noble of you, Nim'sim!"

Sim laughed a confident laugh. "Well, that depends on how you look at it. We're just protecting the figurehead right now. Our real boss is back at Headquarters."

Una. He means Una.

A blinding rage pulsated behind Sturd's eyes, and for a second, all he could see was red. He jammed his crooked finger into Sim's chest. "Let's get one thing clear. You serve one master, and one master alone—me! I'm the one who put you on the Council in the first place, and don't you forget that. I'm the one who's been with you every step of the way in your Brotherhood's crusade. And need I remind you—I *know* things. I've *seen* the things that you've done, Sim Nim'sim. Things that could get you banished to the far reaches of Ice Island for the rest of your miserable days. Or worse…"

A flash of the old Sim flooded into his face— the scared, timid, unsure Sim who followed blindly in his brother's footsteps in the Mines. Sturd saw that glow in his eyes—a strange look of regret and fear and insanity. Sturd smiled as Sim pushed that look away and shook his head.

His eyes came back into focus. "I'm sorry, Sturd. You're right. You're right."

"That's better, my friend," Sturd answered calmly. "Now, Councilman, tell me… how can I be of assistance to you and your elves?"

Sim opened his mouth, but the words got caught up on his tongue. He seemed to hesitate between his loyalty to Sturd and the orders he was given by Una.

"Come on, Sim," Sturd cooed. "It's just me and you. Tell me what's going on and where I'm needed."

Sim hunched forward and leaned in close next to Sturd's mangled ear. "There was an attempt made on Ember's life," he whispered.

Sturd gasped in mock surprise. "You don't say! How is she now?"

Sim pulled back and gave Sturd a twisted look, but Sturd kept his eyebrows raised in shock. Fake shock, obviously, because he was the one who poisoned Ember, but there was a hint of real shock, too because he was unaware that the Council had known.

"She made it out okay," Sim whispered. "Her former Nanny sent a message directly to Madame Claus, but one of my guys was able to intercept it before it got to her."

"And what did you do with this knowledge when you found out?"

"I told Una and Zelcodor," Sim replied with a nervous undertone in his voice. "Una said it was time to invoke the last steps of the original Brotherhood plan."

"Twelve Drummers Drumming?"

"Yes. And they both came as fast as they could."

"Una and Zelcodor? They're here right now?" Sturd asked.

"Yes. They're inside meeting with Madame Claus as we speak."

Sturd took a step back and grumbled something unintelligible. Maybe toying with Ember like that wasn't such a good idea. He just wanted to play with her a little! Just wanted to see her suffer a little for his own amusement. Corzakk had wanted him to completely eliminate her, but he couldn't! When he saw her standing there under the streetlamp—her stupid book tucked under her arm, her blonde hair shocked with gray, her fierce determination and wild disobedience—he couldn't destroy her! He didn't have the heart to. She was lovely and disgusting and cold and enchanting, and she had smelled of the sweetest strawberries that he just couldn't resist. He hated to admit it, but he wasn't ready for a life without Ember Skye Ruprecht. He wasn't ready to have a playful adversarial void in his existence. For who would he be if not for her?

But this slip of his had given Una and Zelcodor reason to move forward. He knew what the intended outcome of the Twelve Drummers Drumming phase meant. *Eliminate the Claus.* And if Una had called for it, then it was going to happen very soon.

And he wasn't prepared.

For the first time, Sturd was fearful of the future, fearful that the grand plan of his own coup was crumbling before him. It was clear to him that he needed to eliminate his true opposition and stop messing around with lesser adversaries. He was tired of being the Mastermind with no satisfying return!

"And the Brotherhood?" he asked when he calmed down.

"Armed and ready," Sim answered with a fresh air of confidence. "A captain and two soldiers are located at each point of the castle's perimeter. They are set to move outward..."

"Or inward?" Sturd interrupted with a menacing glare.

Sim shifted nervously again. "Or inward," he agreed. "They are set to move outward or inward at my command."

"And whose command are *you* to follow?" Sturd grilled.

"Yours, of course," Sim answered without hesitation.

"Of course." Sturd smiled.

The gray sky above them darkened. Coal-colored shelf clouds angrily pushed their way in from the southern part of the heavens bringing a rush of wickedly windy air and making the midday sky turn to eerie night. "Another storm coming," Sturd cheerfully noted.

This time Sim tugged at his coat sleeves. They were too small for his arms and a good portion of his forearm had been left exposed to the cold. "Sturd," he said over a gust of wind, "some of my guys are freaking out a bit. They're not used to this weather, and well, the storms have been getting worse every day."

Sturd chuckled. The diabolical sound rose high into the gray cloud sky and seemed to blanket the castle. "Well, you need to tell them to suck it up. They have one objective, and that objective does not include complaining about anything, especially about the weather! This'll all be over soon…"

His words were interrupted by a deep, low rumble in the clouds. The sound shook the ground beneath them, making Sim unsteady on his feet, but Sturd embraced the tremble. All around them, quarter-sized chunks of hail fell from the black sky. A collective bellow of dread and discomfort arose from the ranks of the Brotherhood.

Sim raised his arm up above his head to shield himself from the onslaught of hail stones. "What's going on?" he cried.

Sturd turned his face up to greet the sky and allowed his face to take the brunt of the pelting ice. "Thundersnow," he replied with a smile.

"Thundersnow? What's that?" Sim said frantically.

"Oh, probably one of the worst types of snowstorms the North Pole has ever seen. Rare, too!"

"What?" Sim screamed in disbelief as the clouds rolled and flashed down bolts of thick, purple lightning.

Sturd looked up and absorbed the sight before him—the sky, the hail, the noise, the lightning. It looked as if the sky would swallow up the entire world. Like it would twist and turn and pull everything underneath it right up into the giant maelstrom. The wind whipped and whirled, and while he absolutely detested the snow, he couldn't help but find comfort in this angry scene. The chaotic sky spoke to his chaotic soul as if they were one and the same. It was a cataclysmic sight—one that spoke of the upcoming elven apocalypse. The end of the world raced across the sky and rained death and destruction upon them all. He was enamored. Entranced. He took this as an omen—a prophetic sign that he would be victorious in his mission.

I will be the Claus.

I will rule at the Pole.

I will be unstoppable in my Reign of Chaos.

The elves in the Brotherhood could stand no more as they started yelling and screaming over the storm. They ran from their posts and sought shelter under the overhanging branches of the Gangler Trees and huddled closely together under the archways of the barbicans. Pulled from his trance, Sturd was disgusted by their cowardly display. "What are they doing?" he yelled at Sim. "Get them under control! A little icestorm never killed anybody!"

Yet...

Sim ran to his elves and rallied them up. He yelled for them to return to their stations before disappearing behind the mansion.

Thunder clapped again. The sky had turned completely black. Sturd wondered what the Aboveground elves in the parishes must be feeling right now. Were they scared? Freaking out? Preparing for the end of days? What did the black sky rolling in during midday look like to them? He imagined them taking shelter from the violent hailstones and peering meekly from underneath the windowsills of their homes and schools and businesses. And when the ropes of violet lightning tore through their backyards and city streets, he envisioned them jumping in terror and letting out cowardly squeals—all turning into elflings again at once. And what about the Underground elves? It might have been worse for them—being able to hear what sounded like the vicious sounds of war coming from above, and not being able to see what was actually happening, or what was lurking in the shadows, or what was lying in wait ready to force its way below. Oh, the horror! Oh, the terror! Oh, the pure, unadulterated fear! The thought of it made him swoon in the storm.

Voices in the distance grew to a crescendo, and Sturd was angered now that Sim was unable to control his Brotherhood elves. Just as he was about to go behind the mansion to take matters into his own hands and regulate the situation, Sim and the entire brigade came forward pushing along a crew of elves who were clearly intruders. Their arms were behind their backs as the Brotherhood held their mining tools close against them like prisoners, forcing them to trek through the ices-torm, parading them closer to Sturd.

Must have come in with the storm, he thought. He squinted his eyes against the blinding wind and hail, trying to make out the marching elves in custody. As they got closer he noticed the blinding white hair of the Reindeer Trainer. Towering over the others, and directly behind her was the trolley-driver. Behind him, Sturd's three brothers came into view, followed by the mouthy wife of Bommer. And of course, it was not a surprise for him to see his disobedient wife, who had prob-ably been the mastermind of their little would-be invasion. Before he could shake his head in dis-gust, he saw behind Ember a shock of orange hair peering out from her waist's height.

His heart stopped, and his face fell when they came into full view. His twin nephews—alive and well and standing before him. It was all he could do not to slit their throats right then and there, and punch the smug smirk off his wretched wife's mouth.

CHAPTER SEVENTEEN

The front doors to Lapis Hall slammed shut in time with another thunderous boom from the clouds. The Brotherhood soldiers poked and prodded at the backs of the nine with their pick-axes and other mining implements, and ushered them into the open foyer of the mansion. Side by side, the soldiers lined them up in a row. From the corner of her eye, Ember stared at the deformed monster Sturd had become and couldn't help but laugh to herself. He hadn't even acknowledged her presence with one of his sarcastic, snide remarks. Just seeing the look on his twisted face when he realized the twins were alive gave her enough enjoyment to last the rest of her life. *What kind of pickaxe had that thrown into the back of* his *plan?* she thought.

Nevertheless, she knew the elves in her party were awestruck at the sight of the palace—the fabled Lapis Hall. She had to admit, it was a thing of beauty—a magnificent sight to behold! She had to remind herself to keep her own composure in order to help quell any of her friends' fears.

"Stop poking me so hard!" Bambam yelled at the soldier behind him.

The gruff Brotherhood elf shoved him harder, and Bambam jolted out of the line. "Hey! Hey! Merck!" Bommer yelled. "Easy on my boy!"

Merck shrugged his shoulders. "I got orders, Bom."

Bommer turned around to face him. "Yeah? You got orders?" he challenged.

"Settle down over there," Sim called over from the back of the line.

Merck removed his pickaxe from Bambam's back and bounced the neck of it into his free palm. "Yeah, Bommer. I got orders," Merck said with a threatening tone. "What are you gonna do about it?"

Bommer clenched his fists and reared back on his right foot. The whole group braced themselves for the first punch, when a clacking sound on the ice tiles drew everyone's attention. Senara Calix bounced noisily down the hallway. "Enough!" she screamed. "What in Claus's name is going on here? Councilman? Sturd?"

Sim approached her from the back. "Miss Calix, we've apprehended some trespassers."

Her black eyes jutted from her eye-sockets. "Trespassers? How did they…?" She craned her neck to get a better look of the line-up in the foyer. Her lip twitched when she made eye contact with Ember. After a brief stare-down, she turned her head and yelled down the opposite side of the hallway, "Madame! Madame Claus!"

"They came in with the storm," Sim continued to explain. "They rode in with the thundersnow. That's why we didn't spot them at first."

Ember smirked. *How convenient.*

Docena raced out from her office, followed by Una and Zelcodor. Senara stepped aside and took her usual position next to Docena. Both Sim and Sturd moved from behind the line and took their positions—Sim next to Senara and Sturd next to Zelcodor. Ember and her crew were now sandwiched in the center of the foyer—the Brotherhood guards behind them, and the establishment of power in front of them.

This is it, Ember thought. *It's now or never for me. For us.* She rang her hands together in anticipation.

Docena's eyes narrowed, and her face darkened. "Ember!" she scolded. "What is the meaning of this?"

Una surveyed the line-up and her face fell—just like Sturd's had. She turned to Zelcodor. "The twins? They're alive?" she said in Elvish, and Kyla gave Ember a wide-eyed look.

"You better have a good explanation!" Docena continued.

Ember stepped forward from her position in the line and inhaled her confidence.

Now or never, now or never, now or… "Madame, I have been hounding you for weeks now. Today, I'm not taking 'no' for an answer."

"Well," Docena huffed. "That's the only one you're going to get! The Boss is tired and weary and…"

"With all due respect, Madame, you told me He needed two weeks to rest from the Big Night. It's been much longer than two weeks."

"This year was different, Ember. You know that! We've had this discussion numerous times!" Docena breathed impatiently.

Ember stiffened her body and kept her focus. "I know, but just look at these elves," she pointed to the group behind her. "They're tired and weary, too! Underground. Aboveground. Hell, look at those Brotherhood guys, too!" Sim's ears quickened, and an irate frown swept across Sturd's face.

"It doesn't matter," Ember continued. "Elves everywhere have felt nothing but pain, and strife, and confusion, and despair for far too long. *He* needs to see this! *He* needs to see them!"

Una straightened out the purple cords on her black robe and chuckled. "Sweet girl, don't flatter yourself by thinking you're the only elf who has ever had to endure difficult times. You're not as special as you think you are."

Sturd sniggered and remained suspiciously quiet. Docena raised her hand to silence Una, and Una respectfully bowed her head in acknowledgment before giving Zelcodor a sly, sideways grin.

Ember ignored Una's remark. "Madame," she said, "We're done. We're done with all the lies and the arbitrary rules and regulations. We need to be unified under a strong ruler. We need to have happiness at the Pole again. We all know what happens when the spirit leaves the hearts of the humans…"

"We cease to exist!" Barkuss blurted uncontrollably.

Ember looked back and smiled at him. A feeling of pride swept up inside her. Barkuss—the scared and timid Ceffle who would rather sweep a problem under his glitter-coated carpet than address it, the Coal Elf who was content to stay in the Mines all his life and endure his existence with a bright smile, the one who had even *feared* the Aboveground—was standing here in Norland, at Lapis Hall of all places, and speaking his voice to the Boss Lady! Her good friend had come such a long way, and his jolt of confidence fueled her own fire.

"We would cease to exist," Ember reiterated Barkuss's words. "But what's happening now, Madame, I fear is far worse. What ramifications will there be if the spirit leaves the hearts of the elves?"

Silence fell over them until another wave of thunder shook the palace. "That's absurd!" Una roared as lightning touched down outside.

"But it's not, Councilwoman! I believe it would be catastrophic, and I believe it's already begun." She turned to Docena. "Please," she begged. "Call Him. Let me speak to Him. Let Him see the impact His non-actions have had on His subjects."

Ember touched the side of her jumpsuit where the death certificate rested comfortably.

And let Him answer some of my questions.

Docena gave her a pained look. She looked over the faces of the elves in custody, staring at them one by one. Her eyes reflected the anguish and guilt in her own heart.

She finally turned to Senara and nodded her head. Senara nodded in response and shuffled out of the foyer. Each *click* and *clack* of her high heels pounded in Ember's chest.

Now or never, now or never, now or…

Ember turned her head and surveyed her group. Faces of anticipation stared back at her. Faces of wonder and awe. Bambam and Juju were huddled together. She got their attention and gave them a thumbs-up sign, and they smiled softly at her.

Ember sighed and tried to stifle back her own tears.

Moments later, Senara's clacking echoed again in the distance. She hurriedly shuffled down the hall to Docena and whispered, "He's coming" in her ear. Docena nodded and Senara took her position again.

A slick sheen of sweat coated Ember's palms when a tall figure manifested from the shadowy hallway.

The Boss.

Ember's heart jumped with wild elfling memories.

"Santa?" Juju said to his mother. "Is it really Him?"

Sturd's eyes widened, and he instinctively tried to straighten his crooked back.

Everyone stood straight up at attention in the presence of the Boss.

Jolenir sauntered down the hallway with a graceful stride, passed the line of establishment elves and met Ember face to face in the middle of the foyer. He was everything she had envisioned, and more. And while He closely resembled the Claus found in popular artwork and human depictions, He was above and beyond the stereotypical jolly ole elf.

He was larger than life! A true vision of an Elf King! He towered over the other elves by at least a foot, and wore dark brown leather boots that came up to his knees. His green velvet cloak was fastened in the front by two large silver buttons and revealed the wool liner inside and a hint of a dark green tunic shirt. Snow white hair peeked from the sides of his green velvet stocking cap, and his snow-white beard was full on his face and extended to the center of his chest. He was old—ancient, in fact—but He looked not a day over 50 elfyears, much like His wife and sister. And He was surprisingly fit and trim, not fat and jiggly like the common portrayal of the Claus. Strong muscles pressed tautly against His shirt and kingly cloak.

I guess when you do the kind of work He does, you have to be in shape.

Everyone in the room was star-struck. Even Sturd's mouth was agape.

"Why are you just standing there?" Una called to the Brotherhood guards. "Protect the Claus!"

A line of soldiers spread out and around them, creating a circle of protection around the elves.

Ember stepped closer and noticed a certain sadness surrounding Him—a certain distance in His eyes that engulfed Him, like He was presently there in the foyer of Lapis Hall, but He was not truly *there*. When He looked at her, He looked *through* her, as if He were lost in a daydream, a fantasy, or maybe even a memory from the past. Her mind raced with all the things she wanted to say to Him—from her elfling years to the present.

"Ember Autumn Skye," He said in a deep, resonating voice. He took both her hands in His and stood there, staring at her.

She looked deeply into His and was entranced. His sapphire eyes were old and had seen centuries upon centuries of sights. His sapphire eyes were sad and regretful and peaceful and calming and very much the same color as…

Ember bowed her head. "Your Grace," she said as she pulled her hands from His.

He lifted her chin with His finger and stared at her again. "No need for that," He smiled, and the sound of His voice rattled deep in her chest.

"Forgive me, Your Grace, but I've been desperately trying to… to… to gain audience with you," she fumbled with the proper words. "My friends and I have…"

"Stop!" His voice raised. "Stop with the formalities, child. It is *I* who ask forgiveness of *you*."

Ember's face twisted. "Your Grace?"

"This meeting between you and me has been a long time coming. I am ashamed to admit that I have avoided you for as long as I could."

"All of us!" Bommer yelled out.

Ember snapped her head back and gave Bommer a "Shut up!" look. Barkuss lightly slapped Bommer's shoulder for her, although she had wanted to hit him much harder.

Jolenir lowered His eyes. "All of you," He agreed. "And you, child. You have strived so hard to right all my wrongs, and I've done nothing but disappoint you. I can only hope that you find it in your heart to forgive me for everything. I am truly sorry."

The fire in the pit of Ember's stomach flared. *Forgiveness? After all these years? After everything He's done, or should she say—hasn't done!* After she basically had to storm the castle in order to come face to face with Him, all He had to say to her was "I'm sorry?" No! No way! This was not going to work! She clenched her teeth and fastened her feet to the ground, bracing herself for the onslaught of words about to come from her mouth. "Formalities aside?" she asked.

He nodded.

She took a step back, creating a few feet of distance between them. "Your apology is no good!" she shouted. "I can't accept your apology, and neither can they!" Her arm shot back behind her, and she pointed at her friends one by one. "You've sat up here in the lap of luxury for years while your loyal elves suffer. While your sister and her cronies warp and change things at will with no rhyme or reason, and with no consequence!"

"Ember!" Docena shouted in admonition.

Ember ignored her and continued. "You're sorry? You're gonna have to do much better than that! Do you see those two elflings?" She motioned to Bambam and Juju who were clutching to their mother's coat. "They are the last of the twins at the North Pole. I have reason to believe they are your true successors. They're Coal Elves, Boss. They'll be getting their Life Assignments soon and will probably be assigned as Coal Miner, or cavern sweeper, or something trivial and mundane like that. Their stupid Life Jobs will be picked out of a cap, right? But I know in my heart they are destined for so much more. You see, they can speak Elvish, Boss. Not only that, but they can do it in their minds!"

"That can't be true!" Una burst in. "How do you know this?"

Ember stepped to the side so she could answer Una directly. "It is true. I've heard them. I don't know how I can, or why I can, but I can."

"Bam? Ju?" Jacinda gasped.

The boys huddled closer to their mother and giggled. "Yep," Juju mumbled. "We hate when she gets in our head."

Jolenir closed his eyes as if her words had stabbed Him through the chest.

Ember looked over at her group. Kyla and Barkuss were holding hands for comfort. Balrion and Bommer both had their arms folded over their chests in a defensive stance. She looked over at Tannen whose smile was a mile wide. He looked at her with pure amazement. With pure pride. With pure … *love.*

Her heart warmed, and she smiled back at him. He winked at her to keep going, and she gave him a quick nod and continued. "It's just that… it's just that…" she stammered again for the right words. "We've lost so much. So many of us. And we've lost so much that we're practically losing ourselves. The chaos is deep and palpable. And there are so many unanswered questions… so many…"

Her head spun, and she was overwhelmed with emotion. Jolenir reached for her hands and tugged on them, snapping her back to His gaze. "What questions do you have, Ember?" He said. His voice was soothing and familiar. Comforting and trance-like, as if He spoke them with His eyes and not His mouth, and she couldn't be sure if He spoke the words in Elvish or the common tongue.

Tears pooled in the corners of her eyes as all her questions mashed and bashed together.

You're blowing it! You're blowing your shot! You have Him in front of you, and you have an open invitation! Ask Him, dummy! Ask Him!

Memories and nightmares blended together. Old wounds from her elflinghood re-surfaced and re-opened leaving her mind a seemingly bloody mess. The weak, elfling Ember cried on the inside, under the surface of a lake of tears.

The strong, adult Ember reached her hand deep below its surface and dragged her out, ready to confront her fears, ready to face down the one question that had haunted her all this time. "I know the truth. I know who you really are to me. So, why?" she croaked, her voice catching in her throat. "Why did you put me down there in the Mines? How could you do that to me if I'm really your daughter?"

A collective gasp filled the room, and Jolenir paused and squeezed her hands. He took a deep breath, and when He exhaled, He smelled of peppermint and hot chocolate—smells that soothed the rage in Ember's heart. "Have you ever wanted something, Ember? Like a present? Have you ever wanted something so bad that it physically hurt when you didn't get it, or knew you couldn't have it?"

Ember's breath hitched in her throat. She paused and looked over her shoulder at Tannen.

I just want something I can never have…

Tannen's emerald eyes spoke volumes. The pained expression on his face—the regret, the sadness, the longing, all rolled into one and told the story of their relationship. The one thing she wanted was right behind her. The one thing she wanted…

"Yes," she answered before returning her gaze to the Boss.

"Well, imagine, nearly 300 elfyears of being the Claus and all that time wanting a present, but never getting it."

The twins stirred. "Oh gee, Santa!" Juju exclaimed.

"What did you want?" Bambam added sadly.

Jolenir cocked his head to the side to look at them. He smiled weakly. "I didn't know. I didn't know what I wanted, I just knew that I wanted something. I always felt like something was missing." He turned and looked back at Ember. "But then it came. The greatest gift I could have ever received in all of my days." He bent his head closer to hers so their sapphire eyes were at the exact same level. Ember scanned them, watching them light up as sadness melted away to joy. She heard the word in her heart before He spoke it out loud. She heard the word, and it sent electric shocks throughout her body, filling her up with a strange feeling—a feeling that had always been there, lying dormant, and had just awakened for the first time.

"You," he whispered. "You were my gift."

Docena approached her husband. She put her hand on his shoulder. "Jole?" she said, confused.

Ember stood frozen, but never once broke from his gaze.

"It was against all protocol of the Claus, but then again, nothing about my reign had been standard."

Una shifted uncomfortably.

"When we found out we were going to have a baby, we were frightened. We were scared of punishment from the Mists. We were afraid that balance and order would be severely compromised."

"We?" Docena cried.

Jole reached one of His hands to His shoulder and placed it on top of hers. "Yes, we, my love," He answered. "The Claus is forbidden to have children, Ember. That's just a simple fact for our kind. It's the ancient order. But the prospect of having a child brought so much love and joy to our hearts. We just knew you would be special and pure and bring happiness to all of our days." His face fell as he continued his story. "Signs from the Mists told us it was not to be—that if other elves found out there would be danger and heartache. Docena and I only wanted to keep you safe. It was a heavy decision, but we knew it was the only choice we had."

"Jole, what did you do?" Docena asked.

Jolenir stepped to the side. With one hand, He held on to Docena's, with the other, He clasped Ember's. "Docena, we decided together that it would be best to hide your pregnancy. We sent you to Ice Island where your father watched over you. He hid you under the ice with a protection spell until the time was right for the child to be born. You begged me you didn't want to remember. You begged your father to erase your memories so that you didn't have to live with the constant reminder of what we had and what we lost."

Tears sprung in Docena's eyes.

"You were born under the ice, Ember."

Ember reached into her pocket and pulled out the death certificate. "This," she said, handing it to him. "What's this, then?"

Jole let go of Docena's hand and took the paper. He looked it over carefully and sighed. "Elden worked for me. He was a good elf. A trusted elf. He became one of my closest friends and advisors. His wife, Amalia, had a difficult second pregnancy. This nearly consumed her, as well. Her fragile mind was unable to accept that she might lose a child. Elden came to me as a loyal subject and friend and begged me to help. And that's when we decided that Elden would raise you as his own if the worst-case scenario happened to Amalia. Unfortunately, it did, and Amalia's daughter was stillborn. But she never knew that, for the child that was born under the ice was immediately given to the Skyes."

But she did know! All those years of discontent and disconnect. It made sense now. "My daughter is dead!" Amalia had somehow known. Somehow, somewhere in her mother's heart, she knew Ember was not of her blood. She knew!

And somehow, Ember knew, too.

Docena put her face in her hands and wept.

"Nanny Carole, Jack Frost, Elden Skye, and you?" Ember said. "You were all in on it."

"Your aunt Carole, your grandfather Jack, your foster father Elden, and me," Jole reiterated. "Yes, we all planned for it. We all had a vested interest in keeping you safe and well."

"And the Mines?"

"Docena's extended absence from Lapis Hall raised many questions. There were suspicions and rumors surrounding why she had been gone for so long. Elden and Jack had suggested that sending you to the Mines would be a diversion. No one would suspect that the Boss would actually send His flesh and blood there."

Ember's heart all but stopped. "But… but…" she stammered.

"I know," He said, His voice riddled with anguish and regret, His eyes filling with tears. "It was one of the worst decisions of my life. And for that I am truly sorry."

"Ten elfyears," Docena cried. "That's how long you have been in this lowly state, Jole."

"Ever since you sent me away," Ember added.

Jolenir nodded and handed the certificate back to Ember. "It's no excuse," He said, the sorrow pumping out of Him. "It's no excuse for anything. I kept the knowledge of you close to my heart, and it paralyzed me—crippled me as a leader. Made me… less of a Claus. But you're here now. Right in front of me. And you are beautiful just like your mother … and a bit of a stubborn deer just like me." He couldn't help but smile. "And you know the truth. All I can do is ask for your forgiveness and understanding. You were the greatest gift I could have ever received, Ember. The only gift I ever wanted. In my heart, I called you Dovana—my gift. My one, true and precious gift. My Dovana." His voice trailed to a low hum.

Docena looked up from her hands, her cheeks stained with tears. "I remember," she whispered. "I remember everything."

Ember swallowed hard. Her mind still unsure about everything she heard. The death certificate, the revelation of her parentage, just being in the presence of the Boss was enough to throw her off balance. She looked back and forth between Jolenir and Docena, studying their faces, trying to make connections, trying to find the words to say to all of this.

A loud thunderclap shook the palace again and lighting flashes strobed in the foyer. Bambam and Juju screamed, breaking Ember's trance. She snapped her head to see them just as Jacinda cried out, "No! Let them go!"

CHAPTER EIGHTEEN

Ember planted her feet on the floor and swiveled her body back and forth as she surveyed the room. Two of the Brotherhood guards had picked up Bambam and Juju from the ground and covered their mouths with their hands. The twins' little legs dangled wildly in the air as they fought for their freedom. The other soldiers who had surrounded them took their cues as well and forcefully restrained the others in Ember's group. Jacinda's captor wrapped a long scarf around her face, muffling her cries. Icy dread worked its way into Ember's body, and a feeling of complete helplessness soon paralyzed her.

Una stepped forward and approached them in the middle of the foyer. "I knew it!" she hissed, her voice grating through her clenched teeth. She threw her hands up frantically in the air, and the black hood of her cloak fell behind her, revealing her tight silver bun. "I knew it! I knew it! I knew you two were hiding something!"

Jolenir ignored her hysterics. "Let them go, Jolevana," He said with a calm, deep voice.

"No!" she cried. "I've heard about as much as I'm willing to hear. Enough of the talking and tears and sappy reunions. I'm going to take back what is mine, Jolenir! You've been given one too many passes over the elfyears. And this? This revelation of a child? Why, it's the craziest thing I've ever heard! It's never happened in the history of the Pole before! You should have instantly forfeited your claim as the Claus!" She pulled on her purple cords again and paced back and forth across the floor. "I was the first born, Jole. I was the one who was supposed to reign!"

Ember looked over at Tannen and Bommer. She searched their eyes for a hint, a clue, an inkling of what to do, but she came up empty. Una became unglued, and with Sturd snarling behind her, Ember knew she and her friends were in a highly volatile situation with no exit in sight.

"Please, don't hurt them!" Kyla cried out. "They're just little boys!" But her captor shoved his glove deep into her mouth to silence her.

Jolenir extended his hand to Una like the offering of an olive branch. "Peace, sister," He said. "Why all of this now? We've discussed at length many times why you were passed over." His voice took a stern tone. "You're lucky they even allowed you to live after…"

"It was an accident, and you know it!" she shrieked. "That was just some trumped up excuse to pick their golden boy over me."

"Una, I was there, remember. I saw it happen. I saw the darkness fill your heart."

She turned from Him and looked around the room. *"One for sorrow, two for joy, three for a girl, four for a boy, five for silver, six for gold…* you remember the song, Jole," she said. There was a strange, faraway lilt in her voice. "I know you remember. We sang it together in Elvish so many Clausforsaken times!"

"Seven for a secret never to be told," He added.

Her eyes lit up, but her face darkened, as his response snapped her back to the present. "Ah, yes," she crooned. "And some secret she was," she furrowed her brow and turned her head toward Ember.

"It's been nearly 300 elfyears, Una. Haven't you been able to let it go and move on?"

She snickered. "Oh, quite the contrary, dear brother. The darkness you say you saw fill my heart? It has festered. It has grown to massive proportions throughout the centuries. So large, that you don't even know!" She made a fist and punched her chest so angrily, so forcefully, that the hollow echoes of her strike nearly drowned out the roll of the thunder outside.

Ember wondered if there even was a heart in her body.

"I was a fragile and helpless elfling, and they turned me lose in that pit of ash and rock," Una continued. "What else was I to feel but anger and despair? What else was I to do? I had to fight every day for my own survival, while you went off gallivanting and *enjoying* life down there." She curled her upper lip in disgust. "What they did to me…" her voice trailed. "What they took from me. I was a scared little girl, and you abandoned and betrayed me. You don't know what it's like to have all your hopes and dreams ripped away from you."

Jolenir looked at Docena, then at Ember, and back to his sister. His gentle eyes struggled to keep from filling with tears. "Actually, Jolevana, I do."

Una threw her hands up in the air. "Let's face the facts, Jole. According to the *Dublix Santarae*, when the appointed Claus is ready to be reincorporated with the Mists of the North, His twin will assume His role as the leader. If there is no twin, the current Claus will begin the selection process. *I* am the twin! *I* am the Dublix! The chain of order goes directly to me. Being that there are no more twins, when you are gone I will take my throne."

"Wait!" Bambam spoke up. "We're twins! There are still twins at the Pole!"

Una laughed wickedly and ignored him.

"Una," Jolenir pleaded. "You know that's not what our arrangement was."

"That was not my arrangement. Yours and the Mists. Not mine. I am the Dublix. I am the Double and the true heir. I will step into your boots and rule for another three hundred, maybe 400 elfyears."

Ember steadied herself as another wave of thunder broke outside. The ice crystal chandelier shuddered from the force. Bommer, Balrion, and Tannen continued to buck wildly against the Brotherhood soldiers who detained them. With her friends restrained, and with no weapons or tools, she knew this fight was going to have to be won with words, and it was going to be a matter of perfect timing before she could inject herself into the conversation.

She did not have a positive outlook on the outcome.

Una circled around them. "You haven't named your replacement yet, brother. And without a replacement, the only plausible candidate is the Dublix. It's time for a new reign here at the Pole."

Sturd's long, forked tongue swept across his upper lip and circled in a roundhouse motion to wet the bottom. Ember shuddered at this vile gesture, at his vile visage.

"There will be a new kind of Claus," Una declared.

"You need help," Jolenir said sympathetically. "Let me help you. You don't have to hurt anyone or cause any kind of crazy destruction. We're all family here, and that's what families do." He stepped up to her and placed His hands lovingly on her shoulders. He stared deep into her eyes and recited, *"Eight for a wish, nine for a kiss, ten for a Graespur you must not miss."*

For a brief moment, her eyes smiled, as if she had been transported back in time to a better place, a better moment. Her arm swept up into the space between them, and she affectionately smoothed her hand down the side of his cheek. Another flash of violet lightning filled the room, and her face darkened once again. She stepped back, releasing herself from His grasp, and growled, "Now? Oh, really? Where was my family when I was an elfling and those Coal Elves…" she stopped mid-sentence and smoothed her hands down her robe. "Where was my family when I cried myself to sleep every night? Where were *you*?"

"I'm here now. I had no idea you felt like this. Let me help you."

"I am beyond help, brother," she admitted. "And the only family I have now—the only family I need—is right here with me. Zelcodor, the soon to be Magnus Claus, and Sturd, the Knecht Ruprecht. Look upon their faces for they will be at my right and left hand sides. Look upon the face of Knecht Ruprecht—the hideous and glorious wonder that he is! In his final transformation as *Krampusfrecht*, he will serve me as my Ultimate Enforcer!"

Ember gave a sideways glance in Sturd's direction, not wanting to make full eye contact. His body hunched forward, showing off the full horror of his twisted and gnarled horns in a threatening way, but Ember noticed a frown on his face—a reaction from Una's words, a frown that exposed his fury and discontent, a frown that Ember had seen during moments of Sturd's outrageous, chaotic outbursts.

He doesn't want to serve! He wants to lead!

At that very moment, Ember's instincts said to her on the inside: *Keep a watchful eye on Sturd. The true danger lies with him.*

"Una," Docena finally begged, "just let them go. Let the elflings go. You don't have to do this."

Una glared at Madame Claus with a dagger-like gaze. She raised her hand and flicked it in the air dismissively. "Kill the boys," she said, matter-of-factly.

Screams went wild in the foyer, and panic took root in Ember's soul, giving her a sense of weightlessness and a feeling of being outside her own body.

Kill the boys? Did she just say to kill the boys?

Bommer and the rest of them shouted and fought hard against their captors. Bommer's eyes glowed with desperate fury as he struggled with every ounce of his being to break loose and save his children. Jolenir whispered into Docena's ear, and she took off running to the corner of the room. She huddled close to Senara, who had been on the floor clutching her knees to her chest the entire time.

The Brotherhood guards looked at each other, unsure of the command Una had given. It was obvious to Ember that killing was not part of the deal for them, and Una's directive had left them confused. They turned their puzzled heads to Sim for a semblance of guidance.

"Councilman," Una said to him. "I gave your men an order. You might want to remind them that…"

Suddenly, Bommer and Balrion broke free from their captors. They disarmed them and knocked them out. Balrion rushed the guard who was holding onto Tannen and struck him across the face with the back of the pickaxe. He quickly went back to Bommer and helped him take down the guards who held onto the twins. They both backed the boys up against the wall of the foyer, out of reach of any of the other Brotherhood members. They stood in front of the children like sentinels—feet fixed in a defensive stance and pickaxes held out at arm's length. "Don't anybody get close!" Bommer screamed.

Tannen freed Barkuss before he raced to the middle of the foyer to stand at Ember's side. He took her face in his hands and moved it back and forth, frantically inspecting her. "Are you okay? Are you okay?" he said over and over.

Ember reached up and held onto his wrists. "Yes, yes," she assured him.

In the wave of chaos, Barkuss took down the Brotherhood guard who was holding onto Jacinda, alongside Kyla who had managed to wiggle away herself. The three of them then stood behind Bommer and Balrion for protection.

Now what? Ember thought.

Una huffed in exasperation. "Fine, fine!" she said and turned her back on the Claus. "There are other ways…"

And just like that—before she could open her mouth to protest, before she could unglue her paralyzed feet from the floor and spring into action, before she could push him out of harm's way—in what felt like a slow-motion movie, Zelcodor swiftly snatched a coal-spear from one of the Brotherhood soldiers and in one fell swoop, shoved it deep into Jolenir's chest.

Jolenir's body hunched forward pushing the spear even further into Him. "Jole!" Docena scrambled back to Him at the very same time Ember instinctively screamed out, "Dad!"

Tannen slammed Zelcodor to the ground, knocking him out. Then he pulled back Jolenir's cloak to reveal the dark red stain that had pooled and expanded over the front of his tunic.

"Tannen! Please! Help him!" Ember begged.

Jolenir's sapphire eyes fluttered in and out of consciousness, and Tannen gripped the end of the spear firmly with both hands. With a single heave, he ripped it from the Claus's body, only to reveal a gaping, mortal wound. He tossed the spear to the ground, and he and Ember grabbed Jolenir by the shoulders and eased Him to the floor, propping His back against Docena's chest. Docena removed his stocking cap and petted his long silver hair as she sobbed uncontrollably. Ember took Jolenir's velvet cloak and covered his wound. "Press, Tannen! Help me press here!" she instructed.

Jolenir coughed and a trickle of blood escaped the side of his mouth. "A scratch, a scratch," He said weakly, waving them away.

"Senara!" Docena called her assistant. "Senara, get the kit! Get the wraps and gauze! Hurry!"

And Senara immediately stood up and ran down the hall.

Jolenir straightened Himself out and sat up on his own. "I'm okay. I'm fine," He said through muffled coughs. "I just need a minute."

Ember and Tannen continued to press on the cloak. She looked at her sticky hands and realized the blood had begun to seep through the thick velvet. Tannen raised his eyebrows at her. He had noticed too. She shook her head with disbelief and pushed all the weight of her body down through her slender arms.

Una stood over them and snickered. "Your daughter was right, Jolenir. It wasn't necessary to harm the twins." She kicked His outstretched legs and laughed louder. "They're not your successors yet, so if you're out of the picture, well… there's no need in harming the innocent, I suppose. They don't matter in the grand scheme of things."

The other elves in the room stood frozen, yet Sturd paced back and forth like an animal waiting to be released from its cage. His every movement made Ember wary and nervous as it divided her attention between helping her father and keeping a close eye on another real and tangible threat.

Jolenir inhaled, His chest puffing out against the bloodied velvet cloak. He waved His hands and pushed both Ember and Tannen aside. Somehow, someway, Jole pushed Himself up on His arms, stood up—hunched over at first, but slowly straightened Himself out. Ember and Tannen quickly jumped up at His sides. Jole breathed in again, and this time, miraculously revealed the cavernous hole that had been in the center of His torso had been sealed—healed up, closed, restored.

Una's eyes went crazy with disbelief, and she clawed at her own face. "How can this be?" she bellowed in despair. "How can you...?"

Ember and Tannen exchanged puzzled glances. Docena shot to her feet and slithered in front of Him to see her husband in His restored state. "Oh my Claus," she gasped breathlessly upon seeing the miracle.

Jolenir was still unsteady, and He rested an arm on Ember's shoulder. She swooped her arm up and across His back to give Him some extra support.

"The twins do matter, Una," He said.

Una again furrowed her brow. "What are you talking about, Jolenir?"

"Oh, they matter, all right. You see, sister, they aren't *my* successors," He paused, catching his breath. "They're *hers*." He turned His head and met Ember's gaze.

"Mine?" she mouthed, confused.

Jolenir's legs wobbled, and He nodded at Ember.

"I don't..." she started to say, but Jolenir's body went limp. Overcome with weakness and pain, He passed out as He stood. The weight of His body crashed onto the floor, dragging Ember down with Him.

CHAPTER NINETEEN

A great clamoring noise rose up in the room, but above all, Sturd emitted a strange, guttural howl from the depths of his being. Like a wild animal's cries, the demonic sounds rang out and above the gasps and lamentations of the other elves within the hall. "Never! Never you!" he screeched, his voice like jagged fingernails across a schoolroom chalkboard.

Docena and Tannen tried desperately to drag Jolenir away from the center of the foyer, and Ember sat up, still processing what the Boss had told her. She looked over at Sturd. His pacing was quicker, and he twitched and writhed as if in pain. He twisted his neck from side to side in an un-elf-like way, and his body cracked and jerked with bizarre movements and sounds. He caught her stare and held it for a few moments.

Ember tried to read his expression—to make sense of his state of mind—but it was no use. It was as if Sturd wasn't even there. His red eyes flashed with pure rage, and he licked his lips furiously. And then, without any warning, he rushed at Una, knocked her to the floor, and pounced savagely on Ember.

Ember's head snapped back and smashed hard against the ice stones. Darkness descended over her eyes like a black veil flowing onto her face and gently then floating away. Her eyes came back into focus. Stunned, it took her a few seconds to realize what had happened. Instinctively, she had brought her arms to her face in a defensive position, but he was slashing at her with his long nails. The flesh of her forearms and hands stung as he clawed and opened up gash after gash after gash. Her head batted from side to side as she tried to avoid his flurry of blows, and in these head jerking motions, she saw a pool of blood on the ice stones by her head—blood from the opening of her skull when her head hit the floor.

Relentlessly, he lowered his head, and bringing his horns closer and closer to her throat—prodding at her like a stag, toying with her before he went in for the kill. The sharpened ends gouged deeper into her opened wounds, sent shocks of blinding lights that burst behind her eyes. It was a bloodying dance—dip and sway, dip and retreat, dip and puncture—a violent choreography set to wailing and sobs and screaming in the background, and the thunderous pounding of her own heart within her chest.

Ember couldn't make a sound, nor could she think clearly. She simply acted on her primal instinct to defend herself. She could tell by the way he bucked on top of her that he was easing his way in to try to open her up. All she could do was find the strength to keep her hands up and cover her neck and face as best she could, but she doubted she would make it out alive.

Sturd pulled his head back for an instant and for the first time, created a foot of space between them. Without thinking, Ember seized the moment, reached her hand up to his pale-skin face, dug into the side of his cheek and pulled down hard. Chunks of his wrinkled, withered flesh curled up under her fingernails like wet wood shavings.

He paused and stopped his assault. He brought his hand to his wound and wiped the blood from his face. A sinister laugh escaped his throat when he inspected his bloodied fingertips, and he smiled at her before licking his own blood and continuing his attack.

In an instant, he was on her again, and the cries from the others once again permeated her ears. She was weak and helpless and fading in and out. A few times her arms dropped on her chest, and his horns plunged close to the corner of her eye.

She was drifting. She was losing. She was fading. She was dying.

Suddenly, Tannen rushed up and wrapped his arms around Sturd's neck—jerking Sturd's body backward and wrestling him off Ember. She sat up as Tannen pulled him farther and farther away. But the ground was red and slick with blood, and Sturd was so strong—so very strong. Tannen lost his footing, and in a split second, Sturd had wiggled out from his grasp, lowered his head, reared back, and charged his pointed horns deep into Tannen's chest.

A sickening *poomph* sound discharged deep from within Tannen's ribcage, and he crumpled to the floor in a heap. Sturd stood back, laughing—a hideous sound of a thousand voices echoed throughout the entire palace.

Ember shrieked and crawled urgently to Tannen's side, but she slid and slipped on the slimy stones. Her heart stopped a thousand times for every 1000 elfyears it took her to reach him. When she got there, she cradled his head in her lap. She petted his hair feverishly, pulling the strands out of his opened eyes. "Come on, Tannen!" she commanded as she pressed on his open wound. "Let's go, man! I'm not playing around, Tannen!

She held the tears in her eyes—refusing to release them, knowing that to do so would be admitting the truth of what she had witnessed. She squinted hard to see through her blurred vision. "Let's go, Tannen! Talk to me!" she implored. But her frantic anger soon turned to a despondent plea. "Say something," she whispered in disbelief. "Please."

Don't leave me like this.

The world stopped when a tear escaped the deep wells of her eyes.

The pallor of his skin was not his normal coal-white color of ash, and the light behind his emerald green eyes had vanished. He was gone. And cradling his head in her lap was like holding on to shards of broken glass, like reaching out for something she could never have. "No, please," she squeaked through the hard lump in her throat and the onslaught of tears streaming down her face. There was no time to think or grieve or process anything, and in her frantic panic, she smothered his cold face with her hot kisses—kissing him back to life, willing him back to life, silently praying to the Claus and the Mists and to anyone else who was listening to make him blink and cough and spit out blood and laugh and smile and… "Don't leave me, Tannen! You can't! We're supposed to go flying again. I promised you it wouldn't be that bumpy. And we got that big ole tunnel to build, right? Who else is gonna build that tunnel? Barkuss?" she laughed through her tears, hoping her unfunny joke would somehow rouse him awake.

Tannen Trayth. Descendant-of-the-Tree-Elves, Tannen. Blond-hair-green-eyes-I-can't-lose-you, Tannen. Love-of-my-life, Tannen. We-never-had-a-fair-chance, Tannen.

A red wave of blinding rage overtook her, and she threw her head to the sky and screeched a blood-curdling screech. In an instant, every windowpane in the foyer cracked and glass particles showered over her. A foggy gray maelstrom came filtering into the hall—shadows from the night sky whipped furiously through the crowd and encircled Sturd in its cyclone, lifting him off the ground.

Una stood up and raised her arms high above her head. "The time is now!" she declared above the howl of the storm. "*Al freeg oft Krampusfrecht! An daig unt Krampusnacht!* The time for the final transformation is at hand!"

The misty tornado continued to swirl around Sturd, and he threw his head back and laughed. Una chanted in Elvish, but Ember couldn't make out her words.

I can't let this happen. I can't let this happen. I can't let this…

From the corner of her eye, she spied the spear that Zelcodor had used in his attempt to kill her father. It was on the ground a few inches from where Tannen's body lay lifeless and cold.

Without thought or hesitation, she glided over and scooped it up in her hands. Without thought or hesitation, she stepped into the space of the gray tornado, face to face with Sturd. Without thought or hesitation, she plunged the spear deep into his stomach.

Sturd's body lurched forward, and a high-pitched screeching wail spewed from his mouth. The fog-storm swirled more violently around them, and she too was lifted from the ground. The rest of the world ceased to exist in that moment as she was entranced by the churning shadows around her, and the image of Sturd suffering on the spear before her. The shadows smelled of sweet vanilla, and she breathed in deeply, filling her lungs with the soothing scent. Voices spoke inside the storm, speaking in that ancient language Sturd had used the night he poisoned her. In her heart, she knew the words, knew the message, and knew the very core of what they sang. They sang of violence and hatred and pain. They sang of regret and remorse.

Sturd's soul is crying, she mindlessly thought.

Sturd struggled with the spear and finally yanked it from his body. All the blood from all his wounds rose into the vortex and swirled among the shadows in a red haze. She looked at her own hands and arms and realized that her blood, too, was being lifted up and sucked into the depths of the storm, as if the shadows themselves were feeding on them both. A fine, red mist rained over them—covering their faces, drenching their clothes, dousing them in their very life-forces. Ember stuck out her tongue like an elfling during a snowstorm and caught the red droplets in her mouth.

Sturd reached out his arm in her direction and mouthed her name. Was he begging her for help? Was he imploring her to end his pain? A black cloud materialized at his levitated feet—a storm within the storm—and wrapped around his body like a cocoon. Sturd screamed an agonizing sound as Ember watched the cloud suffocate him.

Transform him.

There he was—a floating, newborn babe inside the cocoon. A large dimple indented the side of his cheek when he cooed at his doting mother. He was innocent and pure with a head full of jet-black hair and soft blue eyes.

There he was—a floating, happy elfling inside the cocoon. Playing in his rock garden and trying to train his beloved Graespurs. He was care-free and happy with a whole productive future ahead of him.

There he was—a floating, angry young elf inside the cocoon. Scars ravaged his arms from hunching in chinchi holes, and his red eyes distorted and changed from the dark.

Episodes of Sturd's life danced before her like an old-time movie. She saw every incident of major importance in his life unfurl within the vortex. How he stalked her, spied on her, and *loved* her? His self-doubt, self-loathing, self-abuse—all of it, everything, scenes of Sturd's life that made Sturd *Sturd*.

And there he was—a floating, murderous elf inside the cocoon. Flashes of Banter's killing, and the Scarf brothers' killing, and the Book Keepers' killing, and the Councilwoman's killing, and… a rampage of red and blood and squeezing and death and…

Scenes of his life continued like a movie reel, flashing before her and highlighting all of Sturd's crowning moments—both the good and the bad.

All the stages of his life. All the wrongs done to him. All the wrongs he's done to others.

"When will it end?" she screamed to the cocoon. "Is this your end, now?"

Her heart sank when she saw him as a child and remembered him from when they were kids. An uncontrollable thought manifested itself mindlessly onto her lips and she whispered, "It's not your fault."

Because the sad truth was—it wasn't. Sturd had been dealt a raw deal.

Just like me. Just like the rest of us.

And there he was again—a floating, changing, transforming elf inside the cocoon. Horns grown, teeth descended, claws extended, and…

The visions stopped. The maelstrom stopped.

The shadows rose up and dropped both of them onto the floor before collapsing on itself and sucking back into the night air.

Ember and Sturd lay on the ice stone, staring at each other. He gave her a pained look, not one of physical pain, but of heartfelt sorrow and regret. It flashed in his eyes just for a second, and she nodded at him to acknowledge what she saw. For that brief moment, she saw through him and into the remorse of his soul. His shape was the same— horns and all, but his wounds were healed. And his eyes—his red, demonic eyes—were now blue.

Una was hysterical as she and Zelcodor rushed to Sturd's side. She repeated over and over that the transformation had not been complete, and that the Shadows had abandoned him.

"Ember!" someone in the room called.

Ember craned her neck to see who in the crowd had called. It was Docena, who was huddled with

Jolenir in a corner of the room. With great effort, she dragged herself to be with her parents.

"He's ready," Docena said somberly through her tears. "It's time."

Jolenir looked off into the distance, staring into space, focusing on nothing. His sapphire eyes glazed over, and He babbled incoherently. A death rattle rumbled in His chest. Ember took His hand. "I thought He was okay," she said to Docena in disbelief. "I saw His wounds heal before my eyes!"

Docena shook her head. "Yes, physically He is well. But it's time for His spirit."

Ember lowered her head. "It's because of me, isn't it?" she asked regretfully.

"No, my dear. It's because it's His time."

Jolenir's eyes lazily wandered around the room until He caught sight of Ember next to Him. When He saw her, His face lit up into a wide grin. "There you are, my child," He said breathlessly, "I've been searching all over for you."

She squeezed His hand tighter. "Well, you can stop looking, Dad. I'm right here."

Docena smiled at her.

"And Doci?" He asked.

"Doci?" Docena chuckled. "You haven't called me that in centuries… literally!"

Jolenir gave a faraway smile. "We're hiking through the Gable Woodlands. Don't let me fall through the ice on that lake again."

Docena looked at Ember with a pained expression. "I won't, my love. I know you hate the cold water."

"We had a good life, together, didn't we?" He said thoughtfully.

Docena's breath hitched in her throat, and she fought to get the words out. "We sure did. Charmed."

Tears pooled in His eyes. "I'm so sorry for all the hurt I caused."

She kissed His cheek and smiled lovingly through her own tears. "You have nothing to be sorry for, my love."

"Thank you for giving me my gift," He mumbled quietly. "My Dovana. Take care of her. Promise me you will enjoy the rest of your days with her."

"I promise," she whispered and kissed Him gently on the lips.

One last time.

"Child," He said, calling for Ember. "Dovana. My Ember. My Daughter. My Child."

"I'm still here," Ember repeated and rubbed His shoulder.

He wearily turned His head to look at her again. "Can you forgive me? Can you forgive this old fool for everything I've done?"

Ember nodded solemnly.

"I left you with quite a mess, haven't I, kid?" His deep chuckle produced another rattle in his chest.

"No worries, Boss. No worries," she gently assured Him.

He closed His eyes and paused, as if He heard something from far away. "You saved him."

Ember turned her head to Tannen's dead body. Her heart sank when she realized he was truly gone. "I didn't save him, Dad. I couldn't."

"No," Jolenir corrected. "You saved Sturd. The Shadows of the Dark retreated and…" He paused, listening again, "you are bound in blood now."

But I didn't want to save him! I had every intention of killing him! I impaled him with a spear! She thought.

Jolenir chuckled again as if in response to her thoughts. "That's not in you to do that. In the moment, yes. But that's not who you are. You are empathy. You are understanding. You are forgiveness."

Ember paused and reflected on the visions she saw in the vortex. "Is Sturd my Dublix?" she asked.

"No," Jolenir said. "He's the Knecht. The Servant. Restorer of order and balance. Deliverer of pain and justice. He is the one True Coal Elf. Your counterpart. Your mirror image." He paused as if listening to someone unseen. "No longer bound by marriage but bound by blood."

Ember glanced over at Sturd, and he nodded at her. Knots formed in her stomach at the sight of his repulsive visage. She had seen everything he'd done and everything and everyone he'd taken away from her, and for that alone, she hated him with a ferocity that she knew would consume her completely if she let it. She wanted to wrap her hands around his throat and squeeze the life out of him, like how he did to Banter and the others. She wanted to gouge his eyes out with her bare hands and shove them down his throat! She burned inside when she looked at him. Burned with rage and hatred and anger and… *pity? Empathy?* Because, not only had she seen what he'd done to her, she'd seen what had been done to him. And for that, for the things that had been so beyond his control, she couldn't help but feel an ounce of sadness for him. "Knecht Ruprecht," she said across the room to him, the words dripping from her mouth like poison. She was mad at herself for her conflicted feelings. Disgusted that she would feel empathy for such a monster.

"Come here, child," Jolenir whispered.

Ember obeyed and moved in closer to Him.

"Almond tall struthers," He said, and Ember's face fell. She jolted back at his words. *How could He have known? How could He have…?*

She looked over at Tannen's corpse and nearly fainted at what she saw. His clothes piled up in a mound with no body to be found. Puzzled, confused, angered, she opened her mouth to protest, to question, to scream! Jolenir smiled, and with His hand, he motioned in the air back and forth in an upward movement. "Mists," He said, his voice scratchy and dry.

Mists.

The Mists of the North.

The Mists of the North had come for Tannen and given him the highest honor an elf could ever dream of. He was now completely incorporated with the spirit and would always live on in her heart and the hearts of all around her. She smiled with pride and happiness, for he would forever be a part of the universe in a profound way. Ember fought back the tears as she smiled at her father and said, "Thank you."

"Closer still," He commanded as He closed his eyes.

Ember scooted closer to Him, so her forehead touched His. Jolenir ran His hands through her long hair and laughed. When she pulled her head back, she saw her hair fall in stark white locks about her shoulders and down the front of her chest.

Docena and Ember held hands, and each one held onto one of Jolenir's sleeves. He breathed deeply and relaxed his body against the wall of the castle. "Okay," He said and closed His eyes. "I'm ready to go Home."

Docena and Ember closed their eyes as well.

And Ember knew if she closed her eyes long enough she could feel the warm sun beating down on her face. Warm heat intermingled with the frosty nip of a breeze that kissed the pointed tips of her ears. And if she tried really hard, she could smell that scent again. The smell that smelled like white and gray if color had an aroma. If that's even possible. A smell that reeked of wetness in the air and ice patches on the ground and sloshing half-frozen dirt between her toes. The smell that indicated the clouds are just heavy enough to burst open their icy insides.

She knew that if she squeezed her eyes a little tighter, the colorful light orbs that flickered behind her closed lids would transform into the hundreds of butterflies flitting about the garden in her courtyard. Their iridescent wings catching the thin rays of light from the sun as it melts its way off the horizon, moving in and out and back and forth against that gray and white-smelling wind. *Home.*

And there was peace. And there was happiness.

And there was a caring mother, and a doting father, and a gaggle of good friends, and a makeshift family, and a loving elfhusband, and a charmed life to be lived year after year after year after…

All of a sudden, the sleeves of Jolenir's tunic went limp. Ember and Docena opened their eyes simultaneously to see they were holding an empty clothing shell.

Jolenir was gone.

Ember stood up and looked around the room, eyeing every elf. Eyes of the elves who had borne witness to this chain of events stared back at her in awe—locked in place, hands over hearts, tear-stained faces, clutching to each other. She shook out her hair. The white waves flickered in front of her face and sent a shiver of dread through her body. In a moment of doubt, she wobbled on her feet.

How am I going to do this? How am I going to lead them?

A voice inside her head echoed, "Almond tall struthers," and she smiled, crossing her arms authoritatively across her shoulders.

One by one, the elves in the room bowed their heads to her in sincere reverence—each one paying respect to their new Lady Claus.

CHAPTER TWENTY

The Meeting Room on the 13th floor of Headquarters' Main Building was decorated in typical Norland Headquarters fashion—a row of tall picture windows served as the east side wall, providing a glorious, unobstructed view of the city below. The other three walls were painted a light sandy-tan color and were adorned with large black velvet portraits in ornate frames. Filing cabinets in various sizes were meticulously spaced along the walls as well—portrait, cabinet, portrait, cabinet—as if the Decorator Elf had a serious obsessive-compulsive disorder. There was a plush beige carpet that gave a feeling of we're-all-business-but-let's-be-comfortable, and in the center of it all sat the grand mahogany table for the eight elves who were to be present at all the meetings.

Ember shifted in Her seat as She waited for the other elves of the cadre to arrive. *I don't think I'll ever get used to this outfit!* She thought to Herself as she wriggled Her small body from side to side to adjust the folds and buttons on Her red suit dress. The elastic waistband wrapped tightly around Her small frame, and a small piece of plastic from the Designer Elf's tag poked at Her side. And the polyester material of the get-up itched. Badly.

One by one, the elves of her Council filtered in. Each one nodded their head respectfully at Her, and She returned the gesture back to them. Docena took her place next to Ember and squeezed Her leg lovingly underneath the table. Ember gave her a quick side-smile.

"Okay, gang," Ember said once they were all seated. "Quick meeting. I promise. I know we have a lot to get done and the clock is not on our side. This is just a check-in, if you will."

The elves at the table nodded in agreement. "Bommer, what of the tunnel?" She asked.

Bommer opened up the black folder in front of him and removed a stack of papers. "Coming along, Lady Claus. The pre-dig is complete, and the Builders will be pouring cement any day now."

"Excellent. What about the stop-points we discussed?"

He flipped through some of the pages. "Between Crystal Cave and West Valley, there are three. Onyx Alley will be completely shut down for mining and used for the tourist attraction, like you suggested."

Ember nodded.

"Another thing, Boss," Bommer continued, "the Architect made the final blueprints for the renovations on Skye Manor." He slid one of his pages across the table to her. Docena reached out her hand to intercept it and turned it over to Ember. The top of the blueprint read "Skyeway Station." Ember's heart sank a little when She saw the final drawing of what her childhood home was to become but smiled at the prospect of a new day for elves at the Pole. A café, a gift shoppe, turnstiles, direct access to visit the Mines—Skye Manor was now going to be the main terminal, the direct port of transportation between the Above and Undergrounds. *Just how Elden wanted*.

She folded up the paper and handed it over to Docena. "Looks great."

"Eventually, we'll have another terminal in West Bank just like Skyway Station, but the Architect felt it was important to start with this one first," Bommer concluded.

"Agreed," Ember said, and turned Her attention to the other end of the table. "Barkuss, what of the schools?"

Barkuss stood up, tucked his orange curls behind his ears, and straightened out his pink silk tie. As a Councilman, he indulged in every aspect of the role—the title, the reputation—and was intent on becoming a positive role model and liaison for the new Claus. He mentioned once in passing that "If you're gonna play the part, you gotta look the part" and commissioned the Designer Elves to create an upscale wardrobe "fit for a Councilman." He cleared his throat and ran his chubby hands down the front of his suit jacket. "Well, Boss, since the elimination of Life Job assignments, I've been working with the Teacher Elves on creating new curricula for the rising elflings. Because of the openness of it all, we're in the process of designing one month courses the elflings can choose to attend. Whether it be banking, teaching, building, designing, apothecary… they will get a hands-on tutorial to experience different Life Jobs and to determine what would be the best fit. Most elves who are already established have chosen to continue on their Life Path. It's the younger generation that will be impacted the most."

"Great," Ember said clapping Her hands together. "Once the finishing touches are made, send the report back to me."

Barkuss sat back down. "Yes, Ma'am," he said.

Ember rolled her eyes. It wasn't just the suits she was going to have to get used to—it was also the formalities and traditions. Hearing her friends call her Lady, and Boss, Ma'am didn't entirely sit well with her. She shifted gears again. "Kyla, what of the reindeer?" Kyla stood up nervously and fidgeted with her cream-colored pinafore. Ember raised Her eyebrows quizzically at her. "*Claugh sonna*," She told her in Elvish, trying to calm her down.

Kyla gave a nervous giggle. "I think they're ready to go, Ma'am. Marley is the only one I have some reservations about. He's still young, and his flying leaves a lot to be desired, to say the least. I recommend we hold him back this year, just until…"

"No," Ember interrupted. "I want him. He can take the lead from his parents, Asche and Boptail. Baptism by fire, right?"

"But I'm not sure he's ready yet," Kyla protested.

"Are any of us?" Ember said with a smile.

Kyla relaxed her rigid shoulders and smiled back. "Point taken."

"That makes three Shadow-Deer on the Main Team, though," Barkuss injected. "Do you think it will be a navigational problem? Old Red Nose has been retired for quite some time now, and none of his progeny have inherited his unique feature."

Kyla sat down. "Zyklon is up front, and his coat is so... so… *white*! He practically glows, even in the faintest of starlight!"

The cadre all chuckled. When their giggling died down, a serious tone filled the silence in the room. Ember stretched Her arms across the table in Kyla's direction, but Her eyes remained downcast. "How's Holly?" She asked.

"She's well," Kyla replied. "She's been a great apprentice at the stable and has been going back and forth between Fannie and me. She has a natural penchant for working with the deer and they all really love her."

Ember's face twisted. "No. I mean, how's Holly?" She repeated.

Kyla gave her an apologetic look that filled Ember's heart with sadness. She wasn't overly concerned with how Holly was dealing with Tannen's death. It was more of a way to project

Her own struggle, Her own daily battle of missing him and longing for him.

I just want something I can never have.

"She gets better every day," Kyla said, breaking through Her thoughts. "Actually, she made a quick mention of getting married again and having a *stable* full of elfbabies."

Ember smirked. *Some habits die hard.*

Kyla chuckled again. "She actually said that the first elfbaby she has will be named *Skyla*—for you and me."

Of course she would.

"She might have a penchant for training reindeer, but she doesn't seem to have a penchant for naming, does she?" Ember joked.

"No, Ma'am, she does not!"

"Why do we have to sit through these boring meetings?" Bambam muttered.

Juju sighed heavily. "I know, right? This stuff is so pointless and useless, and…"

Ember snapped Her head in the twins' direction. They hadn't complained out loud, but She heard them all the same. Since the Mists gave Her the power of the Claus, the boys' voices in Her head were louder and clearer; She could even when She sat in Her office in Lapis Hall and they played wildly down in the Mines, controlling the volume and frequency was yet another thing She had to get used to.

"Because it's important for you boys to understand what's going on," She said out loud.

The boys stiffened up like bandits caught red-handed. It was as if they had forgotten She could hear them in their heads. The adult elves of the Council burst out into a round of giggles.

Juju's cheeks blazed bright red, and Bambam lowered his face in embarrassment. "'Cause we're next?"

"Exactly," Ember replied.

"Not for a long time, though. Right, E?" Barkuss blurted out.

Ember smiled at his concern, and for the fact that he reverted to his nickname for Her.

"I… uh… I mean, Lady Claus," he fumbled, trying to correct himself.

Ember raised Her hand and waved his "mistake" away. "That's correct, Barkuss. I don't plan on going anywhere anytime soon. And I hope none of you are either. As my Councilmembers, we'll all be together for the long haul."

Ember looked around the table. Her Council. Her friends. Her *family*.

She looked over at the last elf who had yet to report. Senara Calix, former assistant to the former Madame Claus turned Councilwoman #2. "Senara, what news of Ice Island?"

Senara stood to address the cadre. "Everything is okay. Una Ruprecht, Zelcodor Ruprecht, Corzakk Ruprecht, Sim Nim'sim, Trelson Castleberry, Quisto Calix, and Magnus Scorpio are all as comfortable in their cells as they can be. The Frosts are watching over them as they have been instructed to. Jack sends his updates regularly and, well, as far as prisoners go, everything is going smoothly."

"And Sturd?" Ember said with a raised eyebrow.

Senara quickly took her seat. "As expected, Boss," she answered quickly.

"As expected," Ember repeated.

But what was expected? Would his solitary confinement change him? Enrage him? Make him more of a monster? Make him repent? Only time would tell…

"Okay, Council, if there isn't anything else, I call this meeting adjourned." Ember waited a moment, and when no one had anything else to add, She struck the table with the gavel, and they all rose to leave.

They each bid her farewell, and before exiting the Meeting Room, Barkuss gave Her a quick hug, whispered, "Red is a good color on you, E," and left.

The cold never bothered Ember, not the way it bothered Kyla or Barkuss. Maybe that was because She was a Frost by blood, and it was said that pure ice ran through every Frost child's veins. She sat in her office in Lapis Hall enjoying the cold, poring over the two long Lists in front of Her—one labeled *Naughty*, one labeled *Nice*. Her eyes were so mesmerized by the colors and names that they all started to bleed together—*Lori*

Deschnow, Carolyn Stafford, Dennis Rooney, Ashley Caldwell, Donna Martinez, Jacey Regan.

A gentle rapping at the door startled Her from Her daydream. "Come in," She called, and Docena made her way to her desk. She carried a thick, blue leather-bound book and handed it to Her.

"What's this?" Ember asked.

"A Memory Book," Docena replied. "The renovations started on the Skyeway Station, and some of the personal belongings were boxed up and sent here. There were many old photographs from your childhood that I had preserved and made into a Memory Book for you."

Ember opened the book and saw the old pictures from when She was an elfling. Old memories of Her charmed life as Ember Skye, daughter of Amalia and Elden, sister of Ginger, charge of Carole… deceptions, yes, but memories all the same. Happy memories. Charmed memories. She flipped to a page with a picture of Her and Nanny Carole playing in the snow and touched it. She smiled when She saw how Carole chased Her around the hedgebush, wagging her finger in the air, admonishing Her that She'll "Catch her death for not having on her galoshes."

"Look at Nanny Carole," She said wistfully. She paused. "Aunt Carole."

Docena smiled and Ember continued to peruse the pages. "But I don't have any pictures since I went to the Mines," She said.

"Keep going," Docena instructed. "You'll see."

Ember turned to a page in the Memory Book that had a blank piece of notebook paper in the center and two empty slots for pictures. "What's this?"

"Your journal. The Bookmaker made it so that when you touch the blank paper, the words of your journal will appear. From those words, you can create your own pictures. Two for each entry. Two visuals to represent your feelings."

"Did he read it? Did you read it?"

Docena shook her head. "No. Not at all. I made him put a locking mechanism on it before he opened it up. The pages are blank to all but you."

Ember closed the book and placed it on the desk. "Thank you, Madame. This is a very thoughtful gift."

"You don't have to call me that, you know. I know I'm your assistant now, but..."

"I know, I know," Ember interrupted. "It's just going to take some time is all."

Docena breathed in and extended her arms out for Ember to rise. "I understand. We have plenty of time, now, don't we?"

Ember stood up and nodded.

Docena adjusted the thick black belt around Ember's waist and ran her hands down the front of Her red velvet coat. "Not a wrinkle on your suit, my dear. Are you ready?"

"I think so."

"The sleigh is waiting outside." She kissed Ember on the cheek and scrunched up the white pom-pom on Her red stocking cap. "I'm so proud of you."

Ember picked up the Lists on the desk and left the office. She raced to the front of the castle where Her team of reindeer had been waiting for Her. They neighed and whinnied and stamped their hooves in excitement when She boarded her toy-filled sleigh. "Okay, guys!" She yelled to them. "We got a lot of work to do tonight! Are you ready?"

They huffed and grunted their responses.

"Not good enough! I said, Are you ready?" She yelled even louder to pump them up.

They whinnied and bucked against their reins. They snorted and stamped and bopped their thick heads into the air.

Ember snapped the reins to jerk them to attention. "Now that's what I'm talking about!

"Now, Aschen! Now, Boptail!
Now, Marley and Northelyn!
On, Eira! On, Jaspar!
On, Lucian and Seren!
To the top of the porch!
To the top of the hall!
Zyklon, dash away! Dash away!
Dash away, all!"

The team shot into the sky at Her final command, and off they went. But their instructions beforehand told them their night would not start until they made their first stop.

Ice Island.
Sturd.

It had been months since She had seen him last. Months since his sentence of solitary confinement had begun on Ice Island. Months since She had heard the sound of his voice or smelled his un-elflike aroma. He wore a brown buckskin overcoat with knee-high black leather boots, and he carried a brown sack over his back. A thick black beard had formed on his face, yet no hair grew on the top of his head. As part of his punishment, the pointed tips of his horns had been clipped and filed down. Ember imagined that they would still hurt if touched, but they were no longer as lethal as when he…

Sturd climbed up into the sleigh next to Her and grinned maniacally. "Ember," he said, graciously acknowledging her. "Oh, I mean, *my Lady*," he corrected, but there was a hint of the old Sturd's sarcasm in his voice.

She ignored him and handed him the Naughty List, practically throwing it in his lap. He looked at it wide-eyed, and a strange look of pleasure washed over his face.

Ember hated to admit it, but She had always been fascinated with the List, too. "New names?" he asked.

"A few," She said curtly. "A dozen or so repeats too."

His ears perked up and his fangs flashed against the moonlight. "Repeats?" he asked with a sinister tone.

"Yep. Some of them just didn't get it from last year. I guess that was to be expected, though.

There's this one boy who has been on there three years in a row now. And poor Jennifer and Jacey are on there *for real*, for real."

Sturd licked his lips to contain his excitement. He reached into his satchel and pulled out a wooden rod with strands of thick knotted rope attached to its end.

"What are you doing? What is that for?" She screeched at him.

He looked at his weapon and rhythmically thumped the rod in the palm of his hand. His horns glinted in the moonlight, and She thought, *He is the Shadow.*

"You're just going to scare them, right? Coal in their stocking? Monster under the bed? Right?" she pleaded.

He smiled at her.

"Right?" She repeated, Her voice becoming wild.

"If we're going to do this, you have to let me do it my way," he cooed.

She stared at him for a moment in disbelief.

Coal, yes. A few scares, sure. But an actual punishment with beating and torture and…

Jolenir's voice came back into her mind, the message that he received from the Mists of the North themselves—*He's the Knecht. The Servant. Restorer of order and balance. Deliverer of pain and justice. He is the one True Coal Elf. Your counterpart. Your mirror image.*

Sturd's blue eyes sparkled with a renewed sense of purpose. She looked at his switch and back at him and nodded her head because, at that moment, everything was so clear. They were the balance now. Not Nessie Fruit, not blackened names in a magic book, not Double-Coal, Coal-less, or All-Coal Nights, not Christmas in July or Light Lists, not *Dublix Santaraes* and Codexes and rules and regulations. Not Adam's Day or Life Job assignments, or secret passages shrouded in fairy dust. Not Councils and cadres. Not tunnel passageways, or Brotherhoods or Chygas. Not even Shadows of the Dark, or even the Mists of the North.

It all came down to Ember Skye and Sturd Ruprecht.

The Boss and the Knecht.

The Claus and the Krampus.

And as She grabbed the reins and to Her team gave a whistle, She couldn't help but think that this was how it was always meant to be.

BOOK CLUB DISCUSSION QUESTIONS

1. How does Ember's character evolve throughout the novel, especially in her interactions with the Council and Sturd?

2. What do you think about Ember's decision to demand an audience with Santa Claus? How does this decision impact the overall plot?

3. Explore the significance of the All-Coal Night concept introduced in the story. How does it challenge traditional Christmas narratives?

4. Discuss the dynamics between Ember and Mrs. Claus. How does their relationship contribute to the tension in the novel?

5. Analyze the motives behind Sturd's actions, especially in gathering the elf twins. How does this add complexity to the plot?

6. Consider the theme of power and leadership in the North Pole. How do different characters,

including Ember, Sturd, and Santa Claus, wield and challenge authority?

7. Reflect on the symbolism of coal in the story. How does it represent morality and the concept of being naughty or nice?

8. Discuss the role of the elf twins in the narrative. How do they contribute to the unfolding events, and what significance do they hold in the overall resolution?

9. Explore the impact of Ember's decisions on the North Pole community. How does it shape the future of the North Pole, and what lasting changes might occur?

10. How does the author use humor and satire in "Above the Ash" to comment on traditional Christmas themes and characters?

THE LOST TALES OF THE NORTH POLE

Episode 3: The Case of Mauve Thistlewood

The big ole orange ball that shifted in the sky was starting to disappear like it did every day. Its dying light cast shadows onto the snowy ground, and Mauve loved the way it reflected back its dazzling and icy light. It gave the world around her a sparkly look—peaceful and serene. It made the light from the sky kind of stay a little while longer even after it was gone, and that was oh-so-very comforting to her. The more light, the better because Mauve Thistlewood couldn't see very well. The affliction had started the moment she had opened her newborn elfling eyes. Her mother had shouted in awe and wonder that their color was so shocking, so un-elflike, that the elf-babe must have been some kind of miracle. Her father only grumbled in dismay, for having yet another mouth to feed was beginning to take its toll on the family, and that responsibility fell solely on his shoulders.

Mauve's mother named her *Mauve Thistlewood* after the color of the pinkish purple flower that sprouted from the wild thistle in the wood—the same pinkish purple color that matched the elfbabe's eyes. Elves only had one name, but Mauve's mother deemed her so wonderful, so magnificent, so special, that she believed she was deserving of two. Two names. Father was unimpressed. Unamused. Knew the potential mockery she would endure as she grew up.

And unfortunately, Mauve's life was riddled with ridicule, for as she began to get older, Mauve became clumsier. Knocking into things, tripping over things, bumping into things. Her awkwardness and gracelessness soon became the talk of her parish, and the joke of many of her peers. As if being an elfling of seven elfyears old wasn't hard enough in its own right, poor little Mauve experienced derision like no other elfling. But the sweet elfling with the pinkish purple eyes and jet-black hair kept her head held high, pointy little nose in the air, and a smile on her face. "I can't see very well," she would say in her defense. "I can't help it."

It didn't stop the bullies from bullying, though. Her elfling peers would think of new ways to torture and torment her on a daily basis. But Mauve continued to associate with them because she wanted to believe in her heart of hearts that one day, maybe, they would be nice and not trick her, or tease her, or make blind girl jokes. "I'm not blind!" she would scold them. "I just can't see very well."

And now, when the orange ball was leaving the side of the horizon, Mauve knew she had a limited amount of time before she was totally in the dark. And she knew the only reason the other elflings wanted to play "Brimmle Brummle" so late in the day was so they could make fun of her when the sun set. Yet, she agreed to play. Always. Because maybe Stixx would turn around and stick up for her when Bratcher teased her. Or maybe Hrolding would shove Melithoro when he threw snow in her face saying, "Can you see that? Can you see that?"

Regardless, Mauve hid—just like the rules of the game stated. Bratcher was "it," and he was out stalking the other elflings. Mauve heard the sloshing of feet in the snow and ducked down low behind a large magnolia tree so as to not be found. Soon, the footfalls scampered out of earshot, and she exhaled and leaned her back against the trunk. She let her bottom sink into the wet snow and curled her knees to her chest for some extra warmth. The forest was quiet and the sparkle on the snow from the diminishing light seemed to hypnotize her. Mauve marveled at the wonderous wood around her! She ran her hands back and forth in the snow in the space around her and enjoyed the frigid particles between her fingers.

Suddenly, her fingers brushed up against something prickly next to her. She brushed away the snow to see what was there, and when she dug enough, it was a thistle bush growing from the base of the tree. Her heart flashed with hot anger when she saw the pinkish purple tendrils from the spikey green bud. The mauve thistle poked through the white snow, and she grumbled. Aggravated. Annoyed. For this was a reminder of all the teasing and hardship she had endured her entire life.

Mauve Thistlewood. Blind girl with the pinkish purple eyes. Hiding from the whole world out in the snow.

Normally, she would have pushed the anger and hatred down in her heart, but at that moment, it was hard to suppress the overwhelming feeling of despair. Enraged, Mauve tugged at the plant from its thin green stem. She wanted to rip it from the very ground and toss it aside—let that plant feel how she felt every single day.

Only, the plant was either so deeply rooted, or frozen in the hard-packed earth, that Mauve struggled to tear it up. "Of course," she whispered to herself. "Clumsy me can't even uproot a delicate thistle."

She pulled harder, and harder still. She wriggled and wormed, fixed both feet on the ground, and used all her might from the waist down to lift that sucker out of the soil. It was a long battle between elf and vegetation, and in the end, with great strength and determination, Mauve was victorious in her plight and the thistle plant slithered out of the cold ground. Its long roots twirled and curled at the end of it and with everything left in her, she threw it violently into the woods with a *hmmph!*

As Mauve turned to return to her hiding space against the trunk of the magnolia tree, something stirred in the soil. A rumbling sound from deep below grew louder and louder, and the earth itself started to collapse upon itself forming a crevice that stretched wider and wider. Mauve tried to scramble to her feet to get away from the growing hole, but clumsy as she was, she tripped over her own delicate feet, tumbled head-first into the deep pit, and passed out.

She rubbed the back of her head when she came to and looked around the dark hole. The last of the light from above was quickly disintegrating, and panic quickly invaded her heart. "Help! Help!" she screamed as loud as she could. "Help! I've fallen in a ditch!"

The voices of her elfling mates were muffled at first, but as they approached the opening in the ground she could hear them get closer. Soon, the other elflings appeared over the hole, four silhouettes hovering with their heads faced down and the last of the light piercing in between them.

"Bratcher? Hrolding? Stixx? Mel?" she called up, identifying each of them.

"Mauve?" Melithoro sang curiously. "What are you doing down there?"

"I fell! I fell down this hole!" Mauve responded.

"Of course she did!" Bratcher snorted, and the others laughed.

"Can you help me get out?"

"Help you get out?" Stixx wailed. "We can't even see where you are!"

Panic struck Mauve deep again as she heard a faint scratching sound coming from inside the hole. "Oh, please! Please!" she begged. "I can see you! You're not that far up."

The group howled with another round of laughter. "Did you hear what she said?" Hrolding cried. "She said she can see us, but she couldn't see the hole in the ground?"

"Oh, please, guys! Please! I slipped. I tripped. Please! There's something down here, and I'm really scared."

"Uh… yeah, Mauve. I don't know if we're gonna be able to," Stixx snickered.

"Yeah," Bratcher repeated. "It's getting dark."

"But you knew that already," Hrolding chimed.

"We're gonna have to get back soon for supper time," Melithoro added.

Mauve's stomach lurched up to her throat. "No, no, no! You have to help me. At least go back and get my dad. He'll get me out."

The elflings' laughter rose up through the forest, and Mauve's mouth went dry with fear as the scratching sound got louder and closer. Her tongue scraped the roof of her mouth and tears began to swell in her eyes. "Come on, guys," she croaked pitifully. "Please help me. I… I think there's something down here. I have to get out."

"And *we* have to get home," Bratcher declared. "Maybe we'll come tomorrow when it's light out."

An uncontrolled yelp escaped Mauve's throat, and the elflings chuckled and scampered away. "No! No! No!" she screamed with a burst of energy, but it was too late, the last of the light had disappeared and so did the wretched little elflings.

Mauve shuddered in the dark hole; the blackness practically blinded her. She struggled to see her surroundings, struggled to get her bearings, but the cold was quickly shifting to freezing, and what had once been shades of ever-changing tones of grays had turned to nothing but the blackest of blacks.

And the scratching sound moved in on her.

"Huh… huh… huh-low?" she sang out, not expecting a response, and hoping to not get one at the same time.

The scratching got closer.

"Is somebody there?" she said, softer, her voice shaky and weak.

The sound grew closer still, but in the complete void of the dark, something amplified in her ears, and she could hear the sound more carefully—more distinctly. She determined that the sound wasn't scratching at all. It was more like a flutter. Like insect wings but larger. There was movement and noise and a clear humming sound that soon surrounded her completely.

The tears overflowed down her cheeks. "Can somebody help me?" she cried through muffled sobs.

Soon, a circle of pink twinkling lights like a hundred stars illuminated the space around her. Mauve turned and twirled and jerked her body as the hole brilliantly lit up. But as she stared longer and harder, she realized the twinkling lights weren't really lights at all. They were eyes! Pink eyes shining bright and staring her down. Eyes like she had never seen before. Eyes that reflected back her own pink and purple hues. And attached to those eyes were small, winged bodies hovering majestically in the circle. Creatures she had never seen or heard of before. Gray-winged bodies with soft fur and peaked ears much like hers. Miniscule fangs descended over their small black mouths giving them a menacing appearance.

Mauve dropped to her bottom and clutched her legs to her chest. She buried her head in between the space in her legs hoping they wouldn't see her. Praying they would fly away. Fly away. Fly away.

Their humming song only grew louder, and she could feel them closing in—descending upon her, landing on her shoulders, taking a spot on the tops of her knees. Their little feet latched on to her overall dress like tiny pinching spurs, or the spindles of a thistle. She braced herself for the inevitable onslaught of their pin-prickly fangs at her flesh, for she knew they would surely bite her to death. But when the attack never came, she slowly opened her eyes to a sight that both alarmed and mystified her—the curious little creatures were calm and still and had attached themselves to her. They looked at her with their gentle eyes and what looked like tiny smiles on their mouths.

"Hello?" she whispered to them after a few moments of wonder and awe.

The creatures collectively hummed.

"What are you little guys?" she mused. "You're not going to hurt me, are you?"

Fervently, they fluttered their wings like they understood her, like they knew, like they were saying, "Absolutely not."

Mauve was amazed at the way the strange beings responded to her.

"I'm lost and alone," she said to them. "Can you help me?"

Again, they shook and flitted their gray velvety bodies as if to say "yes."

Mauve raised her hand in front of her face and extended her forefinger. One of the creatures perched itself down, and she brought it closer to her face. "You're so cute!" she gushed as she examined it. "Momma and Poppa never told me about you guys. The Trainers never talked about you. In fact, I don't think anyone knows what you are! You're so strange. Different. Like me."

The brood went wild again, their wings flapping with quick bursts—so fast and furiously that they lifted her an inch off the ground. Mauve gasped and smiled wide. Being in their presence gave her so much joy and filled her with a warmth and light she had never experienced before. Then she realized, the pink glowing lights from their eyes helped to illuminate the darkness of the pit and she no longer struggled to see! There was clarity, crispness, and light!

They gently put her back to the ground and the creatures adjusted on her body, but never once left her. "Where do you guys live? Where do you come from?" she asked.

At once they flapped their wings pulling her along the pit. She let their movements guide her until she could see that the hole was not just a hole, but a tunnel—a long passage that twisted and curved underground. "I'd like to see your home, if that's okay with you," she said.

A gust of wind flooded the cavern, sending a chill in Mauve's body. She shuddered with the cold and with surprise when she thought she heard a voice echo throughout.

"W… w… what was that?" her voice quivered.

"Come, child," the voice said clearly. "Come and see."

The creatures flapped their wings in excitement.

"Who said that?" Mauve shouted down the dark corridor.

"Come and see," it repeated.

Mauve looked up to the gaping hole above her. There was no way for her to get out—this she sadly knew. What other choice did she have but to follow the sound of the ominous voice down the pathway of the underground labyrinth?

"No worries, sweet child. My friends will guide you to me." And with a hum of approval, the creatures led her through the tunnel, their eyes lighting the way. The mysterious voice sang a lullaby that was both haunting and soothing at the same time. It comforted Mauve as it reminded her of her mother's sweet bedtime songs.

The creatures brought her to an open space in the middle of a dark corridor, and before her, a plume of smoke rose up from a crack in the rocky ground. It encircled Mauve like a twister and she froze in her place. "What is this? What are you?" she asked it.

"I am Dark," it responded, it's voice like sand-paper on stone.

"Dark? Is that really your name?"

"No. But I am very old. Older than names ever existed. Dark is the only name that you would be able to understand."

She scrunched her nose. It was right. She didn't understand. "You live down here with these flying things?"

"Yes. And no," it said. "But I've been waiting for you for a very long time."

"For me?" she exclaimed. "That's impossible. I'm not very old," she said innocently.

Dark's smoky form twirled around her one last time before transforming itself into the shape of a tall elf. Mauve gasped at its magical-like display. "I know, child. I've been waiting for someone *like* you," it emphasized.

"Mauve. My name is Mauve Thistlewood," she corrected.

"Not for much longer," it said, and reached its long smoky arm around her shoulders and led her deeper underground.

The next day, the nasty little elflings returned to the spot where Mauve had fallen. To their surprise she was gone, so they quickly covered the hole, made a pact to never speak of this again, and ran back to town. Mauve's parents and the entire parish set out to look for her, but their efforts were in vain.

While Underground, Mauve marveled at her new surroundings. The curious critters had an intricate system of tunnels and grottos, and there was much to see and explore. And see she could! Even in the darkness of the tunnels, even with her already poor eyesight, there was something powerful about the creatures that enabled her to see clearly but differently. Her eyes adjusted to the black shadows as her vision altered and changed, and she was no longer clumsy and klutzy and unsure of herself. The little guys had taken a real liking to her, attending to her every need and want. Soon, Mauve became so in sync, so in tune, with them that she was able to command them with the power of her mind. They revered her, practically worshipped her. She called them Graespurs (for their gray velvet bodies and the prickly spurs on their feet), and she became their Queen.

She spent a lot of her time with Dark, too. Every day they conversed by the crack in the ground. Mauve enjoyed the stories it shared with her, no matter how scary, or gruesome, or grim. And every day she felt more and more connected to it, like they were one living, breathing entity. Dark sympathized with her. Empathized with her. Comforted her and told her she wasn't alone. At first, Dark was a plume of black smoke, but as time marched on, the smoke diminished, and all that was left was a voice in her head. Like Dark had somehow incorporated with her—*became* her, and its smoky limbs had begun to darken her heart. Sometimes she felt like she was crazy, like she had been lost for so long that she was just imagining everything, but then Dark would speak loud and clear in her mind, and she would push those silly thoughts aside. And yes, Dark was right about losing her name. As time passed on, Mauve began to forget bits and pieces of her life before the underground, before the Graespurs, before Dark. But what never left her were the images of the nasty little elflings who had teased her so—a thought that haunted her every waking moment. Before long, she was consumed with a lonely, black rage like smoke in her soul and in her brain clouding her thoughts and feelings and worst of all, her judgements.

One day, she knew she had been underground long enough. Dark's voice no longer bounded in her mind, and her thoughts had become none other than her own. It was time to return to the aboveground. Her darkness and loneliness would be no more! She searched the underground maze until she came across the roots of a familiar plant. A thistle bush! Just like the one she had uprooted once upon a time. Only this time, she pulled down hard on it, and within no time, the soil from above crashed down onto the rocks below leaving a gaping hole in the ground.

She commanded the Graespurs to attend to her, and they immediately flocked to their Queen, dug their feet into her clothing, attached themselves to her hair, and simultaneously lifted her out of the hole in the ground. They sent her soaring over the town, and at her request, left her at the front door of her old cottage. She stood upright for the first time in what seemed like forever and realized just how much she had grown. Elves in the parish stopped and stared as she towered over them in her dark and dusty glory. She was a vision of elegance and grace, yet they feared her presence and the presence of the unknown creatures. Some bowed on their knees before her. Some threw rocks and other objects to scare her away. The Queen arched her throat and laughed.

"Who are you?" the elves sang out in curiosity and fear.

"I am the Graespur Queen," she replied. "And I claim this land for me and my companions." She snapped her fingers and set the Graespurs on the townspeople, commanding them to attack, commanding them to tear out the eyes of anyone who would oppose her, commanding them to sentence them to a lifetime of darkness. She no longer cared that her former tormentors were no longer among the living—anyone and everyone was going to suffer her wrath.

The Graespur Queen set up her palace on a mountaintop of one of the coldest regions in the Pole—a land covered in sparkling blueice; a place she had never been to when she was a child. She ruled the elves under a tight-fisted hand of fear, but it was again, a lonely life for her. The Graes were not fans of the big orange ball in the sky, so they would retreat back to their underground domain until the sky was black, so she adopted her companions' circadian rhythm, and became nocturnal like them.

The Queen's reign of madness and terror lasted for many an elfyear. She was ruthless and malicious and was easily sent into a terrifying rage. The elves at the Pole prayed to the sky for help—they prayed to be saved from her villainous clutches.

One morning, a violent storm blew in from the northern most part of the North. The white clouds descended over the entire land, and as The Queen observed from her castle, she saw a glowing mist swirling like a twister in her front yard, so she ran out into the snow to see what was going on.

"What are you?" she bellowed over the vicious wind. "What do you want?"

"I am Mist," it answered, its voice like soft strings being plucked on a harp.

"Mist?" she scoffed. "Is that really your name?"

"No. But I am very old. Older than names ever existed. Mist is the only name that you would be able to understand."

She narrowed her eyes with disdain. "I don't like games," she reprimanded. "And I don't like intruders in my domain."

"This is no longer your domain," it replied. "You've terrorized this land for far too long. We've come for you. To put an end to this."

"For me?" she exclaimed. "That's impossible! My Graespurs won't allow you to touch…" But she stopped herself before she could finish. It was morning, and the Graespurs had flown back to the cave for the day. There was no one and nothing to protect her from Mist.

"Graespur Queen, you are no more," Mist interrupted. "A new ruler will take your place. One who is kind and gentle and will right your wrongs. He will be called the Claus, and no one will remember your time of chaos."

"But I'm righting *my* wrongs!" she cried, and hot tears melted off her cheeks. "I'm righting *my* wrongs!" As she screamed, a thin line of black smoke escaped from her mouth—the last remnants of Dark leaving her soul. "I'm Mauve Thistlewood!" she cried as she seemed to regain her inner consciousness. "Mauve…"

But the twister danced circles around her. Snow blew up from the ground in a frenzied maelstrom and lifted her into the icy vortex. Mist carried her to the eastern side of the Pole, and buried her under snow and rock and stone and granite, deep, deep into the hard-packed earth where she would sleep for the rest of eternity.

That was fine by her. She didn't mind the eternal thoughts of exacting revenge—of righting her wrongs.

That evening when the Graespurs returned to their Queen, they were surprised to find her gone. Lost and confused, they scattered throughout the land to make a new way for themselves without their cruel leader.

The Graespur Queen slept for thousands and thousands of elfyears. It was a soundless sleep with only images of black and white vengeance invading her mind—images of tormenting elves and darkness and caverns and labyrinths and plucked-out eyes and thistle leaves and Graespurs and shadow monsters and snow tornados. It was all jumbled up like a puzzle, all at once. But when a peculiar noise suddenly filtered into her con-sciousness and broke through all her murderous visions, she was unnerved. She heard a voice say, "Skyeway Station," and not understanding what that meant, perturbed her even more.

Unnerved? Perturbed? How could she feel any of that?

A great banging and clanging noise filled her rocky tomb again.

The Graespur Queen opened her pinkish purple eyes, and she could *see*.

AUTHOR BIO

Maria DeVivo writes horror and dark fantasy for both a YA and an adult audience. Each of her series has been Amazon best-sellers and has won multiple awards since 2012. When not writing, she teaches Language Arts and Journalism to middle school students in Florida. A lover of all things dark and demented, the worlds she creates are fantastical and immersive. Get swept away in the lands of elves, zombies, angels, demons, and witches (but not all in the same place). Maria takes great pleasure in warping the comfort factor in her readers' minds—just when you think you've reached a safe space in her stories, she snaps you back into her twisted reality.

Witch of the Black Circle
Witch of the Red Thorn
Witch of the Silver Locust
Witch of the White Serpent
Witch of the Golden Veil

Aestrangel the Fallen
Aestrangel the Chosen
Aestrangel the Risen

The Coal Elf